to

crown

a

beast

r. scarlett

Pictures on the front of the book:

Man: Stock photo ID: 268027562 by ITALO

Woman: Stock photo ID: 262847522 by Svyatoslava Vladzimirska

Cover and book design by Mae I Design & Photography

Photograph on back of book by Lauren Perry

Edited by Bex Harper and Ellie McLove (LoveNBooks)

To the true storyteller, Robert Cousins.

You were the first one to show me the gift of storytelling and each story you tell is magical. Not many people I know have the skill and strength you command simply with words. I am so proud to call you my grandpa and you've taught me so much on how to work hard and cherish every single story. I love you grandpa, to the moon and back.

playlist

Devotion by Hurts

The War by SYML

Become the Beast by Karliene

The Other Side by Ruelle

Cold by Aqualung & Lucy Schwartz

Bones by Low Roar

Hurts Too Good by Ruelle

You Were Never Gone by Hannah Ellis

Ultraviolence by Lana Del Rey

Gemini Feed (Salute Remix) by Banks

"we were both created in chaos,
we were both born to destroy.
you were like death,
and i was like war.
and where we collided,
darling, i loved you."

— born disasters ‖ k.a.

to
crown
a
beast

r. scarlett

chapter one

THE BEAST IGNORED the burn in his veins, thriving off the adrenaline storming through him, and turned to face the court, covered in blood—his own and the former king's.Painted in power, painted in sin, he bared his teeth, licking at the edge of his mouth as he looked over his court.

The court that trembled in his mere presence, and it only hungered him for more power.

A lone figure stood out amidst the sea of snakes and he eyed her. His daemon.

CLOAKED IN WARM darkness, Molly Darling approached the High Court's new king. King of all demons. The man she had married not even a day ago, the man who had told her he loved her mere hours before.

A single glance from his obsidian eyes felt like a thousand daggers slicing across her flesh, letting her drain out and collapse. Those soft lips of his were smoothed into a line of indifference.

Impassive. Fierce. Deadly.

The crowd had dropped to the ground in low bows, like a god to mortals, like a storm sinking mighty ships, sinking the wreckage to the ocean's bottom deep.

Her stomach dropped into a bottomless pit. The man she loved now long gone, replaced by a beast: dark and hungry for pain and suffering. And so Molly's knees bent, bowing to her king like the rest of them.

Tensley's sharp eyes watched her every move, pupils dilating at the spike in her pulse.

She wanted to touch him—to calm her racing thoughts. Two sides warred in her.

The rational—and the irrational.

One knew the damage was done.

The other, hoped—*hoped* that the broken shards in her chest, cutting deep into her lungs, were a lie.

Tensley Knight hadn't died.

Tensley Knight hadn't had his heart ripped out by the king, and then moments later, beheaded Fallen.

Heartless.

Empty.

Not her Tensley.

Not the man she had fallen utterly and deeply in love with.

Her knees hit the cool marble floor and she bowed her head, eyeing the tiny specks of gold glimmering against the white slabs—splattered with Fallen's still fresh blood. The previous king's body lay decapitated a few feet away, lifeless—an ancient body turned to stone.

She breathed through her nose shakily, fallen strands of hair fanning across her tear stained cheeks.

In, out. In, out.

If she kept calming herself with soothing breaths, she wouldn't pass out. She wouldn't sob aloud in pain and let the court see her crushing under the shock.

She couldn't piece the facts together. She wanted to collapse. Ignore everything.

You're in shock.

Tensley's shadow moved across the floor, his boots thudding harshly like cries of war, and with each step forward, she recoiled.

Then two black riding boots stopped in front of her and she examined their weathered texture, the mud and dirt and specks of blood coating the dark leather.

In, out. In, out.

She didn't know what was going on in his head, what would be his next move, and her nerves were eating at her. Seconds, minutes perhaps, passed by painfully slow. No one moved. No one spoke. All she could do was concentrate on her own shaky breaths as she waited. And waited.

Ever so slowly, she tilted her head upward. Her gaze traced up his toned thighs— breeches tight, up his strong chest— the ugly punctured hole there a symbol of what he had lost, and she froze, carefully lifting her gaze further.

She saw the vicious man in parts—first his jaw, as sharp as a deadly weapon, a muscle feathering there under his clench, those full, tempting lips she touched every morning and every night, the feel of his lips the last thing she'd feel before falling asleep at night. And lastly, with eyes blurred by tears due to the crushing pain now residing permanently in her chest, she found his eyes.

A calm storm rippled in the depths of them, controlled by their master.

Dark grey, but with a cold edge of anger slicing through, of rage, and she knew how easily he could snap.

In, out. In, out.

She kept repeating to herself.

Over and over.

His fisted hand relaxed beside his thigh and with one single fluid movement, two fingers touched the soft and fragile skin under her chin.

"Stand," he commanded coolly, his hoarse voice causing chills on her skin. Because she still responded to him. Still craved the man before her, despite the hunger of the beast.

She stood, his fingers still anchored to her chin, and eyed him from underneath her lashes.

He simply stared back, that jaw flexing, those eyes darkening to the point she wondered what he was calculating.

This isn't Tensley.

He's not heartless.

Surely...

Surely he's still somewhere in there.

Far beneath, perhaps. But still there.

Please.

Please...

"Tensley," she whispered, hating how her voice wobbled and cracked. She hated how so much emotion echoed in one single word. His name. His precious name she cried out in the darkness, the name that made her stomach flutter with giddiness, and the name that soothed the fear throbbing in her chest and head.

His eyes narrowed.

Simply narrowed, and she sucked in air fast.

Now it was just a hollow name that echoed through this new emptiness ravaging deep within her chest.

"This is absurd," a lord snapped and Molly flinched at the loud sound when the room had previously been so silent. Unbearably silent. A lord, one she had seen a handful of times, stood out from the crowd, his face red in anger.

Tensley's head turned ever so slowly toward the man, a look of indifference, his jaw finally relaxing to its usual state. Sharp, precise, beautiful...

"A heartless bastard, a bastard that murdered our king," the lord bit out, gesturing to the corpse of the fallen king.

"Remus," another man hissed at him. "Stand down."

"Stand down?" Remus, the lord, took a few brave steps forward, laughing angrily at his fellow court member. "I will not stand to be led by a middle-class bastard," he spat out angrily, eyes blazing with hatred. His focus turned to Molly and he growled viciously at her. "A man who, mere minutes ago, had his own heart ripped out because he fell in love for a worthless piece of woman. A filthy whore with no title."

"Lords," Lilith said, stepping forward, her head high, but Molly eyed her shaking, clenched hands in front of her stomach. Lilith rolled her shoulders back and faced the crowd, her chin high, her eyes curved in dominance and power. "I suggest we do not let him become king. Fallen is dead, and with him so could be his numerous laws. He no longer rules, therefore why should he still dictate our ways? My son deserves to be the king more than this wild beast," she added with a sneer in Tensley's direction. "This is a civilized court, after all. Blood should speak louder than dominance."

A few men roared their agreement.

"Is it not blood that I am covered in, Lady Lilith," Tensley spat darkly, his voice slicing through the room viciously. "Am I not wearing your late husband's precious blood on me? Blood speaks louder, indeed."

"Stand down, Dux," the prince's voice echoed over the vicious crowd, the sound powerful and unafraid. He took a single step forward, people around him stepping to the side immediately. His authority over the court was palpable, king or not, he had power and would stop at nothing to use it. Blood splattered across his sheer shirt, delicate chains looped at the top of it. Born with royal blood, raised in gold and darkness, he was molded into a king. "Now would be the time to honor our bargain," he said, jaw clenched, but the rest of his composure was nothing but a chilling calm.

Molly eyed the prince's cool composure. The bargain. Tensley had promised to kill Fallen and hand over the crown to his son in exchange for safety for the both of them, as well as their unborn son.

Tensley didn't say a word and stared back at the prince coolly.

"A Dux does not become king—one of us, bred from grace and power," Remus hollered, getting brave enough to step closer as he met the stares of each of his peers. Lilith's features pinched into an ugly scowl. "We deserve the crown, we deserve the throne. Your blood is too wild, too tainted by your bride."

Molly stole a glance at Tensley's features, but she only saw perfect composure. A cool expression of steel and strength.

"And you betrayed Fallen's sacred laws whilst he still reigned. His word was still law as you committed that sin," Remus said, jabbing his shaking finger toward Molly. Molly swallowed as the whole court turned to look at her. "A child out of wedlock. Both the bastard child and the whore should be killed for the crime. I will not let this court be tainted by their filth and disgrace." He growled out again, veins pulsing wildly in his neck as his hands shook.

Molly could feel the air in the court thicken and waver, the tension building to a boiling point. A few other members shouted their approval, pushing Remus closer and closer to her. She placed a hand on her stomach, glaring at the man. Everyone cried out their opinions, battling to win against the other voices, but all of their eyes stayed on their new king. Waiting, anticipating his reaction. Calculating the risks, the possibilities.

The lord's features were sharpened in anger and he spoke, but his words were muffled by the voices battling in the court. Of agreements and disagreements.

"You fucking whore," Remus hissed now only mere feet away from her, encouraged by the exclamations of several lords. "You foul excuse of an existence. Perhaps we should hang you for all of this, I would enjoy the sight of your limp, naked and bruised body, hanging loose from a rope. We'd let it on display, to rot under the sun. Perhaps we'll even let the males have a go at the whore before she's hung." He announced, with a monstrous smile creeping on his lips. "How do we feel about that, gentlemen?"

And those were his last words.

Tensley gripped Remus by his shoulders, yanked him back and wrapped a powerful arm around his throat.

The lord's face quickly became purple, his eyes seeming to pop out of their socket.

The crowd hushed.

Tensley's muscles flexed in his arm, like a serpent ready to kill its prey and tightened viciously.

Snap.

It echoed against the cathedral ceilings, the court silenced completely, and a woman fainted in the back of the room, a thud resounding as her body hit the ground.

Tensley stared at Molly, his pitch-black eyes drilling deeply into her, watching her chest fall and rise rapidly in shock.

No remorse.

He didn't flinch, he didn't pause, he simply attacked and devoured.

One second he had been completely composed, and the next he had snapped so fast her head had spun.

She shivered at the realization.

There was no man left inside Tensley. Just a wild, dangerous beast. A predator and a conqueror.

He removed his arm from Remus and the lord's heavy body fell onto the marble slabs.

He turned to the crowd, scanning them like the predator he was, watching for one to flinch, for one to run, for one to attack. None of them moved. Molly wondered if they even breathed. "I am your king," he said, loud and clear, his voice vibrating through the floor. "And anyone who dares defy me will meet the same fate." He growled deep and rough, a powerful arm pointing at the body slumped at his feet.

Molly looked over at the prince, his mouth twisted into a frown, wild fire and deadly ice flowing through his eyes. He looked at her, gaze almost freezing her alive, and she turned quickly away.

The prince was enraged.

Not because his father had died. The prince had hated every breath his father had ever taken. But because Tensley was refusing to hand over the crown as planned. He wasn't honoring their bargain.

Murder the crown, marry the crown.

"Defy you?" the prince spat, his eyes returning to Tensley. "It is my right. The crown is mine." A low growl vibrating through the prince's chest, loud enough for all to hear.

Tensley stared back, far too long, far too calm. "Choose to stand behind me or choose your death." Tensley moved, his boots thundering once more. When he moved, the crowd moved, when he raised his hand, they cowered. Like a god of the sea, summoning vicious waves.

"I do not stand behind others and wait. I take what I want," the prince spat.

And then the prince lunged, their bodies colliding like two freight trains. Molly heard the steel of bones and flesh battling together for dominance.

She watched in sheer horror as the two beasts destroyed each other; each claw, each punch drew more blood onto their skin, bruised and battered, and all she could do was stare.

"Tensley," she gasped. No one heard her though. They weren't interested in what the *filthy whore* had to say. She moved forward, invading their battle ground. The prince dug his fingers into the hole in Tensley's chest and Tensley let out a fractured cry. "Tensley," she screamed, her own voice cracking under the force of her emotions.

The beasts thrashed, further, further into destruction that would end badly for both.

Molly felt the twist inside of her—the ache of power, of strength combusting, and she fisted her hands.

They had to stop. They had to stop fighting before they murdered each other. A desperate need boiled inside of her.

The icy sensation began behind her eyes, the glow, but she could feel the power in her voice, in her limbs.

"Stop," she commanded, her voice iron and steel.

Her strength—her voice alone, tore the two men apart.

The vibrancy, the strength struck her deep—as if it was purely a part of her. Her power like a deadly whip. Something shifted inside of her, something felt different and she couldn't place it.

Tensley stood, his dark eyes focused now on her. She touched her throat, eyeing the court that watched her in confusion and fear.

With a single roar, Tensley marched toward her, a force to be reckoned with.

Her heart warred against her chest as she watched the beast storm toward her. Instinct to protect her rooted deep within himself.

9

Molly caught the prince moving toward them, but he stopped. Both men looked at each other, gazes filled with a battle of their own.

One dripped with undying rage.

The other oozing with cold hatred.

Two trapped, raging beasts.

Two opposite goals.

Only one of them would get what they wanted.

Both men backed off.

Fresh blood now poured from the hole in Tensley's chest and the prince's nose bent and gushed blood into his mouth and down his chin.

Tensley's chest rose and fell fast and she could see the exhaustion. He hadn't fully recovered from his earlier battle with Fallen, the hole in his chest needed more than mere healing powers.

Her hand lifted, debating whether he'd snap if she attempted to touch him.

Tensley eyed the prince once more and turned his attention to the court. "Threaten me—threaten what belongs to me and I will show you how vicious death is. I will be the plague you fear if you try to harm her." His lips pulled back and he growled. "Or my crown."

Molly tasted the power, the thirst for more in the air, and she knew the beast wanted all of it.

The beast wanted the crown, the throne, the court. It wasn't letting go. But the beast also craved the violence, the release. It *wanted* someone to threaten Molly, so it could snap again and drink hungrily from their pain.

He hadn't been poisoned; he'd been destroyed, his vicious heart ripped from him, ripped from her, and she felt it like it had been her own.

Darkness consumed him.

Power ate at him.

Hunger blinded him.

And as she looked at the prince, she saw the same, brewing, sizzling deep within his own beast.

It was only a matter of time... she thought.

He was not done, far from it.

Even through the dark clouds simmering in his gaze, one message rang clear; he would stop at nothing. He would get his crown, no matter what.

With the hushed silence of the court, Tensley turned and looked at Molly behind him. She wanted to catch a glimpse, a moment where all her fears were erased, and to see her Tensley shine through for just a single second. To finally see the proof she had been desperately waiting for since his heart had been ripped out of him. Proof that he was acting, that this was all a trick to fool the court, and Tensley wasn't gone.

Tensley Knight's heart and soul hadn't been torn apart by a mad king.

Looking back at the man before her, she knew the answer and it burnt her insides to embers.

A whisper of breath slithered across the embers, and she felt the sizzling burn, a pain-filled cry almost ripping out of her throat.

And with those pitch-black eyes of power, she knew the beast wanted her.

She was his kiss of strength. She was his weapon.

The man she loved was gone, but a need ached inside of her bones and fueled her.

She wanted his iron heart.

She wanted her husband back.

As she watched him turn away once more, focusing on the court, his features composed, his lips a flat line of indifference, his body posed in leisure, but with a snap, lethal, she vowed to herself.

A vow she'd die with, a vow she'd ruin anyone in her path, destroy gods and burn kingdoms to ashes to keep.

She'd ruin herself—and find his precious iron heart.

The beast before her had no idea she was the true threat.

She'd wage war against him. She'd move mountains and steal stars.

No, she thought, bowing her head, her eyes never leaving the dark lord before her. She would get his heart back for Tensley Knight.

For their unborn son.

She'd make the beast kneel, and save the man.

That, she vowed.

chapter two

TENSION PRICKLED AT Molly's scalp as she watched the heartless king stand at their bedchamber's open balcony.

Posture strong, his wavy dark locks smoothed back in perfection, the blood cleaned from his hair and skin, a new fitted dark suit enveloping his powerful body.

As if nothing had happened.

She took a shaky breath, her eyelids closing softly, and to calm her raging, cracked heart, she remembered.

She remembered when she had first met him when she was four years old. How terrified she had been. How, at her young age, he had seemed so imposing and dark. Yet, somehow, she had known the boy with the dark hair and the stormy eyes would always protect her.

She remembered when he had imposed himself back into her life a few months ago, barging in without warning like a dark, summer storm, and ruined all of her plans. She smiled, laughing softly when she remembered his arrogance. Yet, she would never regret the day he had come to collect her family's end of the bargain.

She remembered the feel of Tensley's soft lips caressing her ear when he would murmur words that would make her stomach flutter, every night until darkness consumed them both.

She remembered the numerous late nights they had spent, talking and laughing freely, back at Tensley's...their apartment, she corrected herself.

She remembered their wedding day and how despite the danger that had been lurking at every corner, patiently waiting to pounce, she had felt like the happiest woman on earth because she had been gifted the chance to marry the man she loved.

She remembered their wedding night, and how he had shown her the power of touch, the power of the bond they shared with one another, and how love could be expressed in so many ways that didn't require words.

And finally, she remembered the day he had told her he loved her, and a tear rolled down her soft cheek.

She wiped it away roughly, taking a deep breath, before turning toward Tensley once more.

A warlock stood in front of him, finishing up healing the hole in his chest. She rubbed a mixture of herbs and ointments, quietly whispering a chant. When Lilith and the prince refused to heal Tensley's gaping hole, this warlock had volunteered. She had shrugged offhandedly and said that her ancestors had been in charge of healing the previous king for centuries and that they were taught since birth that their duty was to the king and that he had to be saved no matter what. And so she did.

Neither Molly nor Tensley had been opposed to the help.

Finally, the warlock stepped back and bowed her head deeply. "You are healed, my king," she said softly, her voice almost a whisper. So soothing, a wave of calm washed over Molly's nerves and sadness. "I would advise you to rest for a few days, your Highness. The hole was much deeper than I anticipated. The healing chants could heal parts of it but not all. It still needed stitches in the end. Within a few days, you should have fully recovered." Tensley nodded once, barely acknowledging her, and she straightened and gathered her supplies.

As the warlock neared Molly on her way out, she whispered softly: "Thank you for healing him." A smile had barely appeared on the warlock's lips, when a frown appeared between her softly arched brows.

"Now is not maybe the right time to bring this forward, milady, but intimacy could also help the healing process," she said, just as a cruel, vicious laugh resonated through the room. The sound a promise of dark lust and sin. Molly shivered as the warlock quickly left the room.

Leaving Molly and her husband alone, for the first time.

Molly watched Tensley's back as he did the buttons of his dress shirt.

She bit the inside of her cheek. The breeze was cool from outside, but Molly felt heat burn her skin. An inferno roared inside of her being. Deep inside the creases of her heart.

A war, a flame, a vow.

He's in there.

You just need to find him.

She grappled with her mixed emotions. He was breathing, he was standing right in front of her. For now, it was enough. He could have died but he hadn't. There was still hope.

"You're staring," that husky familiar voice jolted her out of her thoughts and she gawked at his back. His suit had been so perfectly fitted, it looked as if it had been molded to his powerful body. The fabric seemed to be stretched beyond its capacity, and each time his muscles flexed, it seemed to grow even tighter. Yet, it never ripped.

Molly licked at her dry lips and took a step forward unsure of how she was meant to act around this new, strange man. As she edged closer, she raised her hand.

She wanted to feel him—feel his muscles flex and the movement of his calm breathing. She wanted to believe he wasn't a mirage, a trick to her mind to cope with the grief of his death.

One touch.

One single finger.

The doors of the chamber pounded against the wall and Molly yanked her hand back and turned to see two guards entering the room like they owned it.

"The queen has required your presence in the throne room to discuss matters, Mr. Knight," one of them announced. The name he had used to refer to Tensley had clearly been meant as an insult to the king. Tensley's face stayed ruled by cold indifference, but Molly could sense the wave of anger beneath the surface.

He was King. Or the beast was.

But that didn't mean Lilith didn't still think of herself as queen.

And some seemed to believe the same.

Tensley gave them one long look, an unwavering stare, and his hand clenched at his side. For an instant, she thought he was going to explode once more and let the beast take full control of himself, but to her surprise, he started moving with a graceful stride. Tensley led the way and Molly walked behind him down the darkened hallways, the sun setting, the first day of his rebirth almost done. A nightmare she wished she could wake up from.

To flutter her eyes open and find the man she had fallen so dangerously hard for.

To own his smiles and his delicious scowls.

As they neared the throne room, the vicious voices grew louder with each step. Lilith's voice was twisted into a shriek of anger and wrath. The court was arguing and it was clear what they were debating.

How to overthrow Tensley.

A death wish, she wanted to say as she shook her head.

She swallowed down the thickening emotion in her throat and stepped into the throne room.

A room tight with anger and panic, each court member turning to icy stone as they laid eyes on their new king. The court grew deadly silent, their bravery turning to ashes in Tensley's thudding footfalls.

Lilith sat on her throne next to Fallen's empty one, and with a face full of venom and rage, her hands gripping the golden trim. She acted as if she owned the throne she was sitting on, and every inch of the palace.

"The court was waiting," Lilith said, lowly, but with a razor sharp edge that Molly knew she aimed to make them bleed.

Tensley stood in the middle of the room, chin high, shoulders back, and his eyes trained on Lilith. The longer he stared, the more she fidgeted with her dress, her hands digging deeper into the golden trim of her throne. It was shaped to represent a lion roaring.

Fitting, Molly thought.

"If you wish to see another day, do not dare summon me like this again. I am not one of your pets," Tensley spat, his anger thickening the air around them.

"My lord," Lilith spoke, her head at last lowering in submission. "I apologize for my forwardness." Her tone seemed truthful enough, but it was her eyes that made Molly's stomach twist in rejection. Dark and shining, like smoke under a glass.

Obedient in appearances, but a rage stronger than her common sense fueled her.

Lilith straightened in her throne, gesturing with a flick of her wrist to the rest of the members standing in front of her. "I asked for your presence here because we were discussing what should be done," she said gesturing wildly toward the king. "With this situation."

"Done?" Molly frowned at her, and as if the members had forgotten she existed, they turned to face her.

Lilith's features pinched in a scowl. "Yes. A vote needs to be taken for who will take the throne. The crown. And the chosen one will be crowned after the mourning period has ended after our late king's death."

Molly's stomach dropped into a pit of darkness. If someone else became king…what would that mean for them? Would that new king kill them? If the Prince took the crown, would he let them go?

"A vote." Molly laughed, the sound empty and dry. "If the conversation you were having before we arrived was any indication, it seems to me as if the decision was already made. You decided long ago that the Dux of Scorpios was not your king. Look at yourself, staring down at us like you own us all. I must applaud your bravery, Lilith," she spat and smiled darkly, the name used as an insult. "You don't stop at anything to get what you want. Do you want your son to obtain the throne because you truly believe he will be the best ruler over these people, or is he simply a way for you to give your filthy hands an easy access to power?" she finished, a brow arching in dismay.

Lilith's mouth was nothing but a thin, white line. Before she could speak, Molly cut her off again.

"Speaking of which, where *is* your son? If we are meant to be 'discussing what should be done' as you so gracefully put it," she continued with a sarcastic turn of her lips. "Shouldn't he be present? To cast his own vote." She finished, the last word tasting foul in her own mouth.

Everyone in the room knew there would be no vote. The outcomes had been chosen long before they had arrived in the throne room.

Her eyes shifted from Lilith to the empty throne beside hers, the gold crown that sat on it caught her attention. A symbol of power and fear, of what her future would be if that crown fell upon Tensley's dark head.

Her breath rushed in her head, low and fast.

Lilith's dry voice shattered Molly's dark thoughts. "I was told my son was indisposed," she said, displeasure written all over her face. "But that is all beside the point. We are here to discuss the future of this court, not the whereabouts of the prince," she added with disdain before turning her head toward the king, dismissing Molly. "You murdered our king," she said after a beat of silence, her voice slicing through Molly's anger.

She so badly wanted to reach out whether it was to slice her claws down Lilith's face or to grip Tensley's wrist for support, she didn't know.

So instead, she fisted her hand and punctured the tender skin of her palm.

Patience, she told herself.

Molly bit her lip and moved forward to stand beside Tensley, glaring at Lilith.

"He won by tradition," a lord spoke, stepping up to the throne. A few other members nodded and murmured their agreement. "Tradition created by Fallen himself. He fell on his own sword."

"Tradition?" Lilith's face turned a bright red full of rage and the golden trim under her fingers groaned in protest.

"He is our king now, my lady," another lord said, face disfigured from war and fire, and he held the handle of his long sword.

"He is not our king," one spat back, gesturing to Tensley with a shaking arm.

Tensley, in the midst of the heated argument, was deadly silent. He didn't move and he didn't interject. So, so silent.

Too silent.

"You can give up the crown," Lilith said, her wide violent eyes trained on Tensley. "You have no interest in our politics. Your interests lie with Scorpios. Why sully our court when you hate all who are a part of it. Vengeance? The king's body is now cold and unmoving. You had your vengeance. Leave my court. Let the real king reign."

Silence.

Each member of the court watched Tensley carefully.

"My son should be the king," Lilith continued, standing up in her gown of red, fitted perfectly to mold around her full figure. A madman's craving. "He grew up within this palace. Played with some of your young," she said, looking at the members of her court. "He lived each day of his life a step behind his father, analyzing, calculating, waiting for this day to come. He was born to rule this court. Will we let disdainful foreigners," she continued, the last word making a few people squirm in discomfort. "Lead us? Rule over us? How could you rule us when you cannot even rule Scorpios without them dying? As queen, I must look out for my people, and I tell you all, this wild animal is not the right choice for the future of our court."

Silence.

No one spoke.

Molly didn't want Tensley to be the king. She didn't want him to be tied forever to the High Court. What would it mean for Scorpios? For his family? For her? For their child? If she took him away from here, she could heal him. She could bring him back without any powerful eyes watching their every movement.

This wouldn't be the right environment for him.

It was toxic.

"The crown is rightfully mine," Tensley's voice of steel and venom slashed through the room. "And your pitiful opinion on what is right and what is wrong will not be needed in *my* court."

Molly's knees shook, but she took even deep breaths and raised her chin high.

"You low-bred bastard," Lilith hissed and stepped far too close, her nose aligned with his. Her anger fumed, consuming everything in her path and she swung her arm, her palm open. "I will destroy—"

Tensley moved like a predator, his hand jolting and wrapping so tightly around Lilith's swan-like throat that she choked on a shriek.

The court froze, including Molly as she gawked at Lilith's olive skin turning pale, then very, very dark. A wave of aggressive pheromones stormed the throne room, suffocating them in anger and rage and relentlessness.

Molly gripped her chest, shaking her head at the man before her.

The Tensley she knew, as much as he hated a woman, would never show such violence toward them.

"Tensley," Molly whispered, finding her voice. When he simply stared at Lilith's blue face, her long fingers clawing at his fisted hand, Molly stepped closer to their two bodies. "Tensley, stop," she almost shouted, her eyes filling up with tears as she realized just how far gone her Tensley was. And as much as she hated the woman he was aiming to kill, she would never let him do this. The crowd around them started to whisper nervously, a few guards moving dangerously forward, weapons drawn, ready to attack.

This was all going very, very wrong.

"Don't do this. This is not you. You would never do this. Let her go," she whispered softly, her words meant only for his ears even though she knew Lilith could hear every word. She put her hand on his arm, his muscles flinching under her fingers as if the thought of her touching him whilst in this state disgusted him. She held in her tears. "Please," she said hurriedly, seeing as Lilith seemed to be dangerously close to her end.

"Don'tdothistoyourself.Lethergo,Tensley,"shesaiddesperately,hisgazeand mindstillinaplacefar,faraway. "Lethergo," sherepeated,hervoiceatlastbreaking. Tensley's head snapped to her and she saw the deep darkness of his eyes, a terrifying storm wreaking havoc on his soul. Or what was left of it anyway.

Seconds dragged on until Tensley let Lilith go and she collapsed, bending over as she drew in deep, loud breaths. Her face contorted in pain as the oxygen rushed through her lungs again.

Tensley took heavy, even footsteps forward, eyeing her. "I am your king," he roared, the castle's walls trembling under his wrath.

The beast was ruled by his extreme emotions. One wrong move, he exploded like a bomb.

Lilith nodded viciously and a second later, she gasped out of breath. She found Tensley's hand and pressed her violent red lips to his knuckles.

She tried to smash her worries with a shake of her head.

Lilith's eyes fluttered open and she stared up at him. "I will serve you, my king." Lilith's raspy voice sounded so raw and broken, Molly had the urge to grip her own throat to soothe the ache.

Tensley flexed his hand and slid it out of her grip, moving back. He scanned the room, eyeing his subjects slowly. "Do not cross me and you won't feel my wrath."

Each member bowed their heads, their left hands resting on their chest, a sign of submission and obedience. *What was Tensley turning into...*

"My king," Lilith sung. Molly frowned at her drastic switch. She was trying to get on his good side. Lilith edged closer, her eyes running down his tall frame. "We will have a feast. To celebrate you as our new king. So powerful, so beautiful, so deadly, they will chant."

Two-faced bitch, Molly wanted to spit out.

Tensley stared at her, then nodded, turning to leave the room. Molly caught Lilith's eye, and the sweet smile dropped to one of evil.

Molly's eyes flashed bright and that destroyed any trace of a smile on the queen's face.

She'd destroy her if she thought she could manipulate her man with smiles and sweet words.

chapter three

MOLLY SAT ON a throne of gold, seated next to the new king. Being presented like this, in front of the court, set her on edge. The atmosphere was toxic and heavy.

But after Tensley's earlier display of power, no one fought against him.

Candles flickered high in the crystal chandeliers, darkness creeping across the paintings depicting victories battled by Fallen. Their now fallen king.

The court members sat at long wood tables decorated with white silk tablecloths, dressed in rich gowns to display their power and wealth in court. The more gold, the more beautiful silk, the higher one appeared in court.

Molly watched as Lilith, for the fifth time since they sat down for their feast, leaned toward Tensley, her fingers touching his wrist.

Molly's blood boiled, but she calmed herself. She wouldn't lower herself to Lilith's childish games.

Tensley didn't acknowledge Lilith, staring darkly at the hall before him. Like he was calculating something, like something stirred within him and he vowed to find the cause.

As Lilith, her mouth twisting ruefully, sat back, Molly glimpsed at the people around them. It was when her eyes found one of the royal guards that suddenly, she remembered, and her breath caught deep within her throat.

Seto...

In the midst of everything, Molly hadn't noticed Seto's disappearance when Fallen had caught them trying to escape. What had happened to him? Where was he? Was he...

Her eyes found the prince.

He watched Tensley carefully, his right hand clenching and unclenching on the edge of the long table. His smooth blond hair was tied loosely back by a leather thong, a few wavy strands framing his angular features of a demon and angel mixed to create something ethereally beautiful.

His sharp quicksand eyes darted to her and his jaw quivered under gritting teeth.

Tensley had gone against the prince's bargain and now he was king. A king who wielded complete control over a court of serpents and wolves.

But Molly didn't understand why he hadn't given up the throne.

Was it the beast? Did the beast want absolute power? Did it feed off of viciousness and domination? Was it the reason why he was unable to give up the crown?

Lilith had been right about one thing; Tensley had made it clear time and time again he wanted nothing to do with the High Court.

Yet, here he was, the king of it all.

Molly turned her attention back to her husband, watching him stare at his court. His hand cupped his jaw, a single finger stroking his bottom lip in deep thought.

With a delicate touch, she laid her fingers on his wrist. "Are you okay?"

He glanced at her, those shimmering obsidian eyes slashing into her core, taking the air out of her lungs. A look that told her he was calculating if she was a threat.

"I'm fine," he bit out.

As if he had given her an electric shock, she drew back her hand.

Sadness weighed in her heart, sinking lower into emptiness and despair.

But pride and anger rang louder.

She folded up her napkin, rose from her chair, and strolled away.

Members of the court watched her closely, burning the back of her head, but she continued to walk.

She needed air and she needed to show the court she wasn't affected. That Tensley's heartless self didn't break her own.

Walking through the open balcony doors, she gripped the iron railing and let the cool breeze assault her scorching cheeks.

A thousand thoughts—worries buzzed in her head. Finishing school, Scorpios, the baby in her belly, and her now heartless husband. Only the thought of school seemed so ridiculous now, with everything that had happened since she had last sat in a classroom. Her life had gone to hell and back.

She breathed out shakily and fisted her hand on the railing. She couldn't break down. She had to be strong. She had to be strong for both of them. Her hand touched her stomach.

For all of them.

"My lady," a sensual voice called to her.

She turned to see the prince approaching behind her.

She regarded him carefully, eyeing his own fisted hands and the pinch of his mouth.

"Or should I call you my queen?" There was a bite to his voice and she didn't like it. When she didn't respond, he licked at his teeth and glanced back to the hall. "It seems though my mother has gladly continued that role to your husband."

Her anger flared and she noted his faint smile.

"She is not the queen," she said, calmly, but nothing inside of her was calm. She didn't understand why she was so possessive.

He quirked a brow and moved closer, with the carefulness of a predator on the hunt. "And you wish to be queen? Queen of us cruel demons?"

She exhaled harshly. "I have no desire to be queen, but if he's—" Her eyes dropped to her intertwined hands. "I don't want any of this. I only want him."

"Then we can find a way to return him," the prince said.

Molly's head jerked up. "Return him?"

He now stood in front of her, his chest so close to warring against her own and his warm breath fanned across her fine strands across her hairline. "Return his heart."

Molly's breath seemed to leave her body altogether, she gripped the railing she had been holding on tighter so she wouldn't fall.

"How," she said, the cracked word barely above a whisper. She couldn't believe it, she couldn't…

"After the fight, I realized the beast was in complete control of him. He'll be provoked by anything, once the emotions take over, he can't stop himself. But I am not a stupid man, Molly. I knew your husband, as he used to be, never wanted the throne. So today, I went in search of a solution. A cure. Anything. Anything that could possibly bring back his heart. And I might have found something."

As Molly was about to ask more, a cry was heard nearby as a drunken couple stumbled toward the balcony. Their cheeks were flushed, the woman giggling uncontrollably as the man licked his way up her neck. She stumbled forward crying out, both of them crashing into a wall. They laughed some more as they started feeling across each other's bodies.

Even though the couple hadn't realized they weren't alone on the balcony, Molly knew what she had been about to ask the prince couldn't be discussed near prying ears.

And as she looked back at him, she knew he thought the same.

"I'll return his heart," he whispered, his fingers skimming her bare arm and upward. "And you will return the throne to me."

She swallowed thickly. Her heart propelled her forward, but she hesitated. A bargain with the prince.

"I'll think about it," she said with resolve and a high chin.

The prince's eyes darkened and his fingers moved forward, brushing across her neck, from one side of her collar, all the way to the other. She flinched, the shock of pain almost bringing her to her knees. The prince smiled darkly, a sensual laugh leaving the barrier of his lips. "With pain comes pleasure, little daemon, you only need to embrace it."

She frowned deeply, stepping away from him. Tensley had once explained to her this was an incredibly disrespectful act. It was strictly forbidden for a male to touch the collar on another male's mate.

And he had just touched the collar his king had put on his mate.

"What are you doing?" she snapped.

"Tempting the beast," the prince bit out and let go. "He needs a relief, to let off some steam. I just gave him a reason to," he said, his voice a low rumble in his chest as the sensual smile reappeared on his lips.

A roar rang through the darkness and the prince was brutally thrown against the brick wall of the palace.

His back arched at a painful angle and Molly watched in horror as Tensley, her husband, slashed his hands across the prince's torso.

The prince hissed in pain, but he didn't falter.

He propelled his body forward, his weight crashing into Tensley, throwing them both into the heavy, detailed railing. The force of the impact breaking it down the middle, as the cement crumbled with a thunderous sound.

Members in their fancy silk and diamonds crept into the sight of two members of the royalty fighting with the brutality of two unfed, raging beasts.

They probably thought this was entertaining.

Molly wrapped an arm around her stomach, watching in horror as the two men clawed and nipped at each other like animals.

Eyes dark as ash, bodies radiating those powerful aggressive pheromones like acid, and their teeth elongated and sharpened, ready to slash at any given opportunity.

Wounds still fresh from Fallen's battle reopened and blood spilled down Tensley's side, an ugly streak forming across his white dress shirt.

Tensley snarled and slammed his fist into the prince's nose, an awful crack of bone and blood spluttered.

The force of the prince's following snarl made Molly's blood run cold, she swallowed with difficulty. Suddenly, despite his pain, the prince moved quickly, his hand clawing at Tensley's cheek, deep enough that flesh hung loosely, blood dripping everywhere.

"Stop," Molly screamed, the sound ripping through her throat. She gripped Tensley's bicep with all the strength she could muster before he could lunge for the prince again.

The prince, still on the defense, braced himself, growling deeply.

Tensley stilled, but she felt his muscles flex under her grip. The one thing that told her he was still affected by her was that jackrabbit pulse against her fingertips.

"You have no authority over me, Dux," the prince spat.

"Disrespect me again, touch her, go near her, even glance at her, and I'll rip your throat out," Tensley snapped, his teeth bared in warning.

The prince licked at the blood on his lip and sneered, not saying a word, but staring right into Tensley's eyes, his gaze cold and unwavering.

She glanced at the crowd as they all stared back at her. She made sure they couldn't see how much she wanted to cringe under their weighted stare in that moment. She knew exactly what they had witnessed because she had seen the same.

A possessive beast.

And she, the daemon, his wife.

The only thing that could possibly hurt him, weaken him.

Tensley spun, his large hand wrapping around her bicep tightly, but not enough to hurt, and moved them fast through the gathered crowd. Almost tripping over her own feet a few times as she tried to keep up.

Once they reached their bedroom, he threw open the door and let go of her, stomping into the middle of the large room.

She stayed by the door, trying to decipher his emotions.

She used to be able to tell what he was thinking, how he was feeling. Now, he was nothing but an unpredictable predator, even to her.

"He disrespected me," he hissed, his hands rolling into fists beside him. "When he dared to touch your collar—" He swore under his breath.

Molly's fingertips ghosted over the collar Tensley had put on and shivered. The moment the prince touched her there, she felt the painful shock.

Only when Tensley touched her collar did she feel absolute pleasure.

Tensley paused, noting an envelope on the desk and she watched him rip it open. She eyed his expression as he read it, his brows furrowing and then he slammed the letter down and growled. He punched the wall, making Molly jump.

The letter slipped off the desk and she bent, straightening it to read what it was about.

Tensley,

Ares has attacked again. Twelve casualties, many more missing and injured. Please come home as soon as possible. We need you.

Your mother.

Molly gripped her throat. Ares had attacked again and killed more. She dropped the letter, her emotions weighing her down.

He rolled up his sleeves and popped the two top buttons of his collar. Then he busied himself with pouring whisky and downing it in one go.

Like he was himself.

Like he was her Tensley.

Except, he had blood dripping all over him, and deep cuts that would need to be healed quickly or they would undoubtedly leave terrible scars.

Except, she couldn't forget that he had gotten so bloody to begin with.

How he had gotten so bloody.

Because he had no control over himself.

Because of the heartless beast he had become.

She shook her head, her eyes closing briefly at the thought.

He was there, he was somewhere in there, she knew it.

She could feel it.

And as he drank his whisky, appearing so calm and collected, as if none of it had happened, she couldn't help but want to help him, hold him, love him.

…she missed him so much.

She moved toward him, her shoes the only sound in the room.

He poured more whisky and gulped it down, throwing his head back and gasping afterward.

His eye caught her approaching tentatively and he turned, the ugly marks across his cheek and busted lip sending her stomach dropping.

"You're hurt," she whispered, gesturing to his face and the ugly deep gash across his cheekbone, fresh blood mixing with old, crusty blood deep within the cuts.

She shivered.

He licked along his teeth and stared at her, as if unfazed by the damage.

She warred with herself; her mind telling her to not be unrealistic, and her heart telling her something completely different.

"I can heal it, if you want," she said, softly.

Again, he stared at her longer than she was comfortable with.

After more time passed, his eyes became darker, his lips twisting into a frown as he lifted his short cup and downed the last drop.

He gasped again, slammed it down on the edge of the table so it clanked, buzzing in the room, and turned to face her.

His fingers moved with ease, slow and steady, undoing each button of his shirt, with those sullen eyes unmoving from her.

She didn't look away, but she felt the bloom of heat on her cheeks, down to her chest.

At the sight of his exposed muscular torso, strips of muscles flexing, twisting as he rolled his torn shirt off his shoulders, her mouth grew bone dry.

Damn hormones.

And at the sight of the fresh vicious scar that was left from his heart being ripped out of him, her own heart sunk a little deeper within herself.

"Dolcezza," he murmured, creating an avalanche of shivers across her tender skin. Her eyes darted to his.

This was the first time since he had become the wild beast that he had acknowledged her directly. And he had used the endearment he always used when speaking to her. Not as if she mattered, not as if he cared. Or as if he too remembered and craved what they once were.

No.

As if he was mocking her.

And damned she might be, she couldn't help but feel the burn of attraction, of lust, deep within her belly.

A smirk that drove her insane and fueled her appeared on his lips.

"You still crave me, I see. But you always craved the beast more, didn't you?" he said, his voice dripping with a wild, dark lust that resonated deep inside her, igniting a raging fire.

She knew this was the beast talking. And unlike before, there was certainly no hidden heart deep within him.

She scowled and straightened, ignoring her hunger for him. "Sit down." She gestured to the bed.

He hesitated, not looking away from her, but finally moved to the bed, sitting down on it.

His legs spread out, the fabric of his pants straining against his thick thighs of steel.

She stood in front of him, and with a careful touch, she smoothed her shaking hand across his damaged cheek.

His eyes squeezed shut at the sensation, one she felt, as her energy drained from her and into him.

A stream of seduction, a flutter of want.

When his hands found her hips, she gasped, partly because she hadn't expected the touch, partly because she felt as if it had been so long. Just him touching her, fueled the need to believe it was him.

Maybe, maybe if she kissed him…

She licked her lips and dipped her head. First, she kissed his swollen eyelid, staying there until all the purple and blue had dissolved. His eyes opened and darkened as her lips met his.

Soft, gentle teasing of the familiar.

His hand slipped up her neck and up into her hair.

And it felt like she was finally home.

It's Tensley.

It's Tensley.

And on a single whimper from her mouth, he grew vicious.

The kiss was violent, powerful—and everything she needed.

She needed him—and even if he was the beast, she'd take what she could get.

Tensley.

Tensley.

Her frantic hands clawed against his taut back and he pulled her down on top of him.

She wanted to forget. She wanted to forget everything that happened within the last twenty-four hours and imagine everything was fine.

He smelled the same, masculine and heavy smoke, and he tasted like whisky and sin, and his lips moved like war, conquering and unrelenting, vicious to the core.

And she was overtaken. It felt like home.

She laid on top of his powerful frame, his fingers smoothing down her sides to her derrieve, a soothing, sensual touch of a man who knew her body well.

His fingers dug into her ass cheeks and she groaned deeply. In one single movement, he flipped her onto her back, hovering above her.

She gasped, her heart galloping in her chest. His wounds were healed, the perfect complexion back, the bruises faded, and the skin mended.

His eyes were still dark coals of emptiness.

He stole her mouth in another kiss, but suddenly, it tasted foreign. A mixture of familiar and strange battled in her senses and mind, and she pulled back.

An awful tension expanded in her chest, battling, fighting for her to stay sane.

"No, no," Molly said, and Tensley sat back as she faced away from him, her hands running frantically through her hair.

Her finger toyed with her bottom lip.

She wanted him back—she wanted him to hold her, to kiss her, to whisper her name, but all she had was emptiness.

There was no love in his touch. No care. Only a dark sort of desire.

Like she was simply something to use in order to satisfy himself.

He was an imposter, living and breathing and destroying her heart.

"I can't," she said in a soft breath. She shook her head and turned to face him, hoping, praying, she'd see a different man.

He stood by the edge of the bed, head raised high like a superior, those calculating eyes holding no emotion, no truth, no warmth.

"You fucked me once," he bit out and it felt as if he had slapped her.

Her heart cracked and bled.

Her desire turned to white-hot anger and swept over her body. Sadness seeped into her bones and crushed them to dust.

The pain hit her so deeply, she knew it wouldn't go away.

She blinked back any warmth and settled her wobbling mouth with a scowl. "You are not the Tensley I know and fell in love with. But let me make something very clear here. I do not care what I have to do, I *will* get your heart. I will bring back the man I love. I will do anything, even if I have to bleed for it or go to war. The heart you lost was mine, and I don't like losing things that belong to me."

The corner of Tensley's mouth twitched. "Tame me then. Soothe the rage. Hush the anger. I know what you want—and that you still crave me like the whore you always were for me. Try, and we'll then see who comes out victorious."

And with that, Tensley left the room, shirtless, slamming the door behind him.

Molly sunk into the silk sheets, emotionally bruised. No kiss would heal her broken heart.

She clutched at her dress, the other hand pressed to her trembling lips.

The man she once kissed was long gone.

Denial was dead.

He wasn't in there, but she'd find him.

She wasn't giving up, wasn't giving up hope.

She let her hands fall and fisted the covers, tears fell down her cheeks and onto the silky sheets.

Hell had a new king; and he was bloodthirsty.

chapter four

THE BEAST MARCHED the golden glimmering halls, the darkness seeping into each corner of his being. Infecting his host with his wrath and thirst for power and dominance, pushing the man that once was, deeper and deeper until his voice felt like nothing more than a distant souvenir. It fed the beast, the pain, the fear, the rage...her sweet desire. He wanted more, always more. Rejection sat bitterly on his tongue, but her sweet taste still lingered, making the wrath inside of him stir unresolved.

He wanted something to destroy.

He wanted the chaos inside of him painted on the palace walls. A chaos that would plague and burn a man to ashes. A chaos that left a residue of pain and rage.

As much as he wished to have her, to feel her soft flesh against his own warred skin, the beast knew not to strike her, not to bruise her, or she'd be gone.

She held a power inside of her that kings and gods sought, fought for centuries to conquer, but even the beast knew not to battle that ancient strength. And along with that intriguing power, the beast knew that within the daemon's womb, grew his son. He knew, because he could feel his own power echoing wildly, beating powerfully within the strong heart of his brood. A heart. The beast's son had a heart and it confused him.

Nonetheless, whenever he caught sight of the daemon's womb, fear and possession filled him until it was all he could see and feel. She would have to be guarded, kept safe and well. Any man or woman who threatened her would be met with his wrath.

The beast was getting restless, he was craving her, but he forced himself to stay back because he knew what the woman had done. She had controlled him, controlled his heart. With the thought, he clawed at his chest uncomfortably, a simmering, unrelenting rage brewing from deep within him. He clawed, as if he could still feel the ghost of a heart beating wildly for her and wanted to rip it out himself. The cuts weren't deep, and healed quickly with each swipe he took at himself.

He marched the halls, his chest heavy with a burning anger that only gods held within them.

"He's a bastard king and an insult to our court," he heard a man's voice faintly hiss from somewhere nearby.

He slowed, edging into the shadows, the darkness swallowing him, welcoming him, and he waited.

Monsters lurked in the dark after all, he thought with a dark smile as he watched a group of lords walk into the hallway.

"He's a disgrace, we should lock him up and leave him to rot for his offenses," another snapped.

"He's heartless, is that not what we value in our people?" a larger man spoke, earning hard stares from the previous lords.

"Not one who fell from grace by the likes of a whore," the first said back, his voice carrying through the halls.

"My lords," Lilith's soft voice cracked the tension between the men as she approached, touching one of their shoulders. "Do not fear. If there is one thing we know about heartless demons, it's that they are driven by their purest, most violent emotions. They are blinded by them, controlled by them. Anger, fear, dominance, but most importantly... desire. Need," she said with a vicious smile. "What does a beast need? What does it crave the most? More so than food and water?" She lifted her narrow chin proudly, elongating her neck, and flashed her teeth.

The men murmured.

The answer was there.

A man craved a woman.

"I will control him as I controlled my late husband and I will see to it that the *whore* stays far away from him," she spoke. "We will meet later tomorrow to discuss more of this."

The men spoke lowly to her and ventured off. Lilith began walking toward where he lurked in the shadows, unaware of his presence. Her appearance and posture showing a proper lady, but the beast knew what lay beneath her creamy skin.

A snake.

Just as she turned, she gasped at the sight of him half-hidden in the shadows. Her cheeks lost their color quickly and she fidgeted with her large golden necklace. Her collar—one that the court could see was gone since Fallen's death. She was unmarked, unclaimed now.

"My lord," she whispered, her eyes tracing his figure, want and desire flowing out of her like a deadly poison. He growled darkly, sending aggressive pheromones her way and stepped forward, his entire presence sucking anything happy or light into a dark vortex.

She caught her breath and he noted the slight lick to her bottom lip as she drank him in. "I enjoyed your fury today. Your fierceness to our court. It is refreshing to see a beast so vicious in every sense of the word."

She took a gentle step forward and as soon as she touched his wrist, he felt the disgust, the rage wrap tightly around his throat and chest and he growled again.

He growled lowly enough that Lilith's fingers dropped in shock and her eyes moved back up to his shadowy features. But the woman was not deterred, only want and viciousness could be seen within her eyes.

"Did you know a beast's wrath can consume him if not taken care of?" she asked. "And seeing as you are not with your bride, I must assume she failed to soothe you."

She again went to touch his arm, but he flashed his teeth and growled louder this time, gripping her wandering hand with a tight, bruising clench.

"Do not fucking touch me again, or you will regret it dearly," he snarled in warning, lessening his grip after a while. "I may crave a woman, but it isn't you."

She jerked her hand back, gawking at him. A mean scowl now laced her features, but before she could say another word, he moved past her.

The beast only craved the one thing that was lethal to him, the one thing that could bend and destroy him until he begged her to do it again.

The beast would not be tamed.

Not by anyone and not by his sweet daemon.

Never again.

MOLLY MARCHED THROUGH the ancient halls of the High Court. Women stalled in their steps, turning to watch their king's wife move on a warpath.

She needed answers.

She needed a solution, a fix, and she'd do anything to get it.

A guard stood outside of a set of French doors and he tensed, his suit of armor clanking as he set eyes on her.

"My lady," he said, slightly bowing his head. "How can I help you?"

Molly didn't stop. She moved past him and threw open the French doors, setting eyes on the man inside of the tousled silk sheets.

The prince laid on his stomach, asleep, the sheets tossed across his legs, but hiding nothing. Molly turned away quickly, closing the door behind her so the guard wouldn't hear a word they were about to discuss. She moved to the large set of windows, brusquely opening the rich, embroidered drapes. The light poured in, and she heard a vicious growl coming from the bed.

"Put some clothes on, we have a conversation to finish," Molly demanded, her eyes directed at the high ceilings.

The prince grumbled, still half asleep. From the corner of her eyes, she saw him turning slowly onto his back both of his arms resting lazily over his head.

He was completely naked, staring at her from across the room, his front on display for all to see. He seemed in no rush to do as she had asked and put some clothes on. Molly kept her eyes firmly trained on the floor.

"You certainly know how to choose your moments to make an entry, little daemon, don't you?" he rasped, his voice still low and roughened from sleep. "If you wanted to enjoy my body, you only had to ask."

Molly rolled her eyes. "Put some clothes on."

He laughed, then ever so slowly got up, walking to a chair nearby, on which a pair of trousers had been slung messily and sheathed a dagger on his hip. He offered her his back as he put them on. Once she knew he was decent, she turned toward him fully.

"We have a conversation to finish," she repeated. "About Tensley."

She noted the ugly cut across his jaw, one left by Tensley the night before.

"You mean the possessive bastard?" He tsked. "The entire court saw it. Surely, it's not very wise for the little daemon to be found alone in another male's room the day after he went all beastly on said man?" he said, looking at her with sarcasm written all over his face. He moved slowly, like a lion tracking its prey. But Molly wasn't prey.

She was the predator.

"Perhaps you shouldn't stray too far away from your king," he added, shrugging nonchalantly.

"And why is that?"

"Because now they know what makes the beast tick," the prince spoke lowly, tilting his head as he scanned her face. "The one thing he still values. His mate and his child." His eyes fell to her stomach between them.

She glared up at him. "You said last night you could return his heart."

The prince stepped back, his fingers rubbing along his jaw. "Yes, yes I did."

He moved to his balcony, stretching his arms to soak in the warm morning sun.

Molly fisted her hands and took a deep breath. "What's your plan to save Tensley?"

His arms froze above his sun-bleached hair and he turned, the smugness he usually wore gone. "You do realize this will be incredibly dangerous, right?"

"You want the throne," Molly said, her tone holding enough bite. "I want him back."

The stone of his face melted to welcome his lazy, sensual smile. The smile of the devil. "Shall we then?" He gripped a tossed shirt on the bed and threw it on.

He moved past her, messily shoving his dress shirt into his trousers. When they passed the guard, the guard gave them a hard look.

Together, they walked the halls. An odd sight to some, but she didn't care. Men raised their brows, the ladies sneered at her. After what had happened last night, the prince was probably right, it wasn't particularly wise for them to be seen more or less alone together.

"The court will talk," the prince whispered, and Molly glanced up at him.

"Yeah," she shrugged. "I thought they might."

"The prince escorting their king's wife to and from. That's sure to get their tongues going," he said with a smirk.

She quickened her pace. "I don't care what they think."

He caught her wrist and redirected her down another hall, stopping in front of old wooden doors. Worn down by the years, cobwebs twisting up the carved designs of ivy cascading the length.

"Brace yourself," he said, shooting her a cocky smile as he took out from his pocket a skeleton key, discolored and large. He twisted it, the sound of a dozen lock mechanisms turning and moving.

Then he budged it open.

Inside the massive room were shelves and shelves of books. Dimly lit by the rare sunlight sneaking through the dark heavy curtains, the room looked like it hadn't been touched for decades.

"This was my father's private library," the prince commented as she edged her way through the shelves. "When I couldn't sleep, I used to steal books from here and read them," he continued, looking around the place with a small smile playing at the corners of his lips. Specks of dust were flying everywhere around them, Molly's nose wiggled with the need to sneeze. "Which, in retrospective, was probably a terrible idea. These books have been hidden here, from everyone, for centuries for a reason."

The prince walked around the room, silent in appearance but his mind no doubt racing with thoughts. He approached a particular shelf, his finger ever so slowly gliding across the spine of one of the old novels. "They are all extremely powerful, Molly. Holding too many secrets, too many dangerous threats to my father's life, to our people, to this world. So he banished them, hid them from everyone, even from me. But I found them anyway." He explained with a wry smile. "I will always find what is trying to hide from me, no matter how well they're hidden. I crave the hunt. I always have. And I never come back empty handed. That is, until a month ago." He added after a beat, no doubt thinking about the Hunt that had taken place a few weeks ago when Molly and Tensley had first arrived at the High Court. The prince had tried to capture Molly, but hadn't succeeded.

Molly followed behind him, watching as he started looking for something, his gaze roaming wildly over the numerous dusty books on the shelves. After what seemed like minutes, he started muttering to himself, swearing under his breath, as if he had completely forgotten her presence.

"What are you looking for exactly?"

He didn't answer at first, his abnormally dark brows drawn in concentration. They were a stark contrast to his wild, shoulder length blond hair.

"A curse to demons," he explained, almost whispering the words as if speaking them aloud could cause him great pain. He straightened, swore loudly this time, and moved to the next few rows.

She frowned at him. "A curse to demons?"

"Yes."

She shook her head. "But we don't want to—"

"Here." The prince yanked out a dusty book, the spine tattered and splitting from the rest of the binding, pages wrinkled and torn.

He opened the book, a cloud of dust blowing into the air. When she looked at the words on the page, she frowned. "That's… a different language," she said, looking at the strange swirls on the paper. They weren't even letters, more like strange-looking drawings and symbols.

"To you lowly humans, yes," he explained, shrugging effortlessly, as if saying Molly was beneath them was simply stating the obvious. She scowled at him. He smiled playfully in return before letting his gaze wonder back to the book, and the words that were written on its pages. "It's one of the deadliest curses known to our kind. It's incredibly old, probably older than the existence of humans themselves, but just as dangerous to your kind," he continued, and she could see his eyes growing agitated at the mere thought of being so close to something so powerful, so utterly final. "This spell could mean the end for a lot of people, it could mean heaven becomes hell, and hell becomes nothing but child's play in comparison. It's so deadly, in fact, that even most warlocks, no matter how old, powerful or how vicious, refuse to speak it."

Molly swallowed, trying to decipher the symbols on the page. A lost cause.

"This book is probably the main reason why my father chose to hide this library from everyone," he whispered. "Because not many things can be a real threat to a king, but this... this could crush one into nothing."

Molly frowned. "If you wanted the throne so bad, why didn't you use this against him."

"Because I am not a stupid man, Molly Darling," he explained, shrugging once more. "Some things should never even be considered options."

"Then why now? Why think of using it now?" she asked, feeling herself growing agitated.

"Because we have well and truly run out of options," he said darkly, eyes growing heavy and wild. "And desperation makes even the most sensitive men grow restless, wild. When there aren't any options left, you create them. No matter how crazy they might be," he finished on the same tone, his finger pointing at the book. "Because it would surely be a threat against him."

"If this is so dangerous, maybe we shouldn't..." she started and a thought suddenly hit her. "Oh my god, you can't possibly mean to kill…" she stopped, a hand flying to her chest and her knees buckled. "No…" she whispered, the word cracking completely.

The prince laughed, the sound loud and vicious. A few bookshelves seemed to rattle, as if curling in on themselves. "No. No, Molly. I do not intend to kill your precious king," he said, and Molly finally started breathing again. "At least not with this curse," he added, but his eyes only held playfulness.

"Then…" she started, swallowing with difficulty. "Then how? How is this supposed to help us without killing him?" she finished, glancing up at him and seeing a muscle in his cheek feather.

In a slow breath, his eyes met hers. "Here," he said, his finger tapping at the edge of a particular line of symbols. "I cannot read this language either, they stopped teaching it to the young, long, long ago to insure we could not read this particular book, but from legends and myths I've heard over the years, I know what this here says." He continued, a deep frown taking place between his brows. "It says: The curse of a heart."

"The curse of a heart," Molly repeated. Slowly, it sunk in. "The ultimate sin of a demon. Destroying him. Make him grow a heart." Hope invaded her chest and she gripped his wrist. "We can get his heart back."

The prince's mouth pinched. "Yes, but we need a warlock willing to speak the curse. It can backfire. Like I said, it can completely destroy not only the target, but also everyone and everything that stands in the way of its wrath. It's an old, vicious curse, it's been sleeping for thousands of years now, and I can only imagine how it would react if woken up by someone who cannot control it."

"Then find a warlock," Molly bit out fast, desperation driving her to a deadly cliff.

The prince eyed her. "That child of his is controlling you."

Her free hand touched her stomach. "What?"

"He's half demon; he's aggressive, he's moody," the prince explained. "Not uncommon for females carrying to go through violent mood swings." He shut the book with a loud smack, the sound resonating like thunder through her soul. More dust flew around them, and the prince placed the book under his armpit as if he was carrying just about any novel, not something so final, so powerful. He rubbed his forehead and let out a sigh. "You want a warlock? I have one, but he's lethal and dangerous in his own way. We let him out of his cage, we'll have to kill him once we're done."

Molly tried to swallow, but the thick lump in her throat prevented her. "Kill him?"

"He went on a rampage centuries ago, murdered half the court by using them like puppets against each other," he explained, shrugging his shoulder as if it meant little.

Molly weighed the options, but her heart was heavier.

"The only question I have for you, little daemon, is; are you ready to kill someone if it means saving your Tensley? Are you ready to jeopardize your life and the life of others, to get him back? You've killed before, haven't you? I can see your hands were once tainted by blood. But are you ready to do it again?" he asked, a dark look roaming through his eyes.

At first, she didn't answer. Taken aback by the question, by everything it implied. But in the darkest, most vile parts of herself, she knew the answer. And so did her heart. "I am," she whispered, heart beating wildly. "I am." And the words sounded so heavy. So final.

"Good," he said, the word sounding short, brusque.

"Are you?" she asked suddenly, surprising herself. "Are you ready to potentially kill your own court and die, just for the chance of getting the throne you so desperately want?"

His eyes seemed to cloud over, getting lost in his own thoughts. Then, after a beat, he looked her straight in the eyes, and said: "Of course," and his smile was pure evil, liquid ash and fiery hunger.

A man who had nothing to lose and had sold his soul to the devil without ever looking back.

She shivered. "Where is he?" she asked, voice barely above a whisper. "The warlock. Where is he?"

His teeth flashed, eyes turning almost black. "The deepest pit of hell."

THE FAMILIAR STENCH of the dungeon sunk deep into her heart and made it bleed all over again. Two days before, Molly had been down in the dungeon with Tensley. Trying to escape. It left a bitter, sour taste in her mouth that she wished she could wash away.

The stench was of rotten flesh and feces sat in for weeks. Perhaps even months. Or years, she thought, almost gagging, as she realized the warlock she was about to pay a visit to had been left there to rot for centuries.

Dear lord…

Each cell they passed, a tired groan greeted them. The few that spoke words or cried out were newer to their tiny prison, she realized.

Molly felt along the brick walls, guiding herself through the maze, following behind the prince as best as she could.

It was so dark she could barely see two feet before her.

The prince suddenly stopped and Molly ran into his back, grunting in pain.

"Here," the prince said, gesturing to a dark cell. Molly moved closer, peering inside, but saw no one.

"I don't see anyone," she whispered.

The prince scowled, took out his sword and banged it across the iron bars. An ugly, violent scream vibrated against the walls. Not of the sword, but of a man shrieking.

A crouched figure stumbled out of the darkness of the cell.

He lifted his head, his hair long and knotted like a rat king, and he smiled. He smiled a toothless grin of anger and insanity.

"Dear prince, who is this fine maiden," the man sung, his voice raspy and mauled. Ancient.

The prince stepped forward. "A friend."

"A friend," he repeated, his beady eyes tracing her figure.

"We need your assistance, Saul," the prince continued and he leaned closer. "In exchange for your freedom from this prison, you must speak a curse."

Saul laughed darkly. "A curse. A curse of what, my prince?" a vile smile appearing on his cracked and bleeding lips. Molly could hear a terrible sound and as she looked at the ancient man, she was convinced it was rotten teeth grinding against each other.

She couldn't get out of this place and away from this man soon enough.

Still, she sucked in a breath, the smell making her knees wobble, and spoke to the warlock.

"The curse of the heart," Molly answered, confident, a touch of venom tainted the words.

Saul's wolf eyes narrowed and his joyful, crazy exterior switched to one of darkness. "You wish to wield that curse?"

"Yes," she said sternly and gripped the bars, her daemon eyes raging as Saul balked at her bravery. "And I want you to destroy that demon until his heart beats so loudly the entire kingdom hears it."

Saul scanned her again, more carefully this time and gritted his teeth. "A daemon." He glanced at her stomach. "A pregnant daemon."

"So what will it be?" the prince asked, his fingers flexing across the handle of his sword.

Saul's eyes turned a darker shade of evil. "Say I did not accept your proposition," he said, a filthy hand shooting out in the air as if having an idea, fingers wiggling. His nails were long, and pitch black with dirt. As if he had tried to carve his way out of the dungeon during all those centuries.

"What would you do?" Saul said wickedly. "No warlock in their right mind will help you. And the heart of your beloved will be forever damned."

How he knew about her and Tensley, she didn't know.

"There is great power lurking in the daemon's womb," he said, dirty nails rubbing back and forth against the remnants of his lips.

"Saul…" the prince warned, his clench tightening around his blade.

"Perhaps, I would like to have a taste of the young," he said, eyes zeroed in on Molly's stomach. "Perhaps, in exchange for my help, I would ask for my magic touch upon the power of the thing," he said, speaking of the baby. Molly placed a protective hand over her stomach. "Perhaps, I would ask to be fed the young, to carry his powers within me."

Before he could say anything else, the prince had the warlock's shirt in his fist, pulled against the bars of the cell, his blade dangerously pressed against Saul's neck. Blood dripped, and fell to the already filthy dirt floor.

"I've grown tired of waiting, Saul," the prince said menacingly. "Very, very tired."

Saul's laugh was heard, but it held no joy. No life. "Patience, little prince, patience. Living under the earth for so many years teaches you some things," he said, voice tight.

The prince pressed the blade even harder and the warlock gurgled, more blood gushing from the wound. "Answer the question. Now," he spat, anger evident. "Help us and be free. Or stay here to rot for centuries more."

Saul's eyes found Molly once more, his gaze traveling down to her stomach. The tip of his tongue came out, licking along his dry lips. "My answer is yes," he said after a beat.

The prince nodded, backing away as more blood gushed from the wound. Molly couldn't keep her eyes away as the warlock spat a few strange-sounding words and the wound around his neck started to heal itself.

The prince cleared his throat. "Good. I will come for you tòmorrow. At dawn. If you step out of line, I will make sure those fragments of lips you have left are sealed shut, so you can never speak a spell again, and then, I'll make sure every part of your body hurts equally as much. Are we clear?"

"Very clear, my prince," Saul said, as more rotten teeth grinding against each other could be heard.

The prince grabbed Molly's elbow and pulled her away from the cell. They made their long way back through the pitch-black halls. More moans and cries could be heard.

As they approached the steep stairs, she stopped, suddenly remembering something she had meant to ask the prince the night before. "Wait." She glanced down the hall at each cell she could see, too many shoved together in tiny spaces. "Where's Seto? What happened to him after... everything?"

The prince glared. "He was brought back here immediately after Fallen caught you. My father said he'd deal with the traitor later," he said, eyes narrowing. "Oh, no. No, no, little daemon. Do not let your mind wander there. We do not have time to release that scum."

Molly spun to face him and she felt a cool sensation run down her spine and tingle her scalp. "I am not leaving here until you release him."

The prince's face pinched in anger and he opened his mouth, but just as fast, growled and moved past her. "Fucking—" She followed him through the dark maze, feeling as if he was leading her nowhere until he stopped at a corner.

"Here you go, your majesty," the prince snapped.

"Seto?" Molly called as she rushed to the bars. "Seto?"

His callused hands wrapped around hers and she saw his gaunt face appear from within the shadows. "Molly, you're alive."

"Yes," she said, holding back a whimper.

"But Tensley..." he said, shaking his head repeatedly. "They brought me down here right away, I couldn't... I couldn't..."

She sucked in deeply, her head dropping. "He's alive, but he's not himself."

Seto's dark brows lowered. "What happened? What did the king do?"

"He's heartless, Seto," Molly managed to say with a quivering voice. "Fallen ripped his heart out, and then Tensley killed him. There's a new king now."

Seto's hands weakened around hers. "Tensley—Tensley's the king?"

She nodded viciously. "We need your help." She turned back to the prince who stood to the side, eyeing the scene with impatience. "Open the cell."

The prince sighed loudly, but didn't argue. He produced his skeleton key and unlocked the door. As Seto stood on wobbly legs, Molly wrapped an arm around his chest and helped him out.

The three of them, the misfits of the high court, walked through the darkest pit once more.

"What do you plan to do?" Seto asked, coughing violently.

Molly glared at the stairs ahead, a dim light cascading down the steps. "We plan to curse him."

chapter five

THE PORT WAS packed to the brim with merchants, the high sun beaming down on top of Molly's cloaked head. The smell of the ocean's essence surrounded her and as hot as she was underneath the cloak, she had to hide her identity from the public.

Being the wife of the new king wasn't something she wanted the public to know. She had no clue how the rest of the kingdom outside of the court felt about Fallen's death, but from the scrunched up noses and ugly scowls, she knew the court didn't like her. The prince had warned her as they left on how different the village would be from the palace.

Seto gripped her elbow, making her pause as the dusty street lined by stone buildings of slab filled with people. "Do not wander away from me. You may not officially be the queen, but you are the king's wife."

Molly nodded, fixing her hood so half of her face was concealed. "How do you think these people feel about Fallen? About the court?"

Seto tsked and guided her through the heavy crowd. "They respected his power over them, accepted it, but feared him nonetheless. The court, however..." he began as his eyes wandered to a nearby armory display, its vendor shouting praises at each pedestrian as he tried to get them to buy one of his beautifully crafted blades or various weapons. Seto's eyes came back to hers, his eyes serious, almost sullen. "Most villagers dislike the court. These men and women are slaves to do the biddings of the high court members, to offer them food... and sometimes bring them power."

Seto sneered and Molly remembered hearing of Seto's past. He once lived amongst these people. He was them—once a poor boy surviving here by dueling in vicious street fights. He had seen both the court and this world, a rare perspective to acquire.

In the mid-afternoon light, Molly saw the clear damage the dungeon and the last week had done to Seto's body. The gaunt features, the limp in his step, the sickly pale skin, but his mind, a mind so strong and powerful propelled his weak body to keep fighting, to keep surviving. At the thought of Prim, Molly bit the inside of her mouth. Seto was doing all of this for Prim. He kept moving forward, only so he could fight for what Prim would have wanted; a better world. A world where people could fall in love freely and marry who they wished to marry. A world that wasn't so restrictive with unnecessary laws. A world in which the greatest thing people could experience wasn't seen as a sin or a weakness, but seen as a strength.

Fruit stands displayed fresh berries and harvested tomatoes, red, large and juicy. Molly watched as a woman pulled a fresh tomato from the vine and take a large bite, the juices and seeds running down her chin, but she didn't appear to care. She sucked in the nutrition and savored the food.

The port was a long straight dock lined with tiny boats that fishermen used to brave the ocean beyond. A statue stood erect at the end of the dock, a stone carved figure of a man—holding a sword in one hand and a cresting wave in the other.

"Aegaeon, he was the god of violent waters. He's said to be a symbol to our people to protect them from the ocean. He's both a savior and a villain, but most sailors pray to him for safe voyage," Seto told her when he caught her stare. By his tone, she could hear how fond he was of tales, of their society's myths and legends and she smiled up at him.

"I guess most of us pray, even for the villain," Molly said, thinking back to Tensley. Women singing down the road stole her from her thoughts and she continued walking alongside Seto. "What are they singing about?" Molly couldn't understand the language they sang in, but it was soft and high, a chant that almost sounded religious, and the way they moved, all in white, swaying their hips and throwing their heads back toward the sky was mesmerizing.

She thought of the hunt she had been thrown into, in honor of Sonolios the sun god, and of the white dresses and veils they had worn for the occasion, how pure and pristine they had looked. So innocent and inviting. But as Molly looked at the singing women, she realized their white dresses were dirtied and stained from hard work and weather.

"They're singing the song of the beast," Seto explained, watching just as closely. "About the purest form of our people, how each man wields a beast inside of him and how to cherish the violence and the hunger within him."

Molly shivered at his words and the heated song—almost chanting like a group of sirens luring men to drown.

Molly eyed two boys dressed in shreds of cloth kicking a ball between them. Her chest ached at the sight of their dirty skin, the sand and dirt like a second skin to them, how tiny they appeared, how fragile, but how they still wore genuine smiles. She pinched her palm, restraining herself from touching her own stomach. Seeing such young boys made her think of her own son. Her heart broke at the mere sight.

"Come," Seto whispered and jerked his head toward a wooden cavern wedged in-between a stone lodge, a skull of a large mammal—perhaps a whale, hanging over the top of the door. Seto opened the large door and Molly entered into the shadowed room. A few men sat along a wood bar, red-faced, bent over as they drowned in the whisky that Molly tasted heavy in the air.

"Ah, Seto, Seto," a man behind the bar greeted. He was stocky with a dark full beard hiding the lower half of his face.

Molly followed Seto over to the man and watched as he leaned over the bar. "I am looking for your specialties, Rennad," Seto said lowly, an intense glint in those dark eyes.

Rennad smiled wearily. "For pleasure or pain?"

Molly stiffened and glanced down the bar, but all the men were either too drunk or simply uninterested in their conversation.

Seto side-eyed Molly. "Pain."

Rennad nodded briskly and hummed to himself. With a flick of his wrist, he began walking to the back room. Seto and Molly followed into a smaller room, darker than the last with cupboards of jars and tiny bottles filled with objects and substances she was sure she didn't want to identify.

Rennad hummed to himself, terribly loud as the two of them stood back, watching the giant man rummage through his jars.

"We need a good sedative. Something that would put out even the most powerful of men for a few hours," Seto added after a second.

Molly's stomach dropped, but she knew it was necessary.

"A sedative, huh?" Rennad shoved a few jars from the front and dug into the back of the cupboard. "Ah!" He pulled out his large arm and turned to face them, in his thick hand he held a tiny bottle of clear liquid. "Lather this onto a knife and the bastard won't stand a chance. If used on a strong man, it might put him out for a few hours, possibly a few days. On a weaker man, however," he said with a dark glint to his eyes. "It would be lethal."

Seto dug into his pocket and handed over seven nyxes, coins from the court, as the man handed him the bottle.

"Pleasure doing business with you," Rennad said and patted Seto's shoulder. Seto stared back blankly at him and pocketed the bottle.

"Come," Seto said to Molly and they left the bar, their heads lowered.

Once outside, Molly heard voices battling each other, bids of numbers tossed back and forth.

"Keep moving," Seto whispered when she paused to find the source.

As they moved, she saw a crowd had gathered around a stage and on the stage was a small group of poorly dressed women, the shreds of clothing barely concealing their nudity.

Men gathered around the stage in the middle of the dirt street, battling to outbid the last announcement and Molly's stomach twisted.

"That's sick," Molly hissed lowly to Seto.

Seto continued to walk ahead. "It's life outside of the court," he said, voice cold and dry.

Molly couldn't tear her eyes from the girls, from the angry, aggressive men below, salivating like beasts at the sight of them. One man even reached out and slid his fingers along a girl's bare calf.

Seto gripped Molly's wrist before she could even turn. "Do not involve yourself. Remember who you are tied to."

Molly gritted her teeth. "It's wrong, Seto."

A cry stopped Seto from responding and as Molly turned, her eyes found a new girl brought to the stage.

She stumbled, unsteady on her thin, bruised legs and wrapped her shaking arms around her chest as the men hooted and called to her.

"For the delicate flower," the ringleader sang to the lively crowd.

Molly took a step closer, her heart seizing, her lungs tightening to the point she couldn't breathe. "Seto…"

Seto moved beside her. He didn't say a word, but when she looked up at him, she saw the sulking darkness in his eyes tremble and his jaw became rigid.

Another cry was all it took to spark the fuse in Seto and he shoved himself deep into the crowd.

"Seto!" Molly rushed after him, pushing through as she watched Seto march to the stage.

A few men swore at him or glared, but as soon as Seto climbed up onto the stage, the crowd roared.

"Get off the stage!" the owner of the girl shouted at him.

Seto walked with determination, his eyes set on the girl shying away into the group of women.

He kept advancing nonetheless, only stopping as he reached her. His hand came up from where it had been at his side, trembling slightly as he gently caressed the girl's shoulder. He slid her ratty locks down her back, revealing her neck, and the burnt skin that seemed to run around its complete circumference.

Molly stood at the base of the stage now, her heart thudding deep in her chest.

The burns…

Someone had tried to remove her mark. The mark she had been given by Seto. A claiming mark. One a demon gave to his mate.

Molly touched her own mark, shivering at the mere thought of the pain such burns must have inflicted. If touch sent her to her knees, she couldn't imagine…

"Prim," Seto whispered, unbelieving. The shivering girl, Prim, only stared at his feet, her delicate features hollowed and stained with dirt. The owner shoved Seto back. "Get off my stage! If you want to have her, you bid!"

Seto turned sharply, his hardened features challenging the owner. "She's not for sale."

The owner paused, and then chuckled, wiping the sweat off his bald head with a cloth, and stuffing it back into his shirt. "And I am the fucking king of High Court," he said, laughing hysterically. Some of the men around the stage joined in, the loud noise making the several girls shrink in fear. The owner's cruel smile faded, his face growing serious once more. "She's mine."

That angered the beast inside of Seto and he growled, taking a step to guard Prim from anyone seeing her. "No, she is most definitely not," Seto managed out in a voice of steel and fire forged together.

The owner's eyes bulged and he stalked forward, his finger jabbing into Seto's chest, heaving in anger. "The bitch is mine, beggar."

Molly saw the flash of pure anger in Seto's face and she knew he would kill the man.

She had to intervene. Right now. Before everything went from bad to worse.

"No," Molly shouted and threw down her hood, the icy sensation stinging behind her eyes and she glared at the owner.

The owner staggered when he caught her eyes.

The crowd parted as if she was the devil herself—and maybe she was. A dangerous threat to their own king, even as he strolled through the palace miles away. She heard them whisper as she stood at the base of the stage. "You will let her go," Molly said, not even recognizing her own voice.

The owner swallowed thickly, unable to move as her eyes held him in place.

"Is that the king's wife?" someone whispered behind her. Molly didn't look back to see who had spoken, she kept her gaze firmly placed on the owner's. Controlling him.

59

"Yes," the owner answered, his voice quivering. When she knew the owner would be no further threat to their intentions of bringing Prim with them, she broke their stare, her powers slithering back into her like a poisonous and ancient serpent.

Molly turned to Seto as he grabbed Prim, sweeping her off her feet and into his arms as he marched down the steps and past the crowd.

Molly pulled her hood back up, but every single person watched her, a weary look in their eyes.

They seemed unsure. Uncertain of what the king's wife held within her bones and blood.

"You shouldn't have done that," Seto mumbled, but his eyes were focused on his mate in his arms, his fingers continuing to soothingly stroke her bruised arms.

"I—I," Molly paused and swallowed. "I think what I'm capable of is changing."

Seto frowned. "Perhaps the trauma of Tensley's death and rebirth triggered these changes."

Molly fisted her hands. She hadn't thought of that, but it had begun right after Tensley's heart had been ripped out. Her powers were triggered from the trauma.

Prim didn't move, her eyes shut tightly, her breathing ragged and wild. From the pained look on her expression, she didn't even want Seto to touch her. Molly's heart broke for the girl who had once been so wild and happy.

"Where should we take her?" Molly asked after they left the port town and ventured back onto the short path to the palace.

Seto fixed his grip on Prim, making sure he was particularly gentle with her. She watched him look down at her, the darkness that glinted in his eyes gone and replaced with pure adoration and hope.

"To the cottage," he answered after some time, pulling Prim even closer to his chest if such a thing was even possible.

Molly nodded and didn't say another word. A few minutes later, once they passed through the woods, she saw the cottage the prince had shown her earlier in the day.

The cottage where they would take Tensley.

She brushed off her nerves and focused on Prim.

The cottage was a tiny stone house with a slanted dirt roof. Broken and abandoned, it had gone without repairs and now sat overgrown by the surrounding forest.

The thin wood door opened easily and Seto moved in past her, going into the separate room and placing Prim down on the cot. Water leaked from the ceiling, dripping a rhythm against the dirt floor.

Prim instantly curled into herself, creating a tiny protective ball. Molly stood at the edge of the room, watching as Prim flinched when Seto touched her arm.

Prim whimpered and shook her head, crawling into the corner on the bed, holding herself.

Seto bent down onto his knees and watched her. Molly swore she heard his heart shatter.

"Prim," he whispered, but she only whimpered in return. "You're safe. I'll protect you."

Again, another whimper of pain and agony. He sat there, bent on his knees for a long period time, watching, waiting for a single movement of hope. He brushed a hand along the side of her shoulder, not touching her, but simply being close enough to feel his warmth.

"I will not let anyone harm you again," he murmured. "I vow to you and you alone."

Seto stood and walked into the other room, Molly following behind.

He wiped a hand down his face and sighed, leaning against a table with vines growing up its legs.

"Fallen lied," Molly said, still not sure she completely believed what they had just discovered. "She's…she never died. Do you think he was the one to sell her off?"

Seto swallowed and shook his head in confusion. He too had a hard time believing any of it. His hands turned to fists at his sides.

"What do you think…happened to her?" Molly whispered, her words a knife twisting in her own chest.

Seto stared at the floor, a sadness, a sickness creeping inside of him. He shook his head. Neither of them could speak of the unthinkable acts done to Prim in the past week since Fallen had banished her.

"Tensley killed him, Seto," Molly said, her hand gripping his own. "Fallen's gone. He's dead."

Seto nodded and looked down at her. "I promise you—we'll save him."

Molly's eyes grew hot and wet and she looked back at Prim hidden in the room beside them.

"Tonight," Seto started, lifting his head high. "Tonight you tame the beast."

chapter six

THE LORDS THAT sat in front of the beast held their breaths. He could sense their uncertainty, their fear and also envy. They wanted the throne, they wanted his head on a spike and they wanted to drink to their victory.

He rolled his hand on the table into an iron fist.

He could feel the buzz of his weakness, the sting of his once powerful body faltering. His body was seeking pleasure to gain power, but every woman who sought him enraged the beast.

"The mourning period lasts for three months. It is tradition for the court to wait to crown the new king until the mourning period has ended," Lilith spoke, sitting beside him. She continued to lean over and whispered what she thought of each word that was pronounced by the lords like she believed the beast valued her opinions.

He did not.

He simply ignored her and each time she tried to touch him—a brush of her thigh against his, her fingers skimming his forearm—he'd push her away, and growl lowly.

"Once you are crowned king," Lilith began and he saw the fire in her eyes spark, excited by the idea of him king. "We will discuss a joint house."

"A joint house, my lady?" a lord asked, his entire features hidden by an unruly beard.

"Yes." She nodded curtly and her voice held no room for further discussion. "I will act as his queen."

The beast hissed lowly. "No."

The entire room went silent and Lilith turned to face him, her brows drawn into a frown.

"No," the beast snapped, the word more vicious than he expected it to be but driven by his emotions.

"No?" Lilith inquired, laughing softly as if the beast was delusional. "I am the only lady fit to be a queen. I am a queen," she added, putting emphasis on the last part. Then her eyes turned cold, calculating, the smile of a viper taking over her mouth. "What did you think, your majesty?" she asked, laughing again, the sound meant to be sensual but it only made the beast's teeth snap with aggression. "You thought your little so-called wife was going to be queen? That she was going to reign beside you? Over a court and a world full of demons? I thought our king vicious, not naïve and driven by a slut." Some lords joined in with Lilith's laugh, and victory flashed in her eyes.

The beast gripped the wooden table before him, the wood cracking under his grip, the sound echoing around the room like a dark storm. He may be weakened by the lack of affection he had been receiving, but he wasn't about to let this court think they could outsmart him. Conquer him. Belittle him.

He had conquered Fallen.

He was king.

And he would crush this court full of snakes to nothing if they thought they could control him.

The beast growled, the sound so vicious, the lords stopped laughing immediately. They knew an unpredictable and dangerous beast when they saw one, and if they wanted out of the room alive, they would have to tread carefully. Only Lilith was brave enough to keep her wicked smile.

"I am afraid no one explained to you our ways, my king. Truthfully, it all happened so quickly, the death of my husband, that we didn't have quite the time. But you are after all a foreigner. So perhaps we should make some things clear here and now; No whore or prudish little girls in this court can dethrone me. I am queen. I was born a queen. And I will die a queen."

A few lords nodded their heads in agreement, one of them, seeming younger than the others in the room, stood.

The lord was trying to appear brave and strong, but he fooled no one, the sweet taste of his fear sat heavy on all of their tongues.

The beast breathed in with the slowness of a predator about to pounce, his neck cracking in preparation.

He waited. Waited for what he knew was about to come.

A taste of satisfaction would come at last.

The relief and release he had been so desperately needing.

Perhaps it wouldn't be enough to truly satisfy the beast's needs, but it certainly would appease them for a little while. Or so he hoped.

The lord took a deep breath and opened his mouth ever so slowly to speak. "The queen has been nothing but faithful to the crown and a strong partner to our late king, Fallen. Perhaps, if the new king does not agree with those terms, the court should consider the possibility of taking away the right, and choosing

Queen Lilith herself as the sole leader of this court," he said, as his hands shook slightly. Lilith offered the young man an encouraging nod accompanied with a secretive smile. The kind of smile someone offered their lover, the person they shared intimate moments with.

But the beast was too far gone to analyze the specifics.

All he could hear were the queen's words followed by the lord's.

His jaw ticked. He blinked twice. And just as the young lord was about to sit down, breathing in shakily as he thought he was safe from the beast's wrath; all hell broke loose, and the beast was unleashed.

TENSLEY WALKED DOWN the glistening white hallways. These men were weak. They went with the flow of power and if they sided with Lilith, he had no use for them.

He'd destroy them before they sought to dethrone him.

Power was like a drug, a need so potent it drove the beast crazy. He craved it just as much as he craved sex. It pleasured him, it ruined him and brought him ultimate strength.

Just as he turned the corner, he saw a group of ladies chatting to each other outside in the gardens.

"Where's my daemon?" he asked them as he approached and the ladies froze, their features turning pale at the sight of crimson on his white shirt.

"My—my lord," one girl whispered, her hands shaking. "I do not know."

He eyed each of the girls and each one dropped their head in submission. He turned, ready to search for her around the castle when one girl spoke.

"I did see her. Yesterday morning with the prince, your majesty," she said.

He paused, his anger coming in waves at the thought of her spending alone time with another man. Especially the prince.

"She went to his chambers…" she added hesitantly.

The beast clawed inside of him and before he could do any harm, he marched. She was with another man. As much as the beast wanted to believe she was faithful to him, it made him crazy with jealousy. Every woman he saw revolted him—he only wanted one, and she was spending time with the prince.

He growled at the anger, at the rage, because even without his fucking heart beating in his chest, she still controlled the beast.

THE WARM WATER engulfed Molly and she squeezed her eyes shut. Tonight, she would be damning him. Tonight, she would plague him with a curse that would either make him grow a heart or end terribly, terribly wrong.

Her hands shook and she spread them under the heated water, letting her back rest against the tub. She rolled her neck back and sighed.

And just like that, the heat was consuming her again, as the ache deep in her belly surged. The cravings weren't as regular or often as they had been before, but she still yearned for his touch. Yearned for his hands on her body. And so in the privacy of the bathroom, Molly closed her eyes and pictured her husband's large, callused hands.

So worn, so weathered, her thighs squeezed together tightly in a failed attempt to calm the ache.

She saw his full lips drawn into the rare smile he shared only with her— only for her, and his bulging muscles flexing as he moved.

When her hands smoothed down her stomach, she imagined they were his powerful ones. Caressing, searching, exploring the curves of her body. And when *his large fingers* reached her folds and caressed them lazily, with torturous slowness under the water, she sighed in deep pleasure.

Sometimes, he liked to love her brutally. He fucked hard and fast. Letting his beast come out to play, and giving her a taste of his true essence. And when he did, she always loved every second of it.

And other times, he enjoyed worshiping her body like it was his temple. Like she was his queen and he had to serve her at all costs. Those times, he liked to go slow and deep, taking his time to discover every inch of skin he hadn't yet kissed. Hadn't yet loved.

And she loved those times just as much.

Each stroke stirred the embers deep inside of her and she breathed heavily out. One hand touched her exposed breast, half emerged in the water and she bit her bottom lip.

Deeper the strokes became and she kept her eyes shut, wishing to imagine it was his hands working her to pleasure.

"Tensley," she moaned deeply, the sound almost rough as it passed the barrier of her lips.

Her fingers worked deeper, faster, the water splashing and she felt her orgasm near, so close—until she heard a low, sensual growl coming from behind her and her eyes flashed open as her fingers slowed.

Her head turned, looking behind her, where the sound had come from. And there, in the shadows of the large, dimly lit washroom stood her husband.

His hooded gaze froze her mid-stroke and she felt her body slide down further into the water. Even still, she knew he could see everything. Her breasts peaked like mountains, the water pooled around them, and her hand still cupped her sex.

Flushed and shocked, she went to remove her hand.

"Don't," he hissed out, echoing loudly against the high ceilings.

Molly stilled once more and she couldn't look away from him. His chest heaved, his nostrils flared, and that darkness in his eyes went straight to her core.

He wanted her.

Badly. But all he did was cross the room with powerful strides until he reached the opposite wall, and casually leaned against it.

He stood right in front of her now. Observing her every move as his tongue licked his bottom lip ever so slowly. His eyes devoured lazily as if nothing else mattered.

They started at her eyes, the look in his own making her shiver, the peaks of her breasts tightening painfully.

Then they traveled down to her collared throat, a possessive growl escaping his own lips at the sight.

Then they followed the path down to her breasts, and just with his gaze, she could tell all the things he wanted to do to them.

Slowly, they left her breasts and found her stomach, the tiny bump there reminding them both of the product of the love they once shared. Growing inside of her, protected and cherished by the soft body of a woman.

And finally; his eyes reached the center of her pleasure and she felt herself tighten with desire, deep within. She craved a beast and he craved her too.

Her legs were wide open, her position hiding nothing from his view. She didn't care. As soon as she had seen the pleasure and need flashing in his eyes, she had stopped caring. There was nothing to be ashamed of. The look he was giving her made her feel powerful.

Desirable.

Sinful.

But sin had never felt better.

Fire burned deep within her, pleasure pulsed between her legs, and with his eyes now firmly on her, unwavering, observing, it brought it all to new heights.

She moaned so deeply it was almost imperceptible. But he heard, and his nostrils flared, eyes consumed by darkness and need.

His hands clenched and unclenched beside him and that's when she noted the large bulge in his trousers.

"You don't want me to stop?" she asked, dragging her eyes from his erection back to that shadowed face of his.

He bared his teeth, his eyes narrowing. "*No.*"

She was curious…of how much power she had over him.

She wanted to taunt him—as he had taunted her.

"Is that an order, my king?"

His brow furrowed deeply. "Yes."

So she obeyed his command with a soft smile and stroked deeper, arching her back so her breasts were in plain sight for him.

"Do I please you?" she breathed out, finding his eyes. He stared at her—his eyes dragging across each part of her, but always returning to her features. "Do I please my king the way I should? The way I vowed to when I married you," she added on the same sensual tone, her eyes half closed with pleasure. "I am ready to bare my body to him — his precious temple, his soothing warmth of night, and bitter bite of ice. Obedience and patience will be my oath—carrying the inferno of his power in my womb," she said, repeating the wedding vows she had recited only a few days ago, all the while her hand kept stroking, deep.

He grunted once and she took that as a *yes.*

She rolled her head back, her damp curls falling over one breast. Her skin was pink from the warmth of the bath.

She moaned when she touched her clit and met his eyes. "Do you remember what I taste like?"

His nostrils flared, his gaze fixated on her hand between her thighs. Those powerful hands of his shook as they fisted.

"Do you remember how it felt when you touched me? With a finger…with two?" She smiled softly at him, at the fury battling below the surface. "Do you remember how tight I was? How it felt when I clenched around you?"

to crown a beast

He growled back at her, but she only smiled in return and closed her eyes.

"Oh *Tensley*," she whispered, the heat spreading, the heat devouring reason and fear, and it took her.

It took her in waves and she cried out, the water splattering as she quivered in pleasure.

Once it passed, she relaxed into the warmth and looked up at him, tiredly.

He hadn't moved, but his jaw was clenched tightly and he didn't look away from her.

"Do you remember anything?" she whispered, the water just below her bottom lip now as she sunk back.

He stared back at her, eyes turning cold and hard. There was no pleasure left in them anymore and it made her uncomfortable. Maybe she had pushed him too much, too fast. She sighed and he growled with anger. "The feast is in an hour. You will sit beside me and eat from my hand only. That is also a command," he snapped.

With that, he left, stomping out of the washroom and leaving her alone.

The heat had left her body now. Tonight, she reminded herself, tonight she would curse him to remember.

chapter seven

MOLLY EYED HER king, her husband, as he sat upon his throne, watching the court nibble on their feast. Each time she looked at him, she thought of the hours ago she worked herself to orgasm and he watched her.

She shook herself from those thoughts.

The time was now. The time to curse the beast and bring back the man.

The time to bring back his heart.

Molly's hands twisted beneath the grand table, her heart following afterward.

This would either work or destroy her husband.

She had to taunt the beast, tease him into anger and insanity to succeed, and that was dangerous in itself.

He won't hurt me.

It was the least of her worries.

What worried her more was him figuring out their plan.

Lilith leaned close to Tensley, the tops of her breasts exposed for him to gaze down on, but he kept his gaze ahead. His brutal, death glare that sent any target into a frenzy of terror.

Everywhere Molly had seen Tensley, Lilith hadn't been far behind. She knew exactly what Lilith was doing, or trying to do. She was trying to dig her claws in deep to gain control over Tensley, to use him like she wanted to use her own son.

Throughout the entire meal, Tensley hadn't glanced at Molly or even touched his food. He was simply a statue of indifference, but she noted the way his hands fisted on his thighs, the way his eyes swept across the crowd, he was calculating something.

A glass clinked and Molly turned to see the prince on the other side of Lilith, standing, a clear flute in hand.

"A toast," the prince said, the crowd quieting. He lifted the flute, his head angled downward, but his eyes burned with intensity. Tensley watched him, no change in his expression. The prince's eyes darted to Molly's and he grinned. "To our beautiful queen."

Molly paled.

She heard Tensley's teeth grind against each other and saw his fisted hands shake.

Pissing off the beast now wasn't part of the plan.

The prince nodded at her, that annoying smile still playing on his lips and downed his drink. He slammed it down and took off. His exit.

Hers would be now.

The crowd murmured, but went back to their meals, the music lifting into the cool night.

"I'll retire early," Molly announced as she stood from her chair. Tensley's head snapped so fast she swore she heard bones crack. He didn't move from his seat and she continued down the few steps onto the leveled floor. Each step, she prayed under her breath he'd follow.

Once she passed the hallway to the rest of the palace, she quickened her pace and focused on the balcony.

The cool night air assaulted her flushed cheeks, not a sound of life in the darkness surrounding the palace. When she disappeared onto the patio, she moved down the steps and onto the fresh green grass. The forest in front of her taunted her fears and memories.

"Molly," that cold, masculine voice wrapped around her throat and she glanced over her bare shoulder.

Tensley stood a few feet back, his fisted hands beside him. His brows furrowed. "What are you doing out here?"

Molly sucked in a deep breath. The prince was right. Tensley's beast still was possessive, still needed her close and under his thumb.

That need would be his downfall and her advantage.

"A walk in the woods," Molly said, removing her heels, letting the soles of her feet kiss the chilled grass. The breeze blew her chiffon dress, the fabric wrapping around her thighs.

A shiver spread across her bare arms.

"Come inside," he said and she could, for once, see he was trying to be collected in his rage.

She took a small step back and cocked her head to the side.

His jaw flexed. "Don't test my patience."

"If you can catch me," Molly whispered, lifting her dress. "Then you can have me."

His chest heaved, slow and hard, and his nostrils flared. "You want to play with the beast, wife?" He moved forward, his body a wall of steel and power, one easily able to catch her. A shiver of dread and terrifying promise ran down her spine. "When I catch you, I will more than have you." Those stormy eyes darkened, a raging thunder taking over. "Run, before I sink my teeth into you again."

She didn't waste a second. She ran, her pulse quickening when she felt his footfalls not far behind her.

She ducked into the woods, down the only visible path, swatting stray branches out of her way. And he was so close, making the hair on the back of her neck stand on end.

The branches scratched at her arms, tearing into her skin. Her dress torn and tangled. She had memorized the path, but fear clouded her mind.

She couldn't forget, she couldn't lose focus.

Don't let fear win.

Insects buzzed and Tensley's low hiss surrounded her.

She pushed back a branch and saw the tiny-slated cottage. She moved, shoving more branches out of the way and rushed to the clearing.

A few more feet, just a few more feet.

Two powerful hands clasped her arms and spun her into his arms. She gasped loudly, gawking up at her husband.

His ruthless brow was drawn into a frown, and he grabbed her chin, forcing her to look up at him. "Don't run from me. It drives me mad."

"Tensley—" She tried to glance back at the cottage, but his grip tightened. She stared up at his darkness, at the fuming rage within, and calmed herself. "I will obey, my lord." Her fingers smoothed down his forearm, over ridged scars and sun kissed skin. She hooked her fingers between two of his large ones and pulled gently. The shadows played along his sculpted features, the face of an angel, but there was nothing holy about him.

"I've heard the rumors, of you spending time with the prince," he hissed, dragging a finger over her bottom lip.

"Nothing happened," she bit out. She swallowed thickly at the heat from his eyes scorching her flesh. Even as the beast she still craved him. "I promise."

He laughed darkly. "Because you know only I can satisfy you. No other man can make you wet and aroused with my presence." He moved in closer, invading, and breathed against her cheek, his lips brushing the skin there.

She turned her head, their mouths touching—so close, so close to succumbing to his wicked voice and she let her own breath tangle with his. "I have that same power over you."

A thigh-clenching snarl left his full mouth of sin and power, and he scooped her up. "Now that I caught you, I get to have you," he growled, and before she could even catch her breath, he stole it and moved with ease to the cottage.

Molly's heart pounded against her ribcage. His lips felt the same, the same with his large hands kneading her backside, but it wasn't him.

With one arm, he held her against him and used his free one to slam open the weathered wood door.

His arm swept anything left on an oak table to the cottage's forest floor and he laid her down, settling in-between her open thighs.

His dark eyes went to her throat and his hand slid up her collarbone, wrapping around her trembling neck. Molly's collar tingled, buzzing from under his lethal touch.

"You taunted me tonight. In that water, teasing me with your fingers, with your beautiful, sinful body. Do not taunt—" Tensley growled in pain, his back arching, immediately shielding her, an arm on either side of her head. The veins in his neck bulged and Molly noted the dagger stabbed in his shoulder.

Molly stilled beneath him—and braced herself. She saw the flash of anger, the wrath in his dark eyes, but he turned, swinging his arm back at the prince.

Chaos erupted in the tiny, dark cottage. The earth shook, the roars of the two beasts echoing against the thin walls. Tensley struck the prince's chest with a heavy fist, but Molly noted how he slowed, how his arms grew weak and when Seto emerged from the darkness, the two men conquered him.

"What did you do?" Molly asked, nervously, as the prince hauled Tensley's weakening body to the corner. He dragged him to a worn down oak chair and began anchoring him in with thick chains. They clanked with each yank and pull.

Seto yanked the dagger from Tensley's shoulder and tossed it aside.

"That sedative," Saul said, lounging in a dark corner of the tiny cottage. He wore a cloak that the prince had provided him with that morning, as he had escorted the warlock to the cottage.

Molly fixed her dress and stood, watching Tensley's bowed head.

"You bastards," he wheezed as the sedative was weakening him.

"Three bastards and your bitch," the prince said, smirking, but Molly gave him a hard look. Tensley growled in response. He swung his head back and struggled against the chains.

"Is everything ready?" Molly glanced to Saul. "We have to hurry before someone finds out he's missing."

Saul licked his cracked lips. A nervous tic Molly had noticed. He produced the book the prince had found and a small rock. "Here. For his heart. I've blessed it."

Molly took the rock, tensing its smoothness and the tiny ridges. She cupped it to her chest, taking deep breaths to calm herself.

"Shall we begin?" the prince asked, stepping back, sliding a dagger into his hand. They had gone over the chant, over what was to be done, but her body still shook at the thought of what they were about to do. The prince moved forward to Tensley, but Molly stepped in his path.

"Let me," she told him, lifting her hand.

He cocked a light brow, full of arrogance. "Are you sure? Don't want you getting your delicate hands dirty with the king's blood."

Seto nodded, standing next to the prince. "It may be too much for you, my lady."

She glowered at the prince's condescending tone and shook her hand once. "Blood won't stop me from saving him."

He hesitated, then sighed, dropping the dagger into her hand.

She breathed in shakily, turning to face the fuming demon chained to the chair. She wondered if even the earth floor would hold him.

Those dark, deadly eyes pierced into hers, a warning, a curse upon her as she stepped closer, the dagger by her side.

"Whatever you think you're capable of, think again, *dolcezza*," he hissed lowly. "You stabbed me once before, remember?" And his words stabbed her deep within her own chest. Her heart shrinking with pain. Even if the man had forgotten her, the beast clearly hadn't. She couldn't blame him.

And she was about to do it again. But this time, she wasn't doing it because she was afraid, or because she hated him. She was doing it out of love. To save him.

She wouldn't, couldn't, let the beast change her mind.

Molly stopped in front of him, head leveled, heart in the middle of a war, and her breath harsh and wild.

"I'm more than capable of cursing you," Molly warned, and she noted the flare in his eyes. She ignored it, ignored the pain she felt at the thought of hurting Tensley once more, beast or not, and ripped his dress shirt open, exposing his chest of scars and muscles.

"Start," the prince ordered Saul.

Saul began to chant in a language she didn't understand and Tensley glared at the warlock.

"What the fuck is he doing?" he growled viciously, the sound not as powerful as it would have been, had he not been sedated.

Molly placed the stone on the floor beside her and steadied the dagger in her other hand. When she placed it against where his heart should have been, tracing the freshly healed wound of Fallen's hand puncturing his chest, Tensley turned to steel.

And lighting flashed through his eyes.

At last, he understood why they were all gathered there.

What they intended to do.

"If you wish to keep your hand, back down," Tensley barked, his voice holding so much violence, her body almost did as he asked out of fear.

But didn't.

She had to be strong.

For him.

For their son.

She had to be strong.

"Stay still," she warned, gripping his shoulder, but it didn't help much.

He twisted against the chains, trying to free himself.

The chanting grew louder.

"He's too strong," Seto snapped.

The prince swore and both he and Seto rushed behind the chair, gripping Tensley's bound wrists. "Be quick."

They were playing with death, and she knew the consequences.

Molly took a deep, even breath and looked into his dark eyes.

"I love you."

And then she pierced his chest.

chapter eight

H E HISSED IN pain, his entire frame shaking as she sliced deeper and deeper and deeper. *Oh god!* The warm blood coated her fingertips, running down her wrists. She wiggled the dagger, creating enough space and patted the floor beside her, scrambling to find the stone.

She paused—the heavy leather handle weighing on her wrist, the heavy weight of guilt over stabbing the love of her life, flashing back to that dreadful day.

Months before to the day she stabbed him in the back to save both of them, to save her from tying herself to the demon.

Yet, she ended up tying herself to the man she loved.

The man she ended up losing.

Hatred swam in her veins and her stomach dropped.

Here she was yet again with a dagger deep within Tensley's chest.

No.

She shook her head. She needed to do this to save him. She was hurting him because she loved him enough.

She grabbed the stone and removed the dagger, shoving the stone where his heart would be.

"How can you do this to me?" Tensley spat, his face pure red, the veins in his neck bulging.

All Molly heard was the chanting of a foreign language and her blood rushing to her head, and then another beat.

A heart beat.

The hole in Tensley's chest glowed darkness and she saw his veins protruding and vibrating in his chest and forearms.

Tensley roared, his head thrown back, his throat constricting, his hands turning white as he gripped the arms of the chair.

The mere image of him in utter pain nearly brought her to her knees and she pressed a hand to his forearm. She knew what strength boiled beneath his skin. One so holy and vicious.

His jaw snapped and he tried to lunge, but the chains held him.

Saul chanted, louder and louder, and Tensley growled, his body recoiling, twisting in pain and horror.

It wasn't natural.

His skin turned a bright red, the anger, the blood all rushing to his head. He spat, he fumed, and swore over and over.

"You can't tame me," he growled, his stormy eyes drilling deep into hers.

"It's a curse," Molly whispered and his dark brows dropped lower in a scowl. "A curse of the heart."

His nose wrinkled and he bared his teeth, but before he could roar again, he seized in pain and doubled over.

A heartbreaking noise left his lips and she clenched her chest. "What's happening?"

"The heart's growing," the prince said, circling around Tensley, examining him. "His body's trying to reject it, but the chant is too strong."

Seto still held Tensley's shoulders, keeping him in place with a frown of determination.

Tensley cried out, thrashing against the chains, his body arching from the chair but to no avail to get free. He became wild, like an animal, biting the air, growling. His beast fully awake, fully fighting the heart growing inside.

The chair itself groaned under the strength, under the impact of his body shaking in pain and rage.

The chanting grew. Vicious and violent and only targeted the pain to grow in Tensley's body.

He was trying to reject the heart.

The chair shook, Tensley's chest heaved aggressively, and a strangled cry echoed into the room.

Molly bit the inside of her mouth and held a hand to her lips. When she went to touch him, he thrashed even more and snarled at her.

"Don't touch him, he's unpredictable," the prince warned.

Molly glanced back at Saul; transfixed by his chant, his eyes focused on the page and his hands shaking as he held the book. Like a man possessed.

"How much longer?"

The prince snorted. "It's only just begun."

Molly pressed a fist to her temple and turned back to the shaking demon.

"You want him back, then deal with his pain," the prince said, folding his arms and leaning against the table.

Molly glared at him and sat down beside Tensley, her hands smoothing along his forearms. He jerked, trying to escape her touch, but he had nowhere to go.

"Shush, it's okay," she murmured, hating how her voice shook.

Tensley bared his teeth at her and thrashed.

She swept a finger along the sweat gathering atop of his furrowed brow and kissed his flexing hand. "Come back to me," she said, a few tears escaping from the corners of her eyes. "Come back to our son, Tensley. Come back to us."

The demon revolted against her touch, against her words, and spat.

Blood boiled from his lips and her heart clenched. The redness poured down his full quivering lips and onto his thighs.

"What's happening?" she asked, her voice littered with panic.

The prince rushed over and lifted Tensley's weak head. "His body is rejecting it, it's pulsing inside of him, trying to latch on, but it's foreign and his body is trying to destroy it." Molly glanced up at the prince's sober face. "And it's destroying him along with it."

Molly blinked back the warmth and gripped Tensley's raging hot cheeks. "No," she screamed. "No, no. This can't be happening." She gasped out in pure fear and pain, her thudding heart frantic. "Tensley," she screamed again, shaking him. But no answer came.

Tensley's body went stiff and Molly felt his chest still. Her hands shook.

"Tensley," she whispered, tears choking her. "He's not breathing."

The prince bowed his head and kissed his thumb, a symbol of blessing the dead.

Molly gasped out in a cry and ran her fingers along his flushed cheeks, feeling the rough stubble, the softness of his lips—

"Molly," those lips murmured.

Molly froze.

Those eyes flickered open, growing to a stormy grey—so familiar, she couldn't speak.

Those eyes swung to her and through bloody lips, he spoke for what seemed like ages since she last heard his husky, dark tone. "Molly..."

"Tensley," she gasped again in shock, her fingers spreading across his cheeks, moving closer. "Tensley, it's okay, it's okay. I'm here." The tears spilled down her face and she pressed a kiss to his lips, not caring about the blood.

He looked weak, so dazed as his eyes drunk her in. "Dolcezza."

She choked on a cry and spread her hands across his chest, feeling the weak beat of his new heart. So faint, the gods wouldn't hear it.

He licked at a tear on her cheek and she shuddered in delight and comfort.

"Dolcezza," he again hushed, that Italian hum to his addictive voice.

She combed her fingers through his hair and kissed his half-shut eyelids, his black lashes so dark against his olive cheeks.

"Don't leave me," she hushed back.

"Dolcezza," his voice grew weaker.

She felt his head give, and she sat back, gawking at his closed eyes. Frantically, she pressed a hand to his chest, the hole still open and bleeding. No beat. Nothing, but an empty chest.

He coughed, more blood pouring out.

"No, no, no!" She gripped his face and tried to arouse him from his slumber, but nothing worked. "It's too much for him; he's going to die!"

The chanting thundered in her ears.

She swung onto her feet and stared at Saul. A haunting smile laced his cracked lips and without a second thought, she felt the familiar icy sensation behind her eyes.

Molly marched toward him and with a death grip around his throat, smashed it.

The chanting stopped. Saul blubbered, blood seeping out of his mouth as he collapsed onto the floor.

"Your freedom," the prince stated, standing above a dying warlock.

Tensley sagged in his chair, the chains the only thing holding him up and

Molly began untying him.

"He's too weak," Seto whispered and began unchaining his arms.

"We need to get him back to the palace," Molly said, untying his wrists. At the sight of the tender welts on his wrists, she bit back a cry.

"They'll kill you, Molly," the prince said. "You threatened their king."

Molly shook her head and untied his other wrist. "I don't care. He's— he's dying."

The prince swore under his breath and she heard his riding boots thud against the ground, stomping toward her. He bent down and began untying Tensley's ankles. "I can only protect you so much."

"They can't hurt me," Molly hissed, yanking his other ankle free. "They already took what mattered most to me. And I'm going to get that back."

The prince stilled and when she looked up, he was staring intently back at her. "They said daemons were rare, but I think they mistook it. You are entirely rare."

She swallowed thickly and lowered her gaze, her heart full of flames and embers, but they simply burnt through her bones and strength.

She wrapped an arm under Tensley's and lifted him, the prince gathering his other side. Seto followed after.

And with a heavy heart, she carried him back to the palace.

THE WARLOCKS CURSED at Molly in a heavy foreign tongue as they rushed around Tensley's bed.

Huddled in blankets of the finest silk and furs, the warlocks worked their herbs to ease the fever that had taken his body.

She knew the moment they put two and two together at the sight of his cut chest, the wound deep and exactly where his heart once was.

One gasped and glared back at her.

"You cursed our king," another hissed.

Once the fever had gone down, the warlocks left in their golden robes and Molly moved closer to his bedside.

She gripped his limp hand and kissed it.

The curse had worked, but only by a sliver. A sliver of a heart now beat weakly, tenderly in the steel and iron beast.

All night she stayed by his side, never letting sleep win, and patting down the sweat on his forehead and chest.

When he groaned or sighed, she was there, checking his pulse, soothing him, loving him, even when he didn't know it.

As the sun rose, streams of precious sunlight filtered in through the lace curtains and pooled them in warmth.

"I'm right here," she whispered again, words she had chanted to him the entire night.

The doors slammed open and she sat up, turning to see a guard and the prince.

"My lady," the prince said, bowing to her. "Lady Lilith summons you to court."

Molly frowned and tightened her hand around Tensley's. "She knows."

The prince sighed and nodded. "Yes, the entire court has heard of what happened to their king. She wishes to discuss it."

Molly swallowed and turned back to Tensley, her fingers sweeping across his creased forehead and into his dark mane. She pressed a soft kiss to his cheek and bit back a cry. "I love you," she whispered to him, savoring his warmth against her and stood.

"Let's go," she told the prince and moved past him with confidence.

She'd go to war to protect the tiny sliver of Tensley's heart. She'd bleed for him, and she wouldn't let a rotten queen control either of them.

She was the daemon, and she would crush anyone who threatened them.

chapter nine

THE COURT WAS in a fury of rage as Molly and the prince passed through the doors into the throne room. The room was furnished with white drapes and a white marble floor, so clear, so clean she could see her own reflection perfectly as she moved into the room. A fake mask of purity.

Words of venom spat between the council and bounced off of the cathedral ceilings, fingers jabbed in the air, confusion and anger filling each space of the room.

Molly took a deep breath and steeled herself.

At the mere sight of her, every single member quieted and watched as she approached the thrones.

An empty one, and one filled with the queen of snakes.

"So the daemon has the confidence to show her face," Lilith spat, leaning forward from her throne of gold and bone.

Molly didn't lower her eyes as she stopped in front of the thrones. Instead, she held Lilith's cold stare, and that made the queen snarl.

"You summoned me, Lady Lilith?" Molly's gaze cut to the council on either side of the thrones, watching her with so much interest.

"Address me as your Queen," she hissed, her skin so tight against her angular face structure, she seemed hollow. Possibly even more hollow on the inside though.

Molly's lips twisted ruefully. "You summoned me," she repeated, slowly, not giving into Lilith's pitiful demands.

Lilith's nostrils flared and her long, manicured nails of red tapped impatiently against the gold trim of her throne. Over a lion head roaring in victory. "You have endangered our king, threatened to curse him." She took a deep, shuddering breath and shook her head. "Cursing him from a forbidden book. A curse so deadly, even Fallen never dared to use it against his enemies."

Molly pinched her palm, breathing evenly through her nose.

"You betrayed your king, your court. An act of treason," she said. "The court has come to an agreement."

Molly glanced at the sour faces of the council; their disapproving frowns, their ugly sneers, and switched her attention back to Lilith.

"Execution."

That single word caused a war of shivers down Molly's spine and she straightened.

The room burst into vicious whispers around her, and she eyed the prince's wild gaze.

"You'd kill me," Molly spoke, her voice soft, but capable of silencing the room. "The only daemon known to you?"

Lilith raised her chin, glaring down at her. "I am tired of that excuse. My late husband may have seen value in you, but I only see a hideous, dangerous whore hell-bent on destroying my people and my court."

Molly's confidence wilted inside of her, but she gritted her teeth, not allowing anyone in the court to see her fear, to see her trembling inside.

Like a sharp dagger, Lilith grinned. "Until the king awakes from his slumber, I am in charge of this court. You were a mere pawn, never the queen. You have no right to govern over my kingdom, you *daemon whore*."

"You can't make that decision," Molly fought, letting the icy sensation expand into her eyes and a vicious glow began.

Lilith swung her arm, a whip of gold clenched in her hand and slashed it across Molly's cheek.

The white-hot pain stung her cheek and she stumbled, grasping the side of her face. Her eyes watered, one squeezed shut.

"Do not question my power," Lilith warned and repositioned herself on her throne, wrapping the gold whip around her arm.

"My Queen," the prince's voice echoed like water to a dying man, and Molly half-faced him, her hand dropping to display the ugly red lash across her skin. "As much as the daemon threatened our king, she is important."

Lilith pursed her ruby red lips, but she, for once, stayed silent as her son approached the throne.

"She carries the heir, the son of our king," the prince continued, a voice of calm and power. "We'd be therefore not only executing his wife, but also his unborn son. A son filled with the king's blood and bone."

The court stilled.

Molly could feel their torment. They were debating. Killing her would be like killing their king, especially when she held his child in her womb.

Her hand went to her stomach and she raised her head, catching Lilith's hard stare.

The prince had found a loophole.

A way to protect her and their son.

"May I suggest an alternative?"

Lilith cocked her brow at her son and again, tapped her fingers on the throne. *Tap, tap, tap.* A constant jab to Molly's chest.

Lilith's fingers stopped and she didn't speak but glared at her son. That apparently was an answer of yes.

"Banishment from the High Court," the prince said.

Molly's heart squeezed.

Tensley needed her. Tensley needed someone to protect him, someone to bring him back. If they banished her, she wouldn't be able to see him.

Her eyes darted to Lilith. A finger ran along her bottom lip, her face pinched in deep thought. Judging by the small, cruel smile growing at the corners of her lips, she was no doubt wondering about all the things she could do with the king whilst his wife, his source of power, was banished from their court.

After a beat, she snapped her fingers. "Very well. I hereby declare that Molly Knight is now banished from setting foot in High Court."

Molly wanted to burn the kingdom down while watching the gold trim boil under Lilith's fingers and hear every member scream for mercy.

But she couldn't fight now.

Not yet.

She hoped, she prayed that sliver of Tensley's heart was enough for now.

Molly ground her teeth, feeling the tension burn the lash on her cheek, but it only fueled her more.

"Guards," Lilith called, her eyes never parting from Molly, a sick glint to them that turned her impregnated stomach inside out. Two guards in their suits of gold armor approached Molly on either side.

Molly didn't let them touch her. She turned, her eyes darting to the prince, and walked toward the double doors.

The court watched their king's wife leave with her head held high. They didn't know her insides were burning and fraying. Holding on by a thread.

The guards flanked her, dangerously close to her sides. They knew the threat underneath her skin.

Once outside in the hallway, she saw Seto.

"My lady," he said, glaring at the two guards beside her.

"Seto," Molly said, stopping in front of him. "You need to protect him. You need to watch out for him."

Seto nodded. "I promise, with my life, I will protect him. Do not worry."

A guard gripped her elbow and shoved her. "Move."

Molly scowled and gave one last look to Seto. She knew this may be the last time she saw him so she said what she had told herself not to bring up.

"Prim will come back to you, she may seem far, and broken. But she'll come back for you, she'll fight for love. And so will you. Love wins," she whispered and watched the way his body stiffened.

He simply nodded, his lip trembling as he tried to speak back.

The guards pressed her forward and she obeyed, marching through the large glamorous hallways, paintings of victories and battles, and she felt lost.

Her heart was in her throat. She didn't even have a chance to say goodbye to Tensley.

"Wait!" Molly looked over her shoulder to see the prince jogging after them. He stopped in front of her and shoved the guards to the side. He pressed his cheek to hers and sighed, "You will have that iron heart, just as I will have that throne."

Molly breathed out shakily and the prince stood back, his eyes focusing on her pale expression.

"Protect him," Molly whispered.

He smirked. "He'll be safe with me."

THE RAIN HAD soaked through her clothes and straight to the bone. As she stood in Tensley's dark apartment, her emotions sat in a heavy lump in her throat. Each swallow, it grew larger and heavier. Each swallow, she ached to sob, to release the building tension in her chest and lungs and bleeding heart.

The guards had opened the veil between the High Court and she ended up outside in the street, behind an old Chinese restaurant.

Now she stood alone in an apartment she once called her own.

Their apartment.

She didn't know how long she stood there in complete darkness, still wearing soaked clothes, but a knock at the door shook her from her thoughts.

She turned, staring at the door until another, louder knock propelled her forward.

She opened it to see a familiar face.

"Molly," Illya whispered, stepping into the room and taking in her dripping wet clothes. "The doorman contacted me as soon as he saw you walk inside the building. What—what happened?"

She opened her mouth, but nothing came out.

Illya laid a light hand on her shoulder and his tender eyes searched her face. "I heard, Molly. About Fallen and Tensley."

She swallowed thickly. She could note the pain written all over Illya's friendly face and it crushed her even more.

Tensley's best friend, like a brother to him.

"Is it true? Is he—" he stopped himself.

Molly nodded, her unwept tears burning.

Illya sighed, closing his eyes in pain. He stood silently for a moment, searching for the floor like it held the answers to cure him.

Illya pulled Molly into his arms and wrapped her in warmth and comfort, and she sobbed. Freely, unafraid of the judgment because Illya would never judge her.

She dug her nails into his shoulders. After some time, he pulled back and brushed her hair from her face.

"Tensley," Illya muttered, his features showcasing a battle inside of him. "Tensley had bought you a gift. He planned to show you after you returned from the High Court."

Molly wrinkled her brow. "A gift?"

Illya studied her. "Come. I'll show you."

chapter ten

I LLYA LED THEM down toward Central Park, but for Molly, everything was a fog. When they stopped in front of the Dakota apartments, a famous building in Manhattan, she frowned. The building's high gables and deep roofs with a profusion of dormers gave it a North German Renaissance character, something anciently beautiful to Manhattan.

The Dakota was to be one of Manhattan's most prestigious and exclusive cooperative residential buildings.

"Come on," Illya urged and took her hand. Illya spoke to the doorman and he smiled back at Molly, but she couldn't form one in return.

A short elevator ride later and they exited into a grand hallway of black and white tiled floors.

Illya withdrew a key from his pocket and stopped at a white door.

He opened it and stepped back, nodding at Molly to go first.

Molly hesitated, her hands held in front of her tightly. She took one step inside and glanced at the classic elegance of the room. Painted a light blue, a foyer greeted them.

Molly moved forward, each new lavish room greeting her. A kitchen of grace and French traditional style, a dining room with a crystal chandelier over a long mahogany table, two living rooms, three bathrooms, three bedrooms, and even a study filled with her books and Tensley's.

The last door she entered was a grand bedroom, a large king bed with a master bathroom attached.

"What is this?" Molly asked as she traced her finger along the bed frame. She turned and stepped into the walk in closet.

"It's your new home," Illya told her. "Tensley said he wanted more room. I guess he was thinking of the future."

Her fingers touched the tip of the ironed dress shirts. Ones that still smelled like her Tensley.

She gripped a sleeve and pulled it off the wooden hanger, clenching it to her throbbing chest.

"Molly?"

Her knees buckled and she fell, bending over as a painful sob wracked her body.

"Molly!' Illya's hands smoothed across her back. "It's okay, we'll figure this out."

She shook her head, gasping between sobs that made her whole body shake. "No, Illya. No." She looked up at him through blurred vision, seeing his sad eyes and his concerned expression. "Illya, I'm pregnant."

Illya's brows shot up to his hairline. "Pregnant?"

She nodded, wetness rolling down her cheeks. "We had a wedding in the High Court, but I was already two months pregnant before then. We didn't want to tell anyone, we didn't want to risk it." Her shaking hands went to her stomach. "Then Fallen ripped his heart out. He knew. About everything. He found out, somehow. That I was pregnant long before the wedding, that Tensley fell in love with me and I love…"

Illya pulled her into his arms and held her, allowing her to sob, to scream into his chest. He didn't let her go, he only whispered soothing words and she cried harder, digging her fingers into his back, afraid to let go in case he too was taken from her.

After a long time of holding each other on the floor of the closet, Illya picked her up and laid her down in the bed.

Illya eventually left the room, and as she cried, she grew tired.

At the sound of a knock, Molly jolted out of slumber and stared at September. Her entire outfit was drenched from the rain, including her dark hair, droplets gathering and creating a puddle on the hardwood floor.

Molly tried to keep her face expressionless, but September smiled shakily, and everything broke inside of her.

September rushed to the bed and wrapped her arms around Molly, whispering cherished words of comfort and understanding, and Molly never wanted to let go.

HOURS HAD PASSED and the three of them, Illya, September, and Molly sat in the living room. It was her home now, but it felt foreign and empty without Tensley. He had decorated the apartment complimentary to her tastes, every last detail, even the lace curtains.

"Pregnant…" September repeated for the thousandth time. "And married." She folded her arms and leaned back against the leather chair.

Illya stood by the fireplace, a hand covering his mouth as he watched her.

"And your husband is now king of demons?" She cocked a brow at Molly. September continued to repeat everything back to them, shocked by all the new information.

"And you're sure you're pregnant?"

Molly sighed and held her stomach. "Yes."

September paused, her mouth twisting in the way Molly knew she wanted to say something but was holding back. "Do your parents know?"

Molly shook her head. "I'll tell them tomorrow. After I get settled in." But she wasn't sure how she would ever settle into this giant apartment.

She pressed her hands into the soft white couch and fixed the wool blanket around her shoulders. A warm shower had eased some of her tension, but it all sat on her chest, weighing heavier each second she wasn't near Tensley.

She wasn't sure how her parents would react. They had never approved of Tensley, but this child was hers. It was their blood and she knew they both wanted grandchildren. The other thing that made her stomach twist with worry was their reaction to their only daughter getting married without their knowledge. Without them being present.

Her heart hurt at the thought of Tensley's promise. A promise that he'd give her another wedding in Manhattan. A promise he'd be there.

"And Tensley..." September paused, taking a deep breath. "Tensley's heartless now?"

Molly nodded again. "I tried to get him back, I tried to give him a heart. The prince and I, we found this old, dangerous curse that was meant to make him grow a heart again. We managed to bring part of it back, but it's so small, so vulnerable," she said, her voice weak to her own ears. "I just—I just feel like I failed him. It's not enough. I didn't do enough. Maybe if I had had more time in High Court I could have worked harder to make the sliver of a heart grow some more, but I'm banished. The court banished me. They said I was a threat to their king. A threat to my own husband."

Silence.

Molly saw Illya and September steal a glance. They didn't know how to handle her. She wanted to yell she wasn't breakable, she wasn't delicate, and she wouldn't back down.

But internally, she knew in that instant, she was all of those things. After weeks and weeks of constantly looking behind her back and playing games, trying to decipher friends from enemies in a court full of snakes and wolves, she needed a moment to be vulnerable around friends. Real friends. A moment to live her emotions fully, not repress them.

She did feel broken. She felt delicate and vulnerable. She felt like a failure.

So, she allowed herself to feel that way. If only for that one night.

A knock startled them and all three looked at the white door.

Illya cleared his throat after a moment and moved, opening the door.

Tensley's mother, Daphne, and his sister, Gabriella, pushed their way into the apartment. Both ignored Illya's presence.

"Hey," September said, awkwardly raising her hand.

Both women glanced at her, but they were both more focused on Molly.

"My dear," Daphne said, rushing to Molly's side. She sat down next to Molly on the couch and held her hand. "Are you all right? Illya told us you were back."

"Yes," Molly said, frowning at both of them. Gabriella stood behind her mother, her baby, Isabella cradled in her arms.

"All we've heard were awful rumors. Some even said you were dead," Daphne continued.

I almost was.

"Where's Tensley?" Gabriella asked, her hard eyes focused on Molly. She rocked Isabella as she began to fuss.

Molly's throat grew tight and she bowed her head. "He's still at High Court," she said, her voice almost a whisper.

Gabriella glanced at her mother whose own head lowered.

"Please tell me it isn't true," Daphne whispered, her voice on the edge of breaking. She gripped Molly's hand tighter. Molly looked into Daphne's shining brown eyes of warmth. "Please tell me my son isn't heartless. My son isn't the king."

Molly squeezed her eyes shut and with courage, opened them and met Daphne's begging eyes. "It is," she said, her own voice breaking. "It's true."

Daphne grew pale and her free hand shook violently as it covered her mouth.

Gabriella pressed her lips together and swore under her breath.

"Was he vicious?" Daphne asked through tearful eyes. "Did he hurt you?"

Molly shook her head and her hands fell to her stomach. Daphne's eyes widened and she turned to her daughter who smiled slightly, and back to Molly. "You're pregnant?"

Molly nodded, a small smile curving her lips.

Daphne gripped her hands, her expression hard. "You're safe now, Molly. I won't let anyone hurt you. We will find a way to hide the pregnancy so no one harms you."

Molly's brows furrowed, and then it occurred to her. "No, no. We're married."

Daphne's hard expression dropped. "Married?"

"Tensley asked Fallen to have the wedding sooner, because we were both afraid someone would find out about the baby. Fallen agreed, but only if it took place in High Court. And so we did, we got married there," she explained, her hand lightly brushing her stomach.

Then, she forced herself to tell them everything that had happened to Tensley and herself, from the moment they had set foot in High Court, to the moment she had left. Alone. Leaving the man she loved behind.

Daphne stared at her, and without warning, pulled her into a tight hug. "We're family, and family protects its own blood."

She pulled back, tears streaming down her face and fixed Molly's wet hair.

"I'm going to save your son, I promise," Molly whispered.

Daphne smiled shakily.

"How's Scorpios? Did Ares do too much damage?" Molly asked, trying to switch the conversation.

Daphne's eyes turned haunted with grief and other emotions Molly couldn't decipher. "Ares attacked the pit. Where Beau was. They killed members, but we were able to fight them off. We're preparing to send an attack, but another thing happened while you were away," she said and her own voice broke completely.

Gabriella moved forward, putting her hand on her mom's shoulder in support. "My husband passed away. The doctor told us the chances of him coming back to us were too slim, and so we," she stopped, a sob escaping her. "We let him go."

"I bet the devil is having too much fun in hell," Gabriella said, and Daphne's lips turned into a small, sad smile.

Molly's heart twisted like a dagger to her chest. Tensley's father was dead. "I'm sorry," she whispered. "I'm so, so sorry."

Daphne shook her head and squeezed Molly's hands.

Molly's brows furrowed at a sudden thought. "Who's in charge of Scorpios then? We were gone for weeks he and I. Who has been leading Scorpios?"

Daphne's head lowered and she turned to look at Gabriella, searching for the right words.

"Evelyn Rose has been acting as Dux," Daphne said, not hiding her distaste.

Molly's stomach dropped.

"She's hungry for power and since the news of Tensley's new role, she's been even hungrier on keeping her position as the new Dux of Scorpios," Gabriella bit out and that made Isabella cry.

"That bitch," September chimed in and all eyes swung to her. She awkwardly shrugged.

Molly dug her nails into her thighs. Evelyn Rose, a woman of Scorpios, Tensley's ex fling. The woman had been hell-bent on ruining her relationship with Tensley, and now she had his position.

"She won't stay in that position," Molly said and lifted her gaze to Daphne. "I'll make sure of it."

chapter eleven

THE WHITE TOWNHOUSE stood out in the dark autumn of Manhattan. The leaves had turned into reds and oranges and soon would fall and paint the sidewalks. Molly didn't knock as she entered Scorpios' townhouse, the row of footmen dressed in black suits a familiar sight.

The men glanced at her and their faces dropped.

As her high heels clicked against the tiled floor, passing each member, they bowed their heads in respect.

She walked with grace and power, as if a crown atop her head.

A guard stood outside of the boardroom and when he saw her, he stilled.

"Ms. Darling," he whispered carefully, as if he wasn't sure how she would react to him speaking to her.

"Is Evelyn Rose in there?" she asked, gesturing to the door he guarded.

He glanced back at it, then her, nodding. "Yes, but she's in a private meeting. I can escort you to her office until it's over."

Molly clenched her jaw, took off her sunglasses and folded them into her purse. "No need. She'll see me now."

"Ms. Darling, it may be better to wait," he protested, lifting a hand.

Molly didn't wait though. She pushed past him and shoved open the boardroom door.

In the dark room, the high members of Scorpios gathered around a long oak desk. Evelyn sat at the head of the table, her legs crossed, and her eyes widened at the sight of Molly.

Then those eyes darkened.

"Ms. Darling," Evelyn began, softly, as if any louder it would break her.

Molly glowered at her. "Actually," Molly started, a slow, venomous smile growing on her lips. "It's Mrs. Knight now."

The pen Evelyn had been holding broke in half and the ink flooded her papers. Other than that, she showed no reaction. She simply dropped the pen and sat back in her seat.

"You're intruding in a private meeting," Evelyn said, lowly, on the edge of a hiss. "One where only members are allowed."

"As the Dux's wife, and now also the wife of a king, I am definitely the best fit to manage Scorpios until his return. And so Ms. Rose?" she said, a brow rising up to her hairline as she looked straight at the other woman with a feral smile. "You can expect me to be at a lot of these lovely private meetings."

Silence.

Then one member cleared his throat. "So it's true then, our Dux is now the king?"

Molly nodded, chin raised high. "Yes, he is. In fact, I saw him snap Fallen's neck with my very own eyes."

Murmurs filled the room and Evelyn's hard stare burnt Molly's flesh.

Evelyn slammed her fist on the desk, the cups of coffee jolting. "I will not have a non-demon interfering with our cause."

"Interfering?" Molly's voice rang loud in the room and she took a dangerous step closer. "I am the wife of your Dux. I am the wife of your king. I have every right to be here."

"Every right?" Evelyn tsked. "You're an outsider. May I remind you that you once tried to trade our Dux to hunters."

The members stiffened at her words.

Molly clenched her teeth, remembering a time where she had been so foolish, terrified of this new world Tensley lived in, and had preferred to trust hunters and harm Tensley.

She would hate herself for it until the day she died.

"I will be filling in as Dux until he returns," Molly repeated, sharply, leaving no room for argument.

Evelyn stood from her seat and Molly felt the whip of aggressive pheromones hit her hard.

Molly's eyes flashed, the icy sensation rushing forward, wrapping around her spine and fingertips, as they glowed.

Brilliantly.

Violently.

She was a snake and her venom was lethal.

The dark light within Evelyn's eyes flickered as the woman realized Molly's hold on her, on her strength and body.

Perhaps, Molly realized, she could even control a demon's will. If she tried. If she wished.

Evelyn's head turned ever so slowly to the side, her movements slowed down due to Molly's power over her.

She was strong if she could still move when under a daemon's hold, Molly had to give her that.

When Evelyn's gaze left Molly's, a growl escaped the other woman. She was giving up this fight.

Molly freed her, but not without a warning of her own. "Do not threaten me or my own, or I will do far worse than simply control your body," she hissed.

Evelyn lifted her chin and yanked at her pin straight skirt. "You are an outsider. Do you expect us to accept a daemon to lead us?"

Molly took a single step forward and she felt the tumble in her stomach. Of her son. Of her son's powers. Protecting her. "Let's see." She turned to the table of men who gawked at each of the women. "Would you prefer your Dux, your king's wife?" Molly caught every single eye, challenging any one to speak, to reject her. "Or would you prefer her?"

The men turned their attention to Evelyn's sour expression. She was on the edge of bursting a blood vessel.

Silence.

Evelyn tapped her ruby red high heels against the hardwood and sighed harshly. "Well?" She waved a hand to the men. "Speak up."

The men exchanged glances, hard and long, and then one rose to their feet.

"Mrs. Knight," he said, a man with a wrinkled forehead and heavy brows. Another stood. "Mrs. Knight." The young man bowed his head in respect.

One after the other, they stood, repeating her name like a chant to a god, and her chest warmed, heavy and hot.

If she couldn't save Tensley at High Court, she'd save him at Scorpios.

Evelyn's face grew bright red and her bottom lip shook. Not in sadness, but in pure rage.

Once all the men had stood, all repeating Mrs. Knight, Evelyn slammed her palm down on the desk.

"No, no! I am Dux. It's my position. It's my right!" She heaved violently, unable to catch her breath.

"Ms. Rose," one man snapped at her. "It has been decided."

Evelyn snarled, like a wild animal and turned her deadly, darkened eyes at Molly.

"Fine," she spat and sat back in her chair, shuffling papers. "You think you can handle Scorpios? Be my fucking guest." She smiled viciously back at Molly.

And Molly didn't give her a reaction. Not even a cruel smile back.

One of the men pulled out a chair at the other end of the table and Molly nodded her thanks, sitting down.

She folded her hands and looked down the row of chairs at each man. "First, tell me what we plan to do with Ares."

Evelyn spent the meeting in silence as the men caught Molly up to speed on the events and plans to deal with Ares.

Nothing had been decided. A crew of men had been sent in to spy on Ares in Boston, but no counterattack.

They had been waiting for Tensley to return.

Molly rubbed at her temples, her back aching from sitting so long. Evelyn smirked at her, enjoying her torture.

"Give us time," Molly said. "They'll be expecting us to counterattack. We need to wait until they least expect it, when they're the most unguarded." She fisted her hands on her thighs. "Perhaps, I'll pay them a visit."

"A visit, my queen?"

Molly's head snapped up at the term. "Please call me Mrs. Knight or Molly."

The older man nodded vigorously, as if frightened at the idea of displeasing her.

"I've met the men that run Ares. If I can talk to them, find a common ground."

"Oh, because that'll work," Evelyn scoffed. "The whole reason Ares attacked was because they wanted you."

Molly's shoulders stiffened.

"With all due respect, Mrs. Knight. These men deserve to be slaughtered. They attacked our men and they poisoned Mr. Knight," a man, Richmond, spoke.

Molly stared at the papers in front of her. "We'll bargain with them. For their lives, they will surrender their land and power. And if not, we will slaughter them." Her voice was loud and strong and everything that Ares should fear.

The men were silent, watching their temporary Dux with curiosity and interest.

Her eyes darted to Evelyn and for once, she didn't have a witty retort, but she still wore that ugly scowl.

Molly would protect what was Tensley's and bring Ares to their knees.

She vowed she would.

MOLLY SAT PERFECTLY still in her parents' living room. It felt like ages since she had been home and now both of her parents sat across from her. It felt foreign. Months before Tensley had walked into their lives and now he was her husband. Now a heartless king.

"School's going well?" her father, Derek, asked. His trimmed brows always made her laugh as a child, and seeing him made her heart warm. All she wanted to do was rush into his warm hug and let him take away the pain.

"It's good. I'll be finishing early though. By the end of December," she told them.

Her mother sipped at her tea and hummed in response. "December? Why so early?"

Molly took a deep breath. This was the hard part. Telling her parents everything. From her pregnancy to her recent wedding and the fact Tensley wasn't in the picture at the moment.

"Well," she whispered and lifted her China white teacup. "Tensley and I got married."

Her mother spluttered out her tea and covered her mouth. "Married?"

Her father frowned. "Did he force you?"

Molly shook her head. "No, no. I love him, Dad."

Derek's mouth twisted and he rubbed at his jaw. "You — you love him," he said, as if the mere thought of loving a demon sounded ridiculous, impossible. "My daughter is in love with a demon. Dear lord," he breathed, his hand going to his heart, rubbing vigorously has if to ease some pain. He turned toward his wife, their eyes meeting briefly. "Our daugh— she's... and she wasn't forced. She wanted it." He sat back, stunned, hand still clutching his chest. "Are you happy with him?"

"I...was," she began, lowering her lashes. "A lot happened recently, he has to stay in this place called High Court, it's where all the high born demons live. He's— he's the king now."

Her mother dropped her teacup and it shattered. Neither of them moved to clean it up. "A king?"

Molly nodded. "Yes," she paused, debating whether or not to tell them he was heartless. She decided otherwise at their pale expressions. The biggest announcement was yet to be revealed. She took a deep breath and went for it. "I'm pregnant," she blurted out, quickly taking a sip of her tea.

"Pregnant?" her mother muttered. Her hands went to her face and she stared at Molly, her eyes shifting between her stomach and Molly's eyes. "You're pregnant?"

Molly opened her mouth to calm her down, but her mother began bawling instead. Molly clasped her mouth shut, unsure of how she was meant to react, what she was supposed to say.

"Pregnant," her mother continued to say, shaking her head.

Derek cleared his throat and reached out to touch Molly's hand, his trembling slightly. "Are you— are you truly happy?"

Molly blinked back tears. "I'm very happy with him and the baby. I love him, Dad."

Her mother sobbed and sniffled, her mascara sliding down onto her pristine Chanel suit. "A baby, Derek. We're going to be grandparents. I'm going to have grandchildren. She's pre—"

Molly cocked a brow. "You're—happy?"

Her mother nodded her head fast and yanked out a tissue from a box on a table nearby, patting under her eyes. "Of course I am. You know I've always wanted to have grandchildren. I didn't expect them so soon, I won't lie. But I'm happy nonetheless. We can go shopping now and get everything you'll need. And a baby shower! I can host one here!"

Molly smiled, warmth gathering behind her eyes. It was the last reaction she expected from her family, but the best. Of course it thrilled her mother to organize everything possible for the baby and she'd gladly let her do it.

Molly spent dinner there and everything felt the same but different. She wasn't their little girl anymore. She had grown, she had changed, and now she was a warrior, a wife, and soon she'd be a mother.

On the walk home it rained and she didn't bother fixing her hood. She let the rain wash over her, hoping to cleanse her blistered heart.

When she arrived at the new apartment, she stood in the middle of the living room. Alone in such a big home, she craved him. It was the tiny moments, it was the moments she came home and let the sadness, the pain sink in.

Tonight, she allowed it to win.

chapter twelve

A VIOLENT THROB RUPTURED inside of Tensley's chest and he jolted. The pain, a bright pulse, too intense, too much all at once that he groaned in pure pain.

His fingers dug deep into the white silk sheets and he pulled himself to sit up.

Bad fucking decision.

He felt empty, he felt a rage binding, winding inside of him like a noose.

Tighter tighter tighter—

Until he couldn't breathe and choked.

Someone touched his shoulder and he struck, swinging his shaking arm into the wall of muscle.

More hands wrapped around his arms and legs and held him down, the beast livid, the beast crazed.

Something was missing.

Something was wrong.

He couldn't breathe.

Confusion was a heavy fog over him and the more he struggled, the more he saw the flash of blood and bodies and the sound of cracking bones.

Voices assaulted his aching eardrums and he twisted his head away.

To once again, hide in his darkness.

It was warm, it was silent and safe.

A lightness burnt his eyes and with tiny flutters of his eyes, he saw the bedchamber.

The sheets were torn, the furniture flipped and broken into pieces of wood, a nearby painting of Fallen was ripped open with claw marks.

Another nightmare.

Another vision of something he couldn't grasp, something buried deep inside of him he wished didn't exist, wasn't embedded in his bones and skin tissue.

His body sagged back into the bed.

Night after night, he raged in his sleep.

Night after night, he became worse. When he avoided sleep, the pains in his chest came and went more frequently. Like the embedded part of him knew he was avoiding sleep.

Cold sweats, screaming until his throat burned raw, and thrashing until he woke himself up.

He was riddled with memories of who he was before, but the pieces inside of him didn't connect.

A month since he last saw her. A month of waking and sleeping in constant pain inside of his chest.

He was a night sky without a full moon, and he was warm in the darkness.

He sat up in the bed, the pounding soft, but nonetheless violent in his chest. *Focus on the rage, the anger, not the emptiness.* He bowed his head, his fingers gathering the silk sheets in an angry fist.

Deep breaths clawed through him, trying to ease the pain. During the day, he shrugged it off or rubbed his chest to soothe the ache, but today was worse.

Each day it grew harder to cope.

Harder to ignore the growing heavy weight gathering in his chest like a bundle of grenades.

One he wished to rip open.

He remembered what the daemon had done. Sewn a little pebble enchanted by a warlock to create a heart in his chest. All the warlocks assured him it was a sliver, not enough to harm him or worry the court.

But he didn't tell anyone about the pain or the growing sensation.

Like a phantom heart.

He would never be weakened again, weakened by a human nonetheless or sink as low as wanting her heart.

He growled as his chest burned at the mere thought of her. At the mere thought of her precious, vicious heart.

He wanted it.

He wanted to devour it and destroy it slowly, so slowly she begged him to give it back.

Again the brutal pain of a thousand daggers seized him and he roared, bowing his head and gripping the sheets.

She fucking cursed me.

He wanted her in front of him. Weeks had gone by and he refused any woman who tried to touch him. Even when Lilith touched him, a spark of fury and sting accompanied her touch. As if his body rejected anyone but his precious wife.

A knock at his door roused him from his thoughts, but the pain still vibrated.

He breathed through his nose, glaring up at the double doors. A shield from the court that fawned over him, waited on him night and day, and kissed his feet and hands like he was a god.

He never bought their loyalty and he heard talk of some members disgust of their middle class born king, but all were too afraid of Tensley to ever confront him.

If they could easily show him loyalty and words, how easily they could do the same to the next king if he died.

Molly had been his only advantage over the court. Her touch was power, and now she was gone, and weeks of her absence wore him down.

The last thing he wanted was to give up the throne. The power made him wild. He loved the feeling of control he wielded in the court and it all led back to his wife.

The one who tried to corrupt him once again.

"Come in," he said, gathering a pair of trousers and pulling them on.

Lilith entered, her red hair half-up, ringlets spiraling down her neck. She curtsied, a secret grin on her face and moved forward.

"My king, you overslept," she said, her eyes immediately going to his exposed chest and down to where he fastened his trousers.

He didn't say a word and grabbed a shirt, pulling it on over his head.

"I need you to send me someone," he told her gruffly, tucking his shirt into his trousers.

"Anything for you, my lord." She smiled like she held a secret, like he hung the moon for her.

"Find me my wife," he told her and watched her smile drop.

She swallowed thickly and shook her head. "My lord, as I said before, we do not know where she is."

His temper flared. So easily, he felt the demon side of him, the now more dominant side of him taking control. He fisted his hands and took a dangerous step closer to her, giving her a pointed look. "Find me my wife or I will shatter this palace."

Lilith straightened, her eyes crinkling, a flash of anger, but she swallowed and smoothed her dress down. She pressed her lips into a thin line and glanced up at him. "My lord, I did not wish to tell you, but now you must know," she said, a bite to her words.

Tensley fisted one hand beside him, watching the late queen carefully. He saw a droplet of sweat roll down her tensed temple and the way her chest rose fast.

The beast was attuned to other's emotions, to their nerves, and their desires.

She feared him—and she desired him.

Fear and lust were alike within her.

"Speak now," he said, lowly.

Lilith took a deep breath and stepped forward. "She chose to leave, Your Majesty."

Tensley's jaw locked and he heard the grit of his sharp teeth scratch.

"She did not wish to stay with you. She did not honor you," she added, shaking her head as if judging his powerful wife.

The thorns dug deeper into his warring chest and he fisted his other hand, an attempt to avoid soothing the growing ache.

He twisted away, searching, roaring inside.

She left me...she left...

The ache intensified and instead of a cry of pain, he growled and turned to Lilith.

Lilith jolted as he rushed toward her. "Find her. And bring her to me."

Lilith blinked rapidly. "My lord, she's a criminal. She must not be near you."

"Bring her to me," he bellowed, gripping the bedpost, the wood snapping in half. Splinters and chunks of wood fell to the floor. He met her blank expression and he took timed steps forward. "Bring me my wife or I will slaughter one of your guards every hour until you do so."

Lilith's cheeks bloomed in fury. With a harsh breath, she bowed. "As you command, my lord."

She turned on her heel and stomped to the door, shutting it behind her.

Tensley moved to the balcony, wiping a hand through his hair only to pull back and look at his bloody hands, splinters of wood embedded into his palms.

He gritted his teeth.

Two sides warred inside of him.

He wanted to destroy her—he wanted to protect her.

But both wanted her.

Craved her. Something far too holy for his bloody, tainted hands.

He curled his fists, the splinters digging deeper, the physical pain relieving the pain in his chest.

"Bring me my queen."

COOL NOVEMBER RAIN dribbled over Molly's black umbrella as she navigated out of her anthropology class. The leaves were brittle, clinging to the trees as autumn ended and she thought of Tensley's fall into a heartless beast.

Like the dying leaves cascading down around her.

One month.

One month since his heart was ripped out and she was banished from the court.

One month closer to having their son.

She smiled at the thought of her son, the doctor saying he was strong and large for four and a half months, but that didn't surprise her. His toes and fingers were well-defined and the doctor said he could even yawn now. Her chest felt heavy and warm at the thought. So nervous, so excited, so scared.

If Tensley were here…

She shook her head and moved forward to the little café. She saw Stella had plopped herself in a booth inside, nursing a steaming tea. When Stella's brown eyes caught Molly, she straightened and waved her over.

Molly closed her umbrella and shook off the excess water.

"I got you herbal tea," Stella announced and pushed a large cup toward her.

Molly sat down and stared at the dark, hot substance.

"I heard it's better for the baby," Stella added and sipped at her own cup. "So how is my little guy?"

Molly smiled. "He's a night hawk. He keeps me up, but the doctor said that's normal." Molly flipped over a menu and clasped her mouth shut to prevent drool rolling down her chin. "And he's constantly hungry. I can't stop eating."

"Well, if he's anything like his daddy, he's gonna be a big boy," Stella said, flipping her red locks over her shoulder. Stella paused and leaned forward. "Have you seen him yet?"

Molly cupped her drink and stared at her hands. "No." The hotness warmed her hands, a soothing calm compared to the cool bite of November. "Maybe it's best—for the baby and me to stay away. I don't need more stress in my life right now." She bit her lip. As much as she believed that, she missed him terribly. At night, she woke up crying his name. At doctor's appointments, she wished he were there to see the ultrasound or to hear the baby's heartbeat. "But Illya's been there. He comes with me to doctor appointments, he stays at the apartment and he's just there. That's all I need right now."

She smiled softly at the thought of Illya. He had taken on a father's role right away. He cleaned the house, he bought groceries, he made sure she got to school okay, and when in the middle of the night she woke up crying, he was there until she fell asleep.

She knew he felt a strong loyalty to Tensley and as much as she and he were good friends, she knew he was doing it all for his best friend.

She caught glimpses of him staring out the large bay window that faced Central Park and she knew he was grieving too.

He had lost his best friend, his brother, and he felt it was his responsibility, like a dying wish, to protect and provide for her.

Illya and her—needed each other most right now, and with focusing entirely on the baby, they could escape their heartbreak. From being banned from High Court, she was scared she'd only endanger the baby by trying to go. If something happened to her, if she was imprisoned…

She shook her head, ridding herself of those thoughts.

Stella cleared her throat and Molly jolted out of her thoughts. "And your parents?"

Molly laughed. "My mom is planning this huge baby shower and she comes over everyday with farmer's market goods." She swallowed, rubbing her hand on her belly. "They do want me to move back in with them. They don't want me to do this by myself, but I think I'd rather stay in the apartment."

"I mean, maybe it'll be good for all of you?" Stella shrugged, twisting her features into an unsure frown.

Molly looked out the window at the busy avenue and the falling leaves. She didn't want to say it out loud. It would sound too naïve, too childish and hopeful.

She dreamed that if she stayed in the apartment—one day, maybe one day Tensley would walk in and everything would be back to normal.

He'd say *dolcezza* and kiss her.

One day.

Molly blinked back tears and smiled at Stella whose brows wrinkled. "Now tell me. What's going on with you and Illya?"

Stella pursed her lips and looked down at her tea. "Nothing."

Molly hummed.

Stella glared at her. "Look, I wish something was going on, but he's as dense as—" She blew out a breath. "I think he's still hung up on September."

Molly frowned. "I don't know, Stella. He is going through a lot right now."

"I know." She sighed and pressed a finger to her temple. "I just want him to know he can count on me. Lean on me. I'm not delicate, I'm not breakable." She shook her head and Molly went to say more, but Stella leaned forward and smiled. "Now, show me those photos of my nephew."

Molly grinned and didn't pry into Stella's life anymore before pulling out the black and white ultrasound picture from her purse.

"Oh my god! Look at him!" Stella gripped the ultrasound and gushed, looking at it from different angles. "I can't believe he's inside of you right now."

Molly pressed a hand to her abdomen and breathed through her nose. "Believe me, I for one cannot forget he's in there."

Both girls laughed at that.

The next hour flew by and the conversation became lighter, more carefree and lighthearted and it was everything Molly needed.

September sent a text as Molly walked home that she'd stop by tomorrow— she basically lived at the apartment too.

Molly entered the glamorous apartment building, waving at the doorman and walked up to her apartment.

As soon as she shut the door, she went to the master bedroom and grabbed one of Tensley's dress shirts. She removed her clothes in the bathroom and slipped the shirt on. His thick scent washed over her and she smoothed it down, ending just below her knees. A bad habit now, one she refused to kick. It comforted her at night to smell his scent around her.

She froze and glanced over her shoulder at the bathroom door. "Illya?"

Only silence replied.

Her heart pounded in her chest all the way to her eardrums, a constant reminder of fear, of being in danger.

She sensed it strongly.

She wasn't alone.

She clenched her teeth and moved slowly to the bathroom door, her hand reaching out. As it touched the crown molding of the door, her heart spiked wildly and she pushed it open.

A tall dark figure stood in the darkness of the master bedroom, his back to the large window.

Her mouth went bone dry and on a gasp, she said: "Tensley?"

chapter thirteen

T HE DARK FIGURE turned. The scruff on his jaw glistened in the low lighting and the familiar brown eyes found hers. What she saw in his own hand was a teddy bear Illya had given her. A toy for her son.

"No, my lady," the prince spoke, fully facing her.

Her heart sank, but she made sure he didn't see any trace of it in her features. "Why are you here?"

The prince took a single step forward and stopped, his eyes dropping to her stomach.

A tiny bump now sat there. She hadn't told anyone outside of her inner circle and had yet to tell Scorpios, but she was sure if they knew, they'd find a way to spin the fact to their advantage, saying they didn't need a pregnant, hormonal, woman leading them through a war.

They needed a warrior.

Any business between Scorpios was between members only. September and Stella barely knew an inch of what was going on behind the scenes.

"Molly," the prince began, his eyes leaving her stomach and they held a softness, along with exhaustion. "Are you well?"

Molly watched him closely and after a long moment, sighed and nodded. "I'm fine, but why are you here?" She fisted her hands. "Is it Tensley? Is he all right?"

The prince tilted his head to the side, but when he didn't reject the thought, her heart pounded fast. "His health is declining, but the court is unaware of how severe the situation is."

She swallowed and gawked at his weathered, scarred hands.

"He refuses to allow another woman's touch upon his skin—he refuses to discuss the war inside of him," he said, lowly and she bit the inside of her cheek. "He summons you."

Molly scowled and tossed her purse onto the bed. "Summons me? I was banished by Lilith."

"The king," the prince said and it still gave Molly shivers to hear her Tensley called a king. "Has revoked it. He summons you—on conditions."

"What conditions?"

The prince folded his arms and gave her a long look. "That is something he must discuss with you."

"And if I refuse?" She didn't know if she could. If Tensley's health was declining, if he was ill, she wouldn't let him die. She'd save the beast if it meant saving the man.

The prince's lips became a straight line and his brows dropped low. "I fear the beast will go mad without you near. He already has."

Molly looked away to the dark master bed, the sheets pulled tight and properly. Maybe this was a second chance. A chance so Tensley could come home one day and they could be a family together.

She swung her eyes back to the prince. "Take me to him."

He stood still for a moment and then moved, grabbing a cloak he had lain on his arm and draped it across her shoulders.

The fabric was heavy, a burden on her, but she raised her chin and stared back at him.

"I would warn you to tread carefully," he whispered, a warning to his hard voice. "But you are the one who can control him." Her chest rose fast and hard. "You're the only one who can tame him. You tame the beast; you're the beast's keeper. A title you hold in court now."

She felt the rush of power, the fear and rage storm in her veins and heart, and she gritted her teeth. She'd tame him, she'd conquer him, and save him.

Molly went to her side table and quickly sprawled a note for Illya. That she'd be back soon and she was safe.

She took a shaky breath and turned to face the prince. "Take me now," she said, lowly.

He nodded and pulled the hood of her cloak over her head. With a skilled hand, he yanked the same dagger he once used to take them to high court months ago, and sliced through the air, a foreign chant burning her ears.

Then the fibers of the air burnt and broke open, revealing the dark hallway of High Court.

She swallowed thickly and with fear nipping at her heels, moved forward through the void and into the heart of darkness.

The air crackled around them, the prince following after her and with a flick of his wrist, the passage closed, disappearing as if it was never there.

The hallway was decorated in its signature white and black herringbone floor with crystal chandeliers that glistened, reflecting off of every surface the light caught.

In the darkness, he guided her to the bedchamber. A month didn't erase the painful ache in her chest or the bitter taste in her mouth of High Court.

As they neared the black wood double doors, her heart was in her throat, choking her. She didn't know how he would be. Would he be ill? Would he be in bed?

Angry?

Happy?

The prince knocked three times with his knuckles and glanced down at her.

"As I said," he told her and touched her shoulder. "You are the beast's tamer."

She didn't respond; her throat was too tight, too dry and she watched as he stepped back.

"Come in," a harsh voice spoke beyond the door and her entire body seized in fear.

She couldn't help the shiver that ran down her spine to the tips of her toes that curled.

Her body still reacted to him nonetheless.

With a deep breath, she steeled herself and grabbed the golden handle, opening the door to find the beast.

He sat on an upholstered chair of gold trim and fur, both of his thick legs spread wide open in a pose of power and authority, but she could see from here how pale he was.

How the sweat pooled on his brow and his chest warred violently.

His nostrils flared and those dark, lethal eyes clung to her.

She watched his fingers dig into the gold trim of the chair and the veins in his hands bulge, a hidden rage just below the surface.

"My lord," she muttered, a whisper of acknowledgment. Her voice shook slightly, but she was able to swallow down her fear.

It was the exact reaction he hoped for.

His upper lip curled in anger and his fingers curled into iron fists on his throne.

The beast wanted submission, but she knew with that tiny fraction of a heart beating somewhere deep within him, the man craved his own name on her lips.

The beast was in fact at war with the man, as the prince had said.

A war on himself.

A demon fighting a heart.

"You summoned me?" She glanced at the glamorous bedchamber dressed in heavy red-wine curtains and a large enough bed to fit multiple people.

She stopped herself from going any further.

"Yes," he bit out like it pained him to speak. She watched his chest fall and rise rapidly.

Then she wondered—was she the violent cause to him?

Tensley pushed himself up onto his feet, sturdy, but she saw the slight waver in his step as he moved toward her.

She braced herself, desperately wanting to retreat. She wasn't backing down though. She stood her ground, her head held high.

As he neared, his toxic scent invaded her and she peeked up through her lashes at him.

So near, so close, she saw the sharp edge of his jawbone waver under his tight clench. She breathed shakily out as his long fingers found the tips of her hood and pulled it down, her blonde ringlets cascading freely down the black cloak.

Being this close to him was a deadly game, a lethal intoxicating hum that settled in her chest, in her head, and in her bones.

She was trapped in a love affair of distortion.

With courage, she met his dark eyes, the shadows playing across his features to create a sinful beauty. She searched for a glimpse, a glimmer of hope that perhaps the man was there.

But she wasn't sure what she saw.

His brow bent and shook, his lips a thin line of annoyance, and his cheeks hollowed out.

It was when two fingers stroked down her neck, down the tender jugular convulsing wildly under his touch, her collar tightening around her lower throat, that she came undone for a moment. A gasp left her lips and heat bloomed in her cheeks.

His two fingers bent back the edge of her cloak and his eyes narrowed at the sight of his dress shirt.

"You're lathered in my scent," he spoke lowly, his husky voice going straight to her core. "The entire court will smell me on you."

He stared at her collarbone, the white fabric hiding where her heart beat like a war drum for him. She knew he could hear it by the way he couldn't look away.

She twisted her head to the side, and she felt his eyes drag up her neck to her side profile.

He watched her like this, her cheeks heating under him.

Finally, he turned and she watched him move to the center of the room. He ran a hand through his disheveled dark locks and swore under his breath.

He glanced back at her, his upper lip curling. "You cursed me."

She blinked, taken aback. She cleared her throat and took a step closer. "Yes, I did. To save you."

He fisted his hands. "To save me?" He laughed darkly at that and tsked. "Making me obsess over your glossy hair, over the tremble in that thick bottom lip I want to bite—" He gestured wildly to her and she rolled her bottom lip between her teeth. "The damn heart that beats like a war cry to me every single second. That every single woman disgusts me. That I fucking crave you beside me at all times."

She swallowed thickly, her mind racing, unable to speak, unsure what to say back to him.

"That any male that mentions your name, utters it—makes me want to snap their necks," he hissed out and stepped closer and closer until he stood right in front of her towering over her petite frame. "I'm going to destroy you."

She looked up at him, not shying way, not hiding, and glared. "Then destroy me."

He stared her down, the muscle in his jaw ticking as he clenched it. His eyes scanned her. "You left."

She frowned. "Left?" She shook her head. "Your court banished me when I cursed you." She swore for a moment she saw his features soften, but it was soon replaced with a scowl. "I didn't want to leave," she whispered.

He watched her, his mouth an angry straight line. He ran his fingers through his hair and paced, but he stopped and faced her. He glowered. "Touch me."

Her brows shot up. "What?"

Without clarifying, he grabbed her hand and simply held it. His tanned, powerful hand slotted with her porcelain one.

One single touch. That was all he needed and she saw the bloom return to his cheeks, his muscles ripple as he flexed his arms and rolled his shoulders.

She felt his thumb stroke the back of her hand and she almost burst into tears.

It hit her too hard, too fast.

She hadn't realized how much she missed his touch.

And then he let go and kept his head bowed as he caught his breath.

She brought her hand to her chest and held it there, too shocked, too upset to move or speak.

Tensley wiped a thumb across his top lip and straightened. "You will come to me every fourth night. You stay as long as I wish."

She simply stared at his hand, the hand that had held hers as he unclenched and clenched it continuously. Did he feel it too? The chemistry, the bond, the strength flowing between the two of them?

"You're dismissed. The prince will escort you back," he told her coldly and turned his back on her.

She let her hand drop and couldn't hide the anger storming inside of her. So many things she wished to spit back at him.

That his father was dead.

That Evelyn was attempting to run his Scorpios.

But she held her tongue.

"Don't you want to ask about your son?" she said, not hiding the anger in her tone.

He didn't turn to face her. "I trust you. That pure heart of yours would never let your own son be neglected."

Her mouth dropped open. In a strange sense, it was a compliment, but it still bothered her he didn't even ask.

"He's doing well," she told him, happy he wasn't facing her or he would see the wetness in her eyes. "They say he's strong."

Tensley didn't respond and she was done. She wasn't wasting another moment.

She wanted to go back to their perfect apartment and forget all of this.

"Keep my son safe," he murmured as she turned.

She didn't say a word and left.

Fourth night of every week.

She shook her head.

She wouldn't see it as a sentence, she would see it as an opportunity to honor her vow.

And make his heart grow.

chapter fourteen

"WE FOUND HIM," one of the soldiers told Molly as she glanced up from her pile of papers.

Daphne sat beside her, another pile of papers in her hands.

The soldier—a young man—didn't need to say another word. For a month since she'd directed Scorpios to attack Ares in a warehouse, many of the members were hiding outside of Boston and the members fled like rats, she had been waiting to hear that they had finally found who she was looking for.

She wasn't looking for Fitz Senior, the Dux of Ares, not yet at least.

No, she wanted the most valuable thing to him and that was his son. Fitz Junior.

"Is he in the cellar?" Molly asked and stood.

The soldier nodded.

"Would you like me to come, Molly?" Daphne asked, a deep frown between her manicured brows.

Molly shook her head. "I'll be right back."

Molly left the room and as she walked down the hallway, the soldiers that lined the walls bowed their heads in greeting. They saw her not only as the Dux's wife, but as their queen, even though she had no official title.

It had been three weeks since her first visit with Tensley and every fourth night of the week, the prince returned to escort Molly to High Court. It was always the same—a staring contest and a few words, him simply holding her hand, then she was dismissed. Tonight, the prince would return again to escort her back. She wasn't sure how to feel, but she was going to be prepared to fight for Tensley.

A soldier opened the cellar door for her and she entered into the darkness, descending down the creaky stairs.

In the middle of the pitch-black room was a single chair and in that chair sat Fitz Junior.

As she edged closer, the sound of her heels resonating around her as each step hit against the tiled floor, he lifted his head, a feat in itself.

In the dim lights and shadows, she could make out his nasty bruised and bloody lip, redness coating the front of Fitz Junior's shirt.

His hands were tied behind his back with black cords.

She wasn't staring at the same man she had seen the past summer.

She was staring at a beaten, fuming man who had escaped death only to be caught by the devil's own hand. A man not entirely innocent. A man on another side of the chessboard that wanted her for himself or for her blood to flow freely between his fingers.

She wouldn't be merciful to him.

"Fitz," Molly said, folding her hands in front of her.

He laughed darkly. "Long time no see, Molly Darling. Or should I call you Queen? I'd bow and kiss your holy feet if I wasn't tied up," he spat, barely containing his own disgust.

She tasted the hostility in the air. It was thick and heavy and she knew he was going to lash out. She needed to calm him so she could get answers.

Ares had been the rival of Scorpios for decades and after Tensley refused to give Molly up for more power and land to Ares, they had attacked.

"You declared war on us," she said and took a few steps closer.

Fitz flashed his teeth—painted red, a complete opposite to the preppy-boy look he had been sporting months ago. "Oh, so you're a Scorpion whore now, huh? Figured he'd manage to make you kneel for him at some point." He sneered with a venomous smile.

"There are two ways to do this, Fitz. You continue to spurt out all that garbage about me and Tensley and I make sure to take a very long time ripping you apart bloody piece by bloody piece. Or," she said, a dark smile growing on her lips. "You shut that awful mouth of yours and tell me what I want to hear and I'll try my hardest to remember to end your life as quickly and as pain-free as possible. How does that sound? Good? Good," she continued, not waiting for his answer. Molly dug her nails into her palm and grinned at him once more, innocent and carefree, but it was clear to both of them that she was anything but. "So, one of your men poisoned Salvatore Knight. You're going to tell me who."

Fitz rolled his head and groaned. "I don't know who did that, but fucking good. That bastard deserved to die."

Molly breathed out slowly. "Fitz," she began and moved closer, bending down to face him. When she was only inches away, she repeated his name. "That's not a very nice thing to say now, is it," she tsked reproachfully, her eyes full of fire.

He leaned back, his wrists twisting against the binds.

"Here," she continued, the innocent look returning. "You tell me where your father is, and we'll let you go. Without a single scratch on your body," she said, but then looked at his cut lip and bruised eyes. "Well, without a single new scratch anyway. All you have to do is tell me, and then you're free. Your father is the Dux after all. He's the one to blame for this war. So, tell me, Fitz. Where. Is. Your. Father?"

"Fucking naïve bitch!" Molly jolted at his sudden rage. He moved against the binds, attempting to get closer and she stood. "I have no idea where the fuck he is. My father would let you remove my organs, my bones, even my fucking dick before he'd hand himself over. I'm worthless to you and I'm worthless to him. We're talking about the man who chose to rip his own wife's heart out for his damn Ares. Do you honestly think he gives two fucks about me? He trusts no one, not even me. I know nothing."

Molly folded her arms, thinking over what to do, what to say next.

Fitz laughed and she turned to face him. "Didn't take long did it?"

She didn't answer and watched him, his bloody teeth flashing as he closed and opened his mouth.

"Your almighty king, he got tired of you, didn't he?" he said and laughed violently, his body shaking. "He's probably spreading the thighs of all the court's high ladies as we speak. Wonder if their pussies taste sweeter than yours? They probably do, you're filth anyway."

White-hot rage stormed her and before she could stop, she slid a knife from the holster against her thigh and stabbed it deep into his arm—crushing bones, blood splattering against her pristine lace dress.

Her free hand found his jaw and her fingers bruised his skin.

"I warned you not to cross me, Fitz," she hissed and forced his head further back, his neck straining, his airway blocked by her force. "I have that vicious king's blood inside of me and I will be just as savage as any one of your kind. Perhaps, even worse." She twisted the knife deeper and the muffled noise of a scream escaped his open mouth. "You will tell me where your precious father is and he will come to me or I will kill every person associated with him until he shows himself to me and me alone. Understood?"

He nodded against her hand and all at once, she saw clearly.

She slowly let go, stepping back on shaky legs. Her hands were coated in his blood and he stared at her, wide-eyed, catching his own breath.

She swallowed and turned, moving up the stairs and once she shut the door, she leaned against the wall.

Deep breaths battled inside of her chest and she looked up to see Evelyn standing at the end of the hallway watching her.

She cocked a brow.

Molly calmed herself and continued walking, ignoring the fact that her white dress was splattered in blood.

Her behavior, her violence, her outrage—was all linked to the demon child inside of her.

His vicious loyalty, his powerful anger smoothed through her and wrapped around her nerve-endings.

She excused herself and cleaned the blood off of her cheeks and nose, like red freckles and tried to wash the red from her dress.

She was vicious, she was powerful, she was lethal.

She had to be careful.

She had to be strategic or someone would use it against her.

THE COURT ECHOED with laughter and music, the dancers moving smoothly across the marble slabs in the dining hall.

A token of appreciation from Lilith to Tensley.

One he didn't care for.

The fawning over him had grown past infuriating and as he sat back, his chin rested on his fist, he didn't know how much longer he could stand.

It also didn't help that his daemon would be visiting him tonight. All week he had spent his time outside, under the rain, under the sun, in the snow, beating himself to the point of pure exhaustion. His army questioned him as he pushed them for hours and hours of no rest, of no water.

He wanted to be punished for thinking such unholy thoughts of his daemon.

The threat, the fear of falling under her control again pushed him further.

The entire time he thought of her glossy curls, how soft they were as he ran his fingers through them or those full pink lips of hers. Those lips were deadly to him. So badly he wanted to bite them, devour them, but one touch, one taste, he wouldn't be able to stop.

The last thing he needed was to lose control under her touch.

He needed to keep his mind straight, keep himself from growing weak over a human again.

But he needed her, he wanted her and that drove him to the point of breaking all over again.

Maybe one taste would be enough. Maybe he'd be the one controlling her, earning those mewls as he sucked on one of her nipples.

He clenched his teeth and cursed himself.

At the sudden sound of applause, he realized the dancers were done and moving away.

"I hope that pleased you, my lord," Lilith whispered and dragged a finger along his thigh.

He didn't speak to her. He knew her games and he knew she craved power more than anything and he wouldn't be surprised if she was planning something behind his back.

Tensley stood, Lilith's hand falling back into her lap as he moved to leave his throne.

"My lord?" Lilith's voice hinted at her frustration but he didn't care. She knew who visited him every fourth night and he wondered if the 'token of appreciation' was an excuse to keep him away from his daemon.

Nothing could keep him from her.

He marched down the halls, his boots thumping loudly, and his chest throbbing. The sliver of heart within him pulsed violently, as if searching for more, searching for room to grow.

As he turned the corner to his chambers, he caught sight of a petite figure, a cloak of darkness hiding her head.

She was leaving though.

He stormed ahead and before she could get far, he gripped the back of her hood and spun her so she hit his chest.

She gasped, her wide vivid eyes glowing up at him. Wet lashes, bloodshot eyes.

"Tensley—" The mere sound of his name on those fuckable lips went straight to his cock and he growled. Her shock vanished fast though and she shoved at his chest. "You don't need me tonight. You'll have your hands full."

He caught her bicep and again yanked her flat against his body. "What the fuck are you talking about?"

"Don't act stupid, asshole."

He wanted to snap back, to fucking curse, but he saw her anger was only hiding her pain as she blinked back tears.

She fucking still cared.

Too fucking much that it made the beast wild with need.

He opened his mouth, but the flurry of giggles halted him and he tensed.

He didn't look away from Molly's wet eyes and he jerked her with him as he turned and marched into his chambers, throwing open the doors.

Three women draped in sheer dresses hiding nothing lay on his bed.

"My king," they all chanted sickeningly.

His beast was on the edge and with a deep breath, he pointed to the door. "Get. Out. *Now.*"

The three women paled, but didn't move and that only irritated him further.

"Now!"

He felt Molly flinch at his loud, booming voice.

The women fled, dashing out of the room with bowed heads.

Tensley let Molly go and ran a hand down his face.

"Sit," he commanded, gesturing to his chair.

After a long moment, Molly moved to his gold chair and sat down.

He eyed her bowed head, the light blonde smoothed down her back and—

Tensley moved fast and grabbed a few strands of her hair. She jerked up, confusion written all over her features.

"You have blood in your hair," he said, rubbing his thumb on the few strands tainted with red.

She blinked rapidly and he watched her throat constrict. "I—I might have tortured someone."

He narrowed his eyes at her.

"Your son is just as vicious as you," she whispered, a sad smile playing on her lips. It faded fast.

He let her hair go but he stood above her, watching her carefully. "Why were you torturing someone?"

She folded her hands in her lap. "It's my own business."

Her words were a dagger to his chest, but he kept a cool expression on. "Tell me."

She stayed silent, her hands rubbing up and down her thighs. "They found Fitz Junior. I was torturing him for answers as to where his father could be hiding"

Tensley grew rigid. Those bastards. Scorpios. Ares. All of his old responsibility.

"When I came back a little over a month ago, Evelyn Rose was acting as Dux," Molly added and he glared at her. But before he could rage, she spoke soft and clear and it went both to his forbidden heart and groin. "I, of course, put her in her place and took up the position as Dux. As it should be. As your wife." He couldn't look away from the blonde siren; humming a lullaby only him and the beast heard so he'd crash into rocks and sink deep into the darkness of her. "Your family obviously provides a lot of help too."

There was a strength, a lethal touch to her that hadn't been there the moment he met her and the beast warred inside of him for dominance.

She brought both the beast and the man to the surface.

Tensley sighed and moved to one of his side tables, gripping a clay pitcher of water. He walked back over to her and gestured for her to stand.

She did and he gripped the few strands of red and slowly, carefully, he poured the water onto his fingers and her strands. With a steady thumb, he rubbed the strands, the water turning red on his fingers and rolling down her cloak and pooling on the floor between them.

Once the redness remained only on his fingers, he let go and returned the pitcher to the side, feeling her eyes watching his every move.

He walked slowly back to her, rubbing the redness between his fingers and thumb. When they started to shake from his exhaustion, he fisted them.

"Only my queen would wear the blood of an enemy," he whispered and sat down on his bed. The pain in his chest vibrated, a fist of pain wrapping around his growing heart until he saw black dots.

"Are you all right?" That sweet voice asked and he felt her touch his cheek, but his vision blurred. Inside of him, his body needed her, craved her like an addict.

"Stay," he told her, his voice coming out softer than he wanted.

Then everything blurred and went black.

chapter fifteen

MOLLY RUBBED HER thumb along her trembling bottom lip, watching as the healer worked over Tensley's unconscious, trembling body. Once he had passed out, she panicked at his grunts of pain, his body thrashing as if physically ill.

She had found the prince and he had called for a healer, and now all she could do was wait.

"Hmm," the healer whispered, rubbing a soothing oil onto Tensley's bare chest. The long, rough scar of where his heart had been ripped out an ugly line of remembrance. Tensley grunted again, twisting his head to the side.

"It is his heart?" Molly asked, the question boiling inside of her. What if her curse had actually hurt him more? Weakened both the man and the demon and was just pure poison to him everyday?

"I do not know," the healer answered, frowning as she stood back. She turned to face Molly, her features drawn into a frown. "But his body needs strength of touch. He has starved himself, that I can tell from his body's weakness."

Molly's stomach dropped. He was weak…because he wasn't getting intimacy from anyone. Only a few touches from her and then he sent her off.

Had he been living with the weakness, the pain because he didn't want to push her too far too fast?

"What can I do?" Molly asked, standing up from her chair.

The healer eyed the length of Molly's body. "Lie beside him. Simply make sure as much of your body is touching as much of him as possible, so it speeds up the process. That alone should help feed his body."

Molly nodded and watched as the healer walked away, leaving her alone with the king of beasts.

A groan left his pursed full lips, his shoulders rolling as the pain riddled his body. Molly stepped forward, smoothing down her nightgown. She undid her cloak and laid it on a nearby chair.

His roar of agony took her breath away, another attack of pain ravaging his body.

Her eyes swung to the thrashing king, a scream of anguish vibrating straight to her bones. She rushed to his side and climbed onto the bed, her hands gripping his shoulders.

"Tensley," she said, her own voice shaky, but loud enough for him to hear. "Tensley!" Her hands found his sweaty cheeks and she patted them roughly. "It's okay, it's okay."

On a roar, his eyes flashed open and he stilled, slowly, taking in his surroundings until he focused on her above him.

She continued to stroke his hot skin, hoping to calm him. She could feel the quick beat of his heart on her palm—that sliver of heart, that iron gift.

When she stared down at him, into his grey stormy eyes, her heart stopped.

A glimmer, a glimpse of the man.

So stripped bare and exposed, she almost kissed him. The man—Tensley stared back at her with fear and confusion and then—adoration. He was still trapped in-between that dream stage and waking stage.

"I'm here," she managed to whisper and lay down beside him.

When his fingers touched the inner side of her arm, she swallowed down a shuddered breath.

"Stay." It was a command, softened by his husky voice of sleep. She rested her head on his shoulder and couldn't escape his eyes.

Her hand still massaged his chest, where his heart pounded and he didn't remove it.

She watched for minutes until his eyes fluttered shut and his breathing evened out.

She was so close—she knew she could break down his high walls and find his iron heart.

THE LIGHTS SPRAWLED across her golden hair.

It was the first thing he noticed.

Those strands of spun-gold, cascading down the exposed porcelain back he wished to mark. His fingers pressed to the bottom of her spine, earning a tiny mewl of pleasure, of pain, and he withdrew.

Her hand, that delicate hand that wielded too much power over him, over his court, laid limply on his chest. On his heart. And under her touch, the forbidden organ grew wild, pumping and thrashing inside of him and fear seized him.

She was the blessing and the curse.

When he pulled back, he found his other hand had been resting on her stomach. He paused, staring at her belly and swept his palm across the tiny bump—barely visible to the naked eye, but he felt it.

He felt the energy inside of her. The power, the essence of a daemon and a demon.

His son.

His flesh and blood.

"Tensley?"

He tore his hand away and stood, running his shaking hands through his hair. He yanked a pair of trousers from a nearby chair and pulled them on, only to bend forward in pain as his heart grew wild inside of him once more.

Fucking shit.

"Tensley," that soft voice said, but it stormed his mind and when her delicate hand touched his bare back, he threw it off.

"Don't *fucking* touch me," he hissed, as he felt the beast overthrow the man within him. He hoped his black eyes would warn her off.

She gawked at him, the sunlight outlining her frame and her gold hair. He wanted to kiss her.

He wanted to yank her to him to calm the storm inside of him, but the beast warred forward.

Stay in control.

Stay in power.

Do not let her win.

He clenched his teeth and through deep breaths, managed to leave the room.

He needed air, he needed to destroy, but he continued to march, the court members stopping in the hallway to watch their king.

Even outside, he did not stop.

He stormed through the gardens and stomped into the forest. When he saw the lake ahead, he yanked off his pants and walked into the cool water, the iciness biting his skin as he walked deeper into its depths.

He gasped, from the cold, from the sudden relief and dunked his head under the clear water.

Until the thrashing inside of him settled down and he dragged himself back to the shore, laying his weak body into the hard sand.

The grains of sand clung to his wet torso and cheeks, his hair littered with dots. An ache deep in his chest took his breath away and he coughed, the sky spinning. Hot and cold battled in his body and he squeezed his eyes shut to fight through it.

Fight.

Fight.

Fucking fight.

He heard the sand crunch and he lazily glanced up the shore to find *her*.

The plague of a girl that destroyed him through and through, and fucking hell, he was beginning to want her, too.

Destroy him until he begged for another tender kiss.

One he ached for on his very mouth right now.

He licked at his bottom lip, like the hungry beast he was.

Ravage her, savage.

Just a few steps away and he'd be able to touch her, hold her, let her consume him entirely. He grunted, pushing himself up and staggered toward her.

"Molly," he breathed and she stumbled back. "Molly."

He quickened his pace and when he saw her turn away, the anger grew within him.

"*Molly.*"

She rushed forward as if scared, terrified of him, only to collide with a man.

Seto caught her and held her, his callused hands stroking her with possessiveness and care, as if she was his.

And as Molly turned her head to gaze back at him, Tensley came to a complete stop.

Because it wasn't Molly.

But Prim. The girl who they'd been told was dead. Her brown hair matted, not the platinum blonde that smelled like sunrays, and her skin was freckled with dirt, not Molly's ivory complexion.

"Prim," he whispered, unable to look away from the woman he mistook for his.

She shuddered when he spoke.

"My lord," Seto said, his eyes dropping to Tensley's lower body. Seto pulled Prim closer.

When he remembered he was naked, he turned around and found his pants, slipping them back on.

"Go back to the cottage," Seto whispered to Prim and he pressed a tender kiss to her temple. Tensley couldn't look away, detailing the soft shared moment. The fraction of a heart within him ached at the sight. A sight he envied, a sight he craved. He wanted to be tender with Molly, but the beast roared, only to die out by the beating of his heart.

To be tender was dangerous.

He pressed two fingers to his temple and squeezed his eyes shut. The emotions fought inside of him. For dominance over his mind, over his body.

"My lord?" Seto questioned, moving closer.

Tensley shook his head, trying to ignore the craving, the confusion in his heart and mind. "She was dead…"

Seto grimaced. "Fallen lied. He sold her off."

Tensley looked over the man before him. A man of once power now trying to protect the woman he had thought he lost.

"You've been hiding her out here?" Tensley asked.

Seto squared his shoulders. "Yes. I do not want the court taking her from me again."

The harsh bite of Seto's words told Tensley just how uneasy the man was with him around. The beast was territorial and protective of his mate. Just the thought of Molly alone drove him mad. The sliver of a heart began to ache and he felt the anxiety, the fear slide up his spine. He shifted on his feet, fixing his stance, begging the awful sensation to stop.

Seto waited, eyeing Tensley's frame. "The beast is unsettled," Seto began after a long pause.

Tensley turned to face him and didn't hide his glare. "Be careful with your next words, Seto."

Seto didn't flinch. "You crave her, but you fear her."

Tensley wiped the excessive water from his top lip and grains of sand cut across his skin. "I fear nothing."

"You want her close, but not too close," Seto continued. "But if you want her to stay, you will have to give her a taste of what you can offer her."

Tensley licked at his teeth. He didn't want to admit his fear, his anxiety of her not being here next to him or when she was here, his fear of her sucking him back in.

Tensley threw his hands, gesturing to around them. "I can offer her everything."

Seto stayed silent, his hands cupped in front of him. The look alone told Tensley it wasn't enough. "Give her a taste of the king—court her, soothe her."

"Court her?"

Seto ignored Tensley's bitter tone and stepped closer. "You cannot hide from it, your majesty. You cannot hide from her. She cursed you and slowly, with each touch, each word she speaks, the curse will grow."

Tensley gritted his teeth, glaring at the ground, the roots exposed. Like himself. His heart was growing fast and the war inside of him was destroying the beast, shoving him further back.

At the mere thought of her, he grew dizzy, ill to his stomach, the intensity inside of him burnt and all he wanted was her in front of him. To hold her, to soothe her, to kiss her tenderly on her lips and cherish her.

The beast roared, but his heart spoke louder, colliding inside of him.

He ran, leaving behind Seto and rushing toward the palace. He rushed down the hallways, the court members stepping aside to gawk at his disheveled appearance, his soaked hair and bare chest.

"My lord," Lilith called as she stepped into the hallway, her eyes widening and darkening all at once at his naked torso.

He brushed past her and stormed into his rooms, his heart in his throat, but his stomach dropped brutally low.

The room was empty, the sheets twisted, a sign of their slumber together. Molly was gone and the beast and his heart raged.

"Fuck," he hissed and in his wrath, he destroyed anything in his path. His heart burnt, his beast silenced.

And when the entire room was a wreck like what battled inside of him, he collapsed with torn sheets in his hands and her name panting from his mouth like a fucking prayer.

She cursed him—and he planned to curse her to crave him just as much.

That he fucking promised.

WHEN MOLLY RETURNED to Scorpios, she felt sick too her stomach. Not because of the baby who decided he'd start moving around like a speedboat, but because of Tensley's reaction.

She saw him—she saw the glimpse of the man before he had his heart ripped out, but he was buried too deep inside. Every two steps forward, were five steps back.

She knew one man may be able to help her dig deeper, but she wasn't sure how he would react.

Molly climbed up the stairs of an apartment that should have been vacant. Used condoms littered in the brown carpet. Smoke and the stench of something rotten filled her nostrils.

Maybe this wasn't the wisest decision…

Dark stains faded into the carpet and she cringed. *Definitely blood.*

Each paper-thin door looked exactly the same and as she neared 54, she paused.

With Tensley, she knew where she stood. He wouldn't attack her, but with another beast?

She rolled her shoulders and stepped forward, knocking on the hollow door.

She listened, waiting for movement.

Nothing.

She frowned and pounded on the door.

Footsteps thudded in the apartment and before Molly could brace herself, the door swung open revealing a freshly showered Beau.

His dark eyes shot daggers at her and she swallowed.

"Why are you here?" His voice held no threat, no anger, but annoyance.

She straightened her purse strap. "To see you. About your brother."

His jaw, the same sharp jaw as his brother, flexed and wavered under his death clench. "The heartless king."

She wasn't sure if he was trying to joke, but she simply stared back at him, waiting for a gesture to come inside.

"Just for a few minutes," she urged, stepping closer.

His entire body blocked the doorway and he kept a firm grip on the door, his body language telling her she wasn't wanted.

Too bad she knew how to get under the skin of a Knight.

"Not interested." He went to shut the door and Molly jerked forward, putting her foot inside to stop the door from closing.

"Please Beau," she whispered, her eyes finding his and pleading.

Beau scowled down at her and she felt his hatred storm off of him. He opened his mouth, but another voice spoke.

"Beau? What are you doing?" Lex tipped her head to the side, her damp brown hair falling over one shoulder. Lex's features softened, her cheeks burning bright red. "Molly, what are you doing here?"

Molly bit her tongue and exchanged a look between the two of them. Lex only wore a long t-shirt down to her knees and Beau was shirtless with a pair of jeans on. Were they a thing now?

Lex pulled Beau back by his arm. "Come in, Molly."

Molly stepped inside the apartment—a large enough apartment for a couple, but she assumed only Beau lived here.

It wasn't anything special, but it wasn't awful.

The kitchen was outdated and the couches were worn.

Lex stood in front of Molly as Beau stood in the middle of the room. Molly could feel more of Beau's resistance to being close to Lex.

"Oh my god," Lex whispered and pressed a hand to Molly's stomach. Molly stilled, not used to people touching her belly. "How far are you?"

"I'll be five months in a day or two." Molly smiled and smoothed her own hands along her belly.

When she looked up at Beau, she saw his nostrils flare, his eyes unable to look away from her stomach. She thought of his own unborn child and the human Fallen murdered. What did he feel seeing his brother's wife pregnant? Anger? Fear? Terror? Remorse?

"Beau," Molly began and his head shot up. "I wanted to ask you about…"

She glanced at Lex, who's brows had knitted in a frown. "About being heartless... about... getting better."

Beau simply stared, working his jaw.

Once a demon's heart was ripped out, it could grow back, but it took time and nurturing, and she doubted in this society of demons it would happen so quickly.

Lex stared through her lashes at him, a longing in her eyes.

"Why?" he finally spoke.

Molly licked at her lips and moved closer. "So I can help him. Make it better for him."

Beau tsked. "To save him. For your own selfishness. Maybe he's better as a beast. Maybe he wants to stay that way."

Lex folded her arms. "Better as a beast?"

Beau glared at Lex. "Take a walk. This has nothing to do with you."

Lex blanched and then her delicate features morphed into a scowl. "Fuck you."

Lex grabbed a bag off of the couch and stomped out, slamming the door behind her.

Molly didn't move, staring at Beau as he ran a hand down his face.

A few seconds passed before Molly spoke. "Are you and her...?"

Beau shook his head. "No."

Molly nodded, deciding it was best to steer clear of that conversation. "Beau, how much of a heart do you have?"

Beau sighed and turned to his kitchen. He turned on the tap and poured himself a cup of water. "Over half a heart." He took a large gulp of his water, the droplets littering on his dark beard. With a dark, steady stare he moved toward her. "It took ten years to get there."

Molly's heart clenched. "Ten years?"

He took another gulp and nodded. "Ten fucking years of darkness."

Molly gripped the back of the couch for support. "What if I did something?

To speed the process?"

Beau cocked a brow. "What exactly?"

She swallowed. "I cursed him to grow a heart."

Beau's brow dropped low and he stepped forward, anger in his movements. "You fucking cursed him?"

"I was desperate."

Beau swore and paced. "Well, he better fucking still be alive. You didn't kill him, right?"

Molly shook her head softly.

He shrugged after a moment. "I don't know how it'll work. It may grow back faster, it may still take time."

She fisted her hands. Time wasn't on her side.

She needed him home. She needed to give the prince the throne in exchange for Tensley's life.

Beau looked straight into her eyes, gaze cold. So, so cold. "I had no Molly in my life during those ten years," he said, spitting out her name like it was an insult. "Because I wasn't lucky like my brother. The woman I fell for was long dead and so was my unborn child. No one and nothing helped me, so I don't know shit about helping someone grow a heart. All I know is the darkness and pain that followed me around all those years. And it's still there, it never goes away."

Molly was taken aback by his words. It felt as if he had slapped her. But she couldn't blame him for what he had said, if anything she understood his pain. The pain of seeing how even heartless, his brother still had people fighting for him, loving him, waiting for him to get better.

When Beau had become heartless, no one had fought for him, people had chosen to simply stand back and let the beast do whatever it wished. He had lost everything, he had been stripped of his right to become the future Dux, he had been shamed for his sins and brought darkness and shame upon his entire family. Looking at his brother, a king, a Dux, a man with a wife and a child on the way, a man who had lost a heart but gained everything else, it probably hurt more than Molly wanted to admit. No one had cared if Beau recovered, no one had hoped he would. They had all given up on him.

But when she thought of Lex, and what she had went through, of the darkness that had seeped within the girl after the horrible events from a few months ago, she realized maybe someone who understood the beast had finally chosen to help him. To step up and fight for him. He just hadn't realized that yet.

chapter sixteen

IXING HER HOOD, Molly tiptoed down the silent hallways. She picked at the hem of the cloak, following in the prince's footsteps, her heart in her throat.

The last time she had seen Tensley was a week ago and he had been angry, out of control and left her in his bedchambers. She knew he was struggling, she knew he was fighting the heart within him. She wanted to push him, but she feared if she pushed him too far, too fast, he would end up suffering more.

"I'll be outside waiting," the prince told her as they neared the double doors of Tensley's bedchambers.

Molly paused in front of the doors and shook her head. "I'm staying longer than usual."

The prince arched a brow. "Oh? And his lordship knows?"

Molly rolled her eyes, then glared at him.

The prince laughed, the sound sensual. "I'll wait outside."

Molly ignored his remark and moved to open the door.

What she found was complete darkness, besides the light from the moon streaming in-between the blowing curtains.

The air was chilled and as she tiptoed inside, squinting into the darkness, she wondered if he was even there.

Maybe he was avoiding her...

She sucked in a deep breath, her shoulders slumping.

"I didn't think you'd return," his rough voice sent a shiver of delight down her spine.

She took a step forward, her eyes slowly adjusting to the darkness to make out his large frame leaning against the wall, his forearm resting there, his back bent slightly.

"Of course I'd come back," she whispered, frowning slightly.

He grunted a response. "You should leave. Now."

She swallowed thickly. At the sound of his husky voice, so low, she felt the room heat. The energy around him was anger—pure anger and it was directed at her.

"Tensley," she said, about to ask what was going on with him and why he was so angry but when she moved forward, she finally saw what was happening.

With this new angle, the moonlight that pooled from the window lit his figure enough that she could now see almost all of him.

His large fist held his erection, his trousers unbuckled, exposing the dark hair, the deep lines leading back to that angry length.

She stopped mid-step, her eyes widening, unable to look away from him.

He grunted again and casted his dark eyes over her frame, his hand working slower now, sliding down his length then up to the swollen head.

Neither of them moved, only his hand, and neither looked away.

A blush took to her face and chest and she rolled her bottom lip between her teeth, biting down from gasping at the sight of Tensley pleasuring himself.

Stupid hormones.

Stupid emotions.

"Do you like seeing what you do to me? I can't look at another woman without wanting to kill someone. This," he said, his hand becoming harder, rougher on himself. "This is what you do to me."

Tensley stared back at her, his dark eyes hooded in want and lust, his teeth clenched. Each time he grunted lowly, her own core burned.

"I'm not stopping," he said through gritted teeth and pumped faster. "So leave."

Molly carefully looked him up and down, his powerful stance, his powerful hand, his heavy balls underneath his cock.

She swallowed and slowly glanced back up at him, meeting his heated glare.

She took a step closer and his ruthless brows lowered in confusion. Then she took another and his hand slowed, his gaze traveling up and down as if she held a secret weapon.

She breathed out softly as she stepped into his space, his own breaths fanning her forehead and her hand shakily pressed to his stomach.

His stomach rippled at her touch and a sharp breath hit her skin.

Her fingertips traced his sculpted abs, following his dark happy trail, moving lower and lower and lower—

Tensley grunted lowly as her soft hand wrapped around his shaft.

His hand let go and both hands touched her hips, capturing her so no escape was possible.

As if she wanted to escape.

She eyed the swollen crown of his length and gently stroked upward, her fingers sweeping over the glistening head.

Again, he groaned and dropped his head so his cheek pressed to hers.

"You sweet monster," he hissed and she moaned back as his fingers dug into her hipbones, only bringing her flushed against him.

His head turned, his hot breath hitting her exposed neck and earlobe.

She stroked slowly, painfully slow, feeling every ridge of his hardening length.

"You ran from me," he said into her ear and she felt the hot anger, the lustful desire to punish her in his words. "I returned to the room and you were gone. Fucking gone."

She braved a look and met his dark eyes, breathless. "Did that anger you?"

His eyes narrowed and his hands spread down her sides and dug into each ass cheek, rolling her against him. "It fucking infuriated me."

She gasped at his sudden strength—and realized it was from their intimacy.

"Because?" she whispered back to him, her gaze unwavering from his.

He growled in her face, kneading her flesh as her hand stroked him thoroughly.

"Did you miss me?" she asked again, tilting her head to the side, a vicious, knowing smile on her lips.

His jaw ticked and that dark gaze of his didn't leave hers. "You're destroying me with that damn curse," he snapped and rolled his hips so his length moved faster in her hand. "I'm being fucking ruined by the wicked heart you cursed me with. It beats. It fucking beats when you're near— and it hurts when you're not. It beats when I think of you. And I fucking think of you all the time."

She swallowed thickly at that confession, her pulse quickening and her lips parting. His eyes noted the movement of her mouth and he stared, unblinking at them.

"Those lips I worship in my nightmares," he whispered, darkly. "How they'd taste between my teeth. How they'd swallow my cock."

She heated at his words and she knew he could feel her excitement, feel her tender nipples harden against his chest.

He leaned forward, his nose tracing down her neck, over the collar and he paused at her sensitive mark. Even as his breath simply blew across it, she moaned, rubbing against his thigh and he hiked her leg up onto his hip.

A surge of desire shook through her body. It wasn't enough, she needed more.

She needed...

She...

His nostrils flared and she knew he could smell her arousal. That he could smell what he was doing to her body, to her mind, to her.

When his head came down to the crook of her neck again, Molly almost fell apart. With her hair pinned up in a ponytail, he had complete access to the skin there. Ever so slowly, he licked her throat, her collar, from the front, all the way to the back.

Molly's vision blurred completely, and she saw black dots dancing around as a cry of pleasure escaped her lips. Her body was shaking violently, her only support was the wall next to them and the powerful steel thigh he still held firmly tucked between hers. Her lower half moved on its own, rubbing shamelessly against him.

The sensation was too much.

The need was too much.

She couldn't think straight, she couldn't breathe.

"Is it nice to feel the burn of the fire but not know how to extinguish it, Molly? Is it nice to crave something you can't have because as soon as you get your claws on it, it runs away from you? Do you think it's nice to never be fully satisfied?" he asked darkly, his voice barely above a sinful whisper.

And she felt it. Oh, how she felt it. The burn. The craving. The unsatisfied need.

It felt like heaven and it felt like hell. Like the two were colliding within her, and it was about to destroy her.

And in that moment, she wanted it to. She wanted it to burn her, to destroy her, to break her.

Tensley laughed darkly, mockingly. "Be rough, dolcezza," he breathed out and his teeth nipped at her earlobe, sending another shiver through her so she curled into him, tightening her grip. "Make the beast kneel."

Slow licks caressed her neck and shoulder, rubbing over the collar and she couldn't stop gasping, couldn't stop rubbing against him like a cat in heat.

He wasn't even fully touching her. All he used was his tongue against her neck but somehow it made her drunk on pleasure. Drunk on him.

"Tame me, dolcezza," he hissed.

She bent her neck to rest against his shoulder and licked.

The way he had done to her.

As if he too had been collared by her.

And in a way, he had.

But her ownership was in the form of a sliver of vicious, wildly pumping heart, hiding deep within his powerful chest.

And she wouldn't have it any other way.

Her teeth dug into his shoulder and he jolted against her, his length quivering as his warmth splattered onto his chest and her hand.

"*Fuck!*" His fingers bit into her skin, not allowing her to move, not allowing her to even rub against him.

His length stopped pulsing and his heaving chest slowed.

She lifted her head, only to see he was watching her.

Watching her so closely, and if the glint in his eyes was any hint, the beast already wanted more.

He took her hand in his, bringing her fingers to her slightly parted mouth. Then, with eyes as dark as the night, he applied them roughly to her plump lips, rubbing his warm pleasure into her soft skin.

Marking them as his.

With deliberate slowness, he pushed her ring finger through her parted lips. Her lips closed around it out of reflex, and he growled, and a frown appeared between his brows.

And just like that, he took her hand away and let it drop to her side.

His gaze was hungry but cold.

Her eyes darted to his parted mouth of sin and she leaned forward—

The doors swung open and they both tensed, Tensley pulling her back against him.

"Fucking hell," he hissed at the intruder.

"I apologize, your majesty," Seto's voice echoed in the dark room and he turned away.

"Seto?" Molly asked and tried to pull away, but Tensley dug his fingers into her hip and growled lowly. She glared up at him and after a moment, he let go.

"What is it Seto?" He snapped, his back turned to them as he fixed his trousers and swiftly cleaned himself in the darkness of the room. When he was done, he turned, stepping beside Molly.

"I need Molly's help," Seto said, carefully and when he turned back toward them, his eyes were dark with worry. "It's Prim, she… I think she's having a panic attack. I— I don't know what to do. She's confused," he said, then frowned. "Terrified, actually. Of me," he whispered, and Molly could see his hand shake violently. He was terrified for her that much was evident.

Molly's heart dropped in her chest. "Is she still at the cottage?"

Seto nodded. "I wouldn't leave her alone like this but there was no one and I didn't know—I didn't know what to do. She won't let me near, she won't talk to me. I just thought you could…We need to hurry," he stopped, head shaking. He seemed so lost, so troubled.

"It's okay. Take me to her, I'll try to calm her. She'll be okay, Seto. I promise,"

Molly said, nodding reassuringly as she went to move, but Tensley caught her arm. "You're not going," he hissed.

Molly frowned. "Prim needs me. She needs help." His glare didn't falter. Frowning up at him, she tried a different tactic. "If I needed help and you couldn't help me, wouldn't you want someone to?"

He worked his jaw and his gaze flickered over her head to Seto. "Fine," he bit out. "But I'm coming with you. I'm not letting you out of my sight. You already escaped one too many times."

chapter seventeen

IN THE DARKNESS, Seto guided them through the woods. Tensley stayed by her side, his hand every so often skimming Molly's body. A reminder he was there. Minutes before, they had shared such an intimate moment and even though she knew the beast still thrived inside of him, she felt her man was fighting his way back to her.

"Here," Seto said and lifted the lantern, the only light guiding them. Molly eyed the slanted cottage and noted some tiny repairs had been made. Not much, but enough she knew Seto was trying to make a better life for Prim.

Her heart warmed at that.

He would do anything for her.

She understood that need inside of her, too and glanced at Tensley.

He scowled at the cottage. "The place where you cursed me."

She stayed quiet and moved forward.

"She's been having nightmares. She wakes up screaming and kicking. She keeps repeating 'You're one of them, you're one them' over and over… and she's… she's shaking like a leaf and I… I think she thinks I'm… I'm one of them, one of the men who…" Seto's eyes turned black, hands turning into tight fists. "One of the men who tried selling her. I don't know what they did to her, she won't say. But…" his voice was tight with anger, his fury and self-hatred over what had happened to Prim evident in the tone.

"The… the lashes… from the whip," he said and his voice choked on a sob. He breathed in shakily, and swallowed with difficulty. Molly's heart broke for the man who clearly couldn't forgive or forget what he had been forced to do to the woman he loved. "They… they didn't heal properly. I think it might be infected, but she won't let me close enough to touch her. Help her. And now she woke up screaming again and I just…" he stopped abruptly, and pushed the door open for Molly.

When Tensley made to enter with her, Seto's arm shot out and blocked his path, growling at his king. A harsh contrast with the sorrow he had been feeling mere seconds before. Molly could almost taste his possessiveness over Prim on her tongue.

"I think it's best for Molly to go alone," he said, teeth snapping, gaze dark as Tensley flashed his teeth in return. His body breathing aggression.

Molly stayed unmoving, unsure of what she should do.

"Get your arm out of my way, or I'll rip it off myself," Tensley snapped.

Seto's aggressive expression fell. " Please," he said, the word full of emotion. Emotions that were rarely heard coming from a demon. "She's… she's clearly frightened of males. I… please."

Molly glanced back at Tensley and touched his fisted hand. "I'll be fine. Wait for me outside."

His jaw ticked and he simply grunted back. His fisted hand relaxed and his fingers skimmed her palm, and her pulse quickened.

Her eyes snapped up to his stormy gray ones.

"I'll be fine," she said again to calm him.

Finally, he let her go and Molly stepped inside, letting her hood roll off her head. She tiptoed further inside and heard a faint whimper.

She followed the scrapping noise and peeked into the small cabin's closed room.

Prim sat in the dark corner, her fingers scratching at the walls.

Like a caged animal.

Molly's heart twisted painfully in her chest at the sight.

Sweet, gentle Prim. What had happened to her when she was with those disgusting men. *What had happened to her...*

"Prim," Molly whispered, afraid that if she spoke any louder, she might frighten the girl further. Prim stopped mid-scratch, nails broken and bleeding from scratching so much. Her small body started shaking heavily and Molly was positive she could hear teeth rattling. Prim's head bowed, her bloody-crusted hands going to cover her ears as she dropped her head between her knees.

She looked like a ball of trembling bones and bloody skin. Molly's stomach turned when she saw the girl's back... or what was left of it anyway.

Her back was nothing but shreds of twisted skin, infected scars and dried blood.

No one had taken care of it, despite the fact that the owner had intended to sell her for what Molly was sure had been a good price. She used to be so full of life, bubbly even. Now she was...

But even through her scars, Prim was still a beautiful woman. Delicate but courageous. Her selfless had been her strength.

She tried being selfish once, she tried listening to her heart, letting her heart beat freely, and it nearly cost her her life. Molly had no doubts it would take a long time before Prim ever allowed herself to live and love freely again. To be selfish and take what she wants. What she desires. And that made Molly's blood boil with rage. Prim hadn't deserved any of this. She had deserved the moon and the stars and Seto loved her enough to try and bring them to her. But Fallen had to ruin it for them, to make them pay for their love. Lilith had to make them pay for their offense. And Seto had to be the one inflicting the punishment.

And the lord knew what the things her friend could have gone through after that. They all had thought her dead. What had happened to her? What had happened to generate such fear in her. Seto hadn't been lying, she was well and truly terrified.

Molly moved slowly, lowering herself so she wasn't towering over Prim. She tried making herself as small as possible.

"Hi," Molly said hesitantly with a soft voice. "I'm Molly, do you remember me?" she asked, inching a bit closer to the trembling girl. "We were friends."

Through Prim's dark glossy locks, her eyes scanned Molly carefully. As if debating whether she was a threat.

"Friends?" Prim's soft voice cracked with the word and she sounded sick.

Molly nodded frantically. "Yes, we were good friends."

Molly waited, for what, she didn't really know. She licked at her lips nervously, as Prim continued examining her from behind the shield of her long, dark hair.

After what seemed like hours, Prim's eyes changed. They stopped being fearful, careful, and recognition flashed through them. Molly smiled softly at the girl, and scooted closer, hoping not to startle her.

Prim didn't flinch at her movements, but kept watching closely.

"What's wrong, Prim? What are you afraid of? You can tell me. I'm not here to hurt you, I'm here to be your friend. To help you," Molly said, pressing a hand to her chest.

Prim looked at her hand, and then slowly, her eyes dropped to her stomach. Her eyes stared at the bump.

Prim's cracked voice broke the silence again. "I'm scared," she started, and a heavy shudder tore through her body. "I'm scared of the... of... of the men re...returning for me."

Molly shook her head, her eyes burning with tears for the girl. "Oh no. No, Prim. Seto won't let anyone touch you. He'll protect you. You're safe here."

Prim's head shook vividly, eyes growing wild and frightened again. "They'll find me," she breathed out, choking on a sob.

"Which men are you afraid of? The men Fallen took you to?" Molly asked, softly.

She didn't want to push Prim back into her dark nightmare, but how could they help her if they didn't know what had happened to her in the first place?

Prim paused on a sob. "Fallen didn't sell me to the men." She wiped at her dirty cheeks and finally, straightened. Molly still saw the same beautiful girl, but this girl now held a sharp, deadly edge. "Lilith sold me to them. Lilith took me from the prison. She... she let them... tou—" she paused, breathing with difficultly. "Touch me in front of her and didn't stop them. They..." she stopped again, shaking her head as if she couldn't say the words. Couldn't voice them. Prim's cheeks reddened in anger and she dug her long, broken nails into her thighs, breaking flesh. "They... ruined me. Lilith ruined me."

Molly's chest ached in pain for her. Lilith...Lilith had done everything. Fallen was the king, but Lilith controlled him. Lilith did everything to gain more power so she could destroy everyone around her who was a threat.

Prim and Seto had gone against the king's laws, but in Lilith's twisted mind, Prim had disrespected her. And she had wanted to make the girl pay for it... A wrath Molly didn't know she was capable of started simmering deep within her.

She would end this snake queen.

She would destroy her the same way Lilith had destroyed so many others.

She was a monster.

And she would die for her actions.

Then the tears streamed down Prim's cheeks and she didn't wipe them away.

Molly slowly reached out and stroked her dark hair and scooted closer, wrapping her in her arms. "Shush." She kissed her temple as she sniffled into her chest. "Don't worry, Prim. Lilith will pay dearly for everything she's done. I promise."

They stayed like that for a while, the girl crying in Molly's arms. When she was calm again, Prim lifted her head slowly.

"Where's Seto?" she asked, a dark, troubled look returning to her eyes.

"He's outside, waiting. He didn't want to frighten you again. He's worried you know," Molly said, with a small smile. "He loves you very much, Prim. He hasn't forgotten what Fallen made him do to you and it's breaking him inside. He just wants to help you, but you have to let him. He brought me here because you wouldn't let him near. But please trust me, Prim. You're safe with him. You're safe here. You need each other to heal, because I know he needs you as much as you need him. Can you try to let him help you, Prim?" Molly asked softly. "Do you think you can do that?"

After a beat, Prim nodded almost imperceptibly and Molly let out a relieved breath.

They would be okay. They would heal.

There was still hope.

TENSLEY DIDN'T LET his gaze wander too far from the cottage or Seto who leaned against the wall, foot tapping nervously against the stone path.

Over the sound of Seto's nerves, all he could hear were the faint voices in the cottage of his dolcezza and Prim, but he didn't bother listening in.

At the sound of footsteps, he fully turned to face the cottage and watched as Molly stepped out, a gloomy expression darkened her features. Tensley moved fast, reaching her side and spreading his hand across the back of her neck.

He wanted her close.

Molly looked up at him, her brows wrinkled.

"How is she?" Seto asked, his voice thick with anxiety.

Molly pressed her lips into a thin line. "She's scared of the men returning. I told her you'd protect her."

Seto's gaze dropped to the ground. "I keep telling her the same thing, but it's like she doesn't hear me. Like she's blocking me out."

"Give her some time, she'll open up. She..." Molly started, brows wrinkling, as if she was unsure of how to say her next words. "She also mentioned that it wasn't Fallen who sold her," Molly continued softly, as if it would lessen the blow. She looked at Tensley before she spoke. "She said Lilith was the one who did it. She... she said Lilith let some of the men touch her. I think," she stopped, and they both heard her swallow. "I think they might have..."

But she didn't need to finish her sentence. Seto's face turned into a mask of dark fury, an expression he had never seen on the man, and he knew Seto understood very well what Molly had been about to say.

Tensley clenched his hands. That wicked bitch.

Seto shook his head, turning away from the both of them. "I want her dead. I want her throat between my hands and—" He paused, catching his breath, the wilderness buzzing loudly. Out of uncontrollable rage, Seto's fists connected with the side of the old cottage, making it rattle. When he saw the blood on his knuckles, his brows furrowed, and his eyes turned tearful once more. He breathed in, but it seemed hard. "Thank you, my lady."

Molly nodded, smiling softly back at him and watched as he tried collecting himself, calming himself down, and returned inside the cottage.

Molly sighed, rubbing her forehead. Tensley's fingers massaged the nape of her neck.

"I have to go home," she whispered to him. "To your family and Scorpios."

His fingers paused, his chest aching at her words. "Of course," he whispered back, not allowing her to know how much that pained him. How much his instincts screamed at him not to let her. To keep her close to him. Always.

But he felt exhausted, the small amount of intimacy they had shared earlier was quickly disappearing. And he knew that even close to him, in a court full of snakes, she wouldn't be truly protected.

So he'd let her go back to earth, where he knew his family was no doubt taking good care of her, protecting her.

Eventually, he'd need to get more energy, or it could be deadly. And already he knew that time wasn't as far away as he liked to believe. He was reaching his last straw, he was drained, but he knew she'd need to feel in control when he slid inside her warmth again.

They moved in the darkness, silent, together, but so apart.

His beast rumbled in his chest, but his heart pounded more violently than ever before.

The daemon was slowly taming the beast.

AS MOLLY ENTERED back into her dark apartment, her chest felt so heavy. She couldn't stop thinking about Prim, about how destroyed she was, and how she wept into her shoulder until she fell asleep.

Tensley had seemed cold again as she left, as if the heat between them had returned back to the bitter resentment like before. She wanted to stay, but she knew everything with Scorpios was not good enough that she could leave them alone for long.

They needed a leader. They needed someone to refer to.

And she intended to do her job.

Her phone buzzed and she scrambled for her purse on the kitchen counter. "Hello?"

"Molly," Evelyn's sharp voice came through the line and her voice sent chills down Molly's spine. "I've been calling you for hours. You need to come to the townhouse now."

"Why?"

"If you want to trap Fitz Senior, be here in five."

And the line went dead.

chapter eighteen

MOLLY WRAPPED HER wool coat around her middle and shuddered from the cool wind. Snowflakes, so tiny, floated across the dark night sky and painted the cement parking lot. The few lamp lights did nothing to lighten the dark area and Molly breathed out to see her breath in the cool air.

"When you see him, don't act weak, got it?" Evelyn said, turning the car light's off so they sat in complete darkness. "He's Ares and you—" Evelyn paused, her dark eyes scanning Molly's frame, her nose scrunched in disgust. "Well to be quite frank, I'm not sure what the fuck you are."

Molly kept her stare blank, but she dug her nails into the middle of her palms and breathed through her nose. *She's trying to rattle you.*

"Let me give you some advice," Evelyn said, sighing as if speaking to a younger sister. "Don't let him see through you. If you feel weak, act strong.

If you feel sad, act as if you were indifferent, if you're afraid, act as If he was nothing more than the dirt under your shoe. That kind of man—the ones like Fitz, they'll eat you alive. They thrive off of all the emotions they're forbidden from feeling. You may be the Dux's fuck-buddy, but give them one reason to harm you and they won't hesitate. Especially that asshole's father," Evelyn said, pointing at the backseat where Fitz Junior sat.

Molly sighed, trying her best to ignore Evelyn's pointless rant. It was nothing new to her. She knew what she was capable of, and she knew how to deal with snakes. She had been around a court full of them for longer than was bearable. If the Dux of Ares thought he could mess with her, he had another thing coming.

She hadn't told Daphne or anyone else where she was going, and that did make her nervous. Daphne continued to stress she had to think of the baby inside of her and rest. She couldn't keep trying to do so much—school, baby classes with September, beast taming, and dealing with frightening men in Scorpios.

But keeping busy kept the awful pain in her chest away. The pain she felt whenever she thought of Tensley, the man she loved, and the number of enemies that were out to kill him or overtake him. If it wasn't Ares, she was pretty sure the High Court would try something of their own. They acted as if they had accepted their fate, but she knew better. And she hoped Tensley did too.

"This is where he said he'd meet us?" Molly asked, turning to face Evelyn in the driver's seat.

Evelyn had rolled down her window and was now smoking, the end of her cigarette a faint ember that flicked in the cool wind. She took a puff and slowly blew out smoke from the side of her mouth. "Yes. Why? The little daemon doesn't believe me?" She cocked a brow at her.

Molly kept her mouth shut. She didn't completely trust the woman, but it was her only lead to Fitz Senior. A step closer to meeting with him and hopefully finding a middle ground, a bargain. If not, Molly didn't doubt blood would be spilled, and she'd make sure it wasn't her own. When Evelyn called and told her she had intercepted a call meant for Fitz Junior, she said she was able to convince Senior to meet as long as Molly was there too.

"Jesus Christ," Fitz Junior hissed in the back of the car. Molly eyed him in the rearview mirror, watching as he shivered in his thin cotton sweater.

"Shut up, kid," Evelyn spat back at him and took another drag of her smoke.

Molly twisted her lips and unwrapped her wool scarf, passing it back to him.

His permanent scowl softened and with chained hands, he took the large scarf and wrapped it around his neck, engulfing his chest.

"And what does the king's wife carry in her purse?" Molly turned to the sound of Evelyn's mischievous tone and found her rifling through her Gucci purse.

"Evelyn," Molly snapped, snatching her purse back.

But Evelyn held a bottle of pills and her features fell into an expression of shock. She turned to face Molly, lifting the prenatal pills. "Why do you need these?"

Molly grabbed the pills back and stuffed them into her purse, her anxiety twisting around her chest tighter and tighter. What if Evelyn told someone? What if she told all of Scorpios? What would they do? Would she use it against her? To gain back the power Molly had taken from her?

"What is it?" Fitz Junior chimed in, trying to lean forward to see what they were talking about.

Molly went to speak, but Evelyn's harsh tone cut the car into a dead silence. "Nothing," she hissed. "You stay in that backseat and you don't say a fucking word."

Molly glanced at her, watching Evelyn for once look deathly ill. After a minute of no one speaking, Evelyn shifted and looked at Molly, her mouth a straight line, but her eyes soft. "Does he know?"

Molly swallowed and she knew who she was talking about. "Yes, he does."

Evelyn sighed heavily and rubbed a hand along her tensed brows. "Fuck me." Evelyn stubbed her smoke and ran her hands through her hair, groaning. She paused, leaning her head back, then she turned to face Molly and twisted the key, the car coming to life. "I'm taking you back."

Molly glared at her. "What? No! I'm staying."

Evelyn chuckled angrily. "Not under my watch."

Molly's brow creased in confusion. "But—"

Lights flashed in front of them and Evelyn paused, watching as a dark van parked in front of them and Fitz Senior exited the car.

"Shit," Fitz Junior whispered behind them.

"C'mon," Molly said, and opened her car door.

Evelyn stared at her, immobile in her own seat. "Molly..."

Molly didn't listen though. She exited the car and walked toward Fitz in the darkness, the snowflakes and his shock white hair the only thing visible.

"Ms. Darling," he greeted her, his voice low and brittle. He smiled at her.

She scowled at him. "Knight. It's Mrs. Knight. Good to see you too, Fitz. It hasn't been long enough." she said, her tone dry.

Evelyn appeared beside her, her mouth set in a thin line as she held Fitz Junior in place.

Senior examined his own son, a wave of emotion flooding his features for a mere second and then vanishing. "Son."

"Father," Junior said back, his throat bobbing.

Senior turned to Molly and that eerie smile turned back on. "It was so kind of you to accept my invitation to meet, Mrs. Knight. And your husband is now king of the demons." He whistled lowly. "And here you are, with little old us. An honor. Truly," he said, not even bothering to hide his lack of honesty.

"You've been killing some of our men, Fitz. I don't appreciate that. But I came here to discuss matters. Perhaps make a bargain. To save a few lives," Molly said, her tone indifferent but clear and strong.

"Ah, yes," he said, and turned to look at his son again. "To come to a truce. My son in exchange for no attacks on my part?" he said, clearly not convinced by the terms of the bargain. If anything, Fitz Junior had been right, his father didn't care for him at all. But even as she thought it, she remembered the few emotions that had passed over the older man's face as he had seen his son, beaten and bruised. There was something there. Something she hoped was somewhat close to affection.

"You don't look convinced, Fitz. You'd sacrifice your son's life, your one and only heir, just to win Scorpios over?" Molly arched a brow, not hiding her disgust. "Can't say I'm surprised, you did kill your own wife after all…"

"I did indeed, but I had reasons a naïve little girl like you would never understand," he snapped, his chest rumbling with a suppressed growl. His eyes shifted quickly to his son, then to Evelyn, something dark and dangerous passing through his eyes before settling back on Molly. "I agree to your bargain. No more attacks on Scorpios. Now release my son."

Molly studied the older man, his strict posture, his black leather gloves as he clenched and unclenched them.

"Swear on your own life," Molly bit out. "If you lie, I'll make sure it's the last one you'll ever tell."

Senior flared his nostrils. "I swear on my life," he said slowly, his voice thick with unspoken emotions.

Molly took a deep breath and nodded to Evelyn.

Evelyn let go of Junior and he limped forward, his body still recovering from the torture Scorpios had inflicted on him.

Fitz Senior smiled warmly at his son and cupped his cheeks. A long look passed between them.

A laugh escaped Senior's thin mouth, mixed with happiness and sadness.

Then Senior snapped his son's neck, the sound echoing in the darkness and straight into Molly's bones.

Molly let out a breath of shock, her eyes widening as she watched Junior's body collapse onto the snowy cement.

Senior rolled his shoulders and wiped his leather gloves on his coat. "Well, now that's done, let's truly discuss business."

Shit.

THE BITE OF winter made Tensley's body shudder violently as his men and him marched inside. The heat of the palace breezed over his numbed cheeks and he made his way up to his chambers. Hunting for large animals took patience and skill, and some of his men held neither of those inside of them.

Once they had caught enough to feed the court, they had returned to the palace. But it had taken them all day and it was now late at night. Not that Tensley minded, he had needed the release. The chase. But as with everything else, it hadn't been enough. It never was.

His body now craved a warm bath, but his mind, his beast craved the sting of brutal ice, of the numbness spreading through his body.

Each time he saw Molly, his beast warred inside of him. He wanted her body, he wanted ownership over her, but that damn heart thudding inside of him wanted something different from her.

Her affection.

Her love.

Anything she'd be willing to give him.

At even the simple thought, he felt his body seize in rejection, revolt against his desire. But the more he suppressed it, the more it consumed him. He felt the pull, the damnation that even after his heart was ripped out, it still beat for her.

His heart sped up and the nerve-endings convulsed.

The rest of the court—Lilith especially, did not need to know what he now hid inside of his chest. A weapon and a curse she'd use against him. He would show her nothing else other than the beast. No tenderness or soft underbelly. He'd bare his teeth and tear the court apart. From the ground up.

As he entered his dim chambers, he unlaced his breeches, only to stop mid-stride and glare at the fire crackling in the fireplace, red and orange flames eating at the stacks of oak wood. His gaze then landed on the silhouette standing by the fire, her back to him.

Her red waves draped down her back and he noted her thin housecoat concealing herself from him. Barely.

"I waited for you," Lilith whispered, her voice husky.

Tensley gritted his teeth. He didn't need to say a word; he simply fisted his hands as the aggressive pheromones lashed against her skin and she jolted.

Her sharp eyes found his in the darkness and instead of frowning, she grinned. Wide and menacing, like a wolf.

"Are you frightened of me, my king?" She moved, the bottom of her nightgown floating gracefully across the marble floor.

"My chambers are not your own," he snapped. "You are not welcome here."

Her fingers played with the laced ribbons above her chest, loosening them to reveal her creamy flesh and the tops of her breasts.

The beast revolted at the sight of another woman.

"I know you have been lacking intimacy. Your wife has forgotten her sole duties to you. She's a failure and a shame," Lilith hummed, but it came out more like a hiss of a serpent swaying its way into its prey. "You're above those little wolves now, my king,"

Tensley didn't bother to look at her. "Never underestimate a pup, Lilith. They grow, they evolve and eventually, they conquer the ones who had thought them too weak."

"I have watched you move, watched you murder lesser men. I must admit, I am a woman of power. I thrive on it. I crave it. And I crave you. More than I ever craved my husband—or any beast in this court," Lilith said, her smiling eyes scanning his rigid form in appreciation. She moved closer, her warm breath hitting his clenched jaw, the scent of roses and sweetness surrounding him in a ball of anger. "You need to fuck and I must serve my king." At the moment her fingers touched his wrist, simply skimming her thumb along the hollow of his wrist, he struck.

He gripped her by her throat, Not enough to crush the air out of her, but enough to hurt. To send a message.

To send a threat to stand down.

"I am not your play toy, I am not fooled by your sweet words or your soft touches. I have a queen that satisfies all of my needs and more, I have no use for a traitor in my bed," he hissed lowly, his dark eyes drilling into her own wide ones.

He let go, Lilith stumbling to catch her balance and he turned away. "Your queen—your queen loathes your existence. She will only weaken you—along with that child she carries." She whipped her violent red hair off her shoulder and smiled wickedly at him, too confident for his liking. "If I reject you, if I show the court how I truly feel about your authority, they will side with me. They will destroy you. I am your only key to them."

He balled his hands, imagining them around her neck, crushing the bones until he heard them crack. "Leave my chambers before I force you."

Lilith hummed, as if scolding a child. "Wrong choice, my brutal king. Wrong choice…"

Tensley waited until she closed the door behind her and listened to her footfalls fade. Until all he heard was the damn beating deep in his chest, a cry of battle and chaos.

He marched to the fireplace and gripped the mantel, digging his nails into the oak wood and hissed out in pain. The flames licked at his skin and he let them. Feel the burn, feel the pain, ignore the twist of desire inside of him.

He wanted to go to his wife, to lay beside her and just hold her. Anxiety controlled him. Anxiety of seeing her again. Anxiety of how to behave around her.

A beast never craved the heart, never bowed to another, but here he was, battling himself to stay within this world.

The heart was growing too fast, too powerful, and the beast was fighting, roaring, but failing.

If he saw her, he'd bow, if he smelled her sweet essence, he'd cave, and if he tasted her, he'd beg.

If she knew, if she had an inkling of how much power she had over him again, she'd win, but he was done fighting what the beast, what even the fucking gods couldn't stop him from wanting.

And he wasn't letting her slip through his bloody fingers again.

chapter nineteen

ITZ SENIOR'S LEATHER gloves squeaked as he flexed his fingers, overstepping his son's dead body and smiling at Molly as if nothing had happened.

She curled her hands into fists beside her, doing anything to not touch her own stomach. How could a father kill their own son with no remorse? Nothing?

"How?" Molly managed to speak, her voice shaking, the last thing she wanted him to hear, but his callous actions dug into her core.

"He was becoming dead weight," Senior answered, a slight shrug accompanied his cool tone of indifference. "You said it yourself, daemon. I killed my own wife. With my bare hands."

Evelyn stood to the side, her features pure stone and unreadable.

All Molly felt was her own rage though, burning the back of her eyes. "He was your fucking son." She didn't care that Evelyn had warned her. To be cool, to be indifferent. All she felt was a burning anger and she wanted to unleash it on the white-haired man in front of her.

He laughed softly. "You may be living in our society, but you have not learned a thing from us, have you, Mrs. Knight?"

"Don't offer me advice," Molly spat, her entire body shaking with rage. "I've dealt with power-hungry kings and queens who wanted to control the way I should act, saying I should submit. But they mean nothing to me. Their words and wants mean nothing to me. Because I'm not a demon. I'm not part of your sick culture."

Senior's lips thinned and he flexed his fingers out again. "Watch your words, honey. You have no idea what you even are. You're still a mystery, even to yourself."

Honey?

Molly squared her jaw and hated that he was right. "I know enough to be able to be a danger. Even to a Dux like you. You think I'm so clueless, so naïve. Keep thinking that, underestimate me, Fitz. It'll only make for a better surprise when I have a front row seat to the last seconds of your miserable existence."

Senior paused, his entire body freezing. The months since the last time he had seen her had changed her greatly. She wasn't the same woman anymore. She definitely wasn't naïve or innocent. She had battled the court, she had watched her husband's heart get ripped out, and she was still fucking standing.

"Back to the bargain," Senior bit out, his anger rolling off in waves at her. "You seem to have forgotten that I too once made a deal. With your then fiancé. You in exchange for Ares. For my land. I think it's time I collect my reward, don't you?"

"Your reward?" Molly scoffed and laughed bitterly. "I'm not an object of exchange."

"But to save Scorpios? To save that dear fiancé of yours and his family?"

He grinned wildly. "Salvatore was only the beginning. Each day you refuse my offer, I'll murder another person close to your Tensley."

Molly bit the inside of her mouth, trying to keep her expression blank. She thought of Daphne and how heartbroken Tensley would be. She thought of Gabriella and her kids, if Donovan was killed. He was just a boy. So tiny, so young, so pure.

"And if I come with you?" Molly began, curious of his response.

Senior's eyes lit up at her words. "No more war. No more blood. No more."

"No," Evelyn's voice was steel and iron and Molly glanced up at her. "The bargain's not happening."

Senior's heavy brows furrowed. "You did your part, Ms. Rose. You're not needed now."

Molly frowned. "You did your—what does that mean?"

Senior smiled, but his eyes never left Evelyn. "How do you think we were able to slip the poison into Salvatore's drink, sweet Molly?"

Pure shock mixed with horror swept over Molly's entire body and she glanced over at Evelyn.

"They threatened us," Evelyn argued. "If I didn't do it, if I—he was going to murder my father. They've been threatening him."

Molly couldn't handle what she was hearing. Evelyn had poisoned Tensley's father. She had known all along. She had killed, murdered, her own Dux.

"Not to mention she told us every little detail about Tensley and your love life," Senior added. Molly's fisted hands shook. "And she made sure this entire meeting took place. Alone. Out here. In the middle of nowhere." Molly couldn't process any of this. It was too much. She couldn't... she couldn't. "What—" she stopped abruptly, not knowing what to say. "I thought..."

Fitz took a step closer, his shiny leather loafers glimmering in the low light. "Yes, yes, well you thought wrong, Mrs. Knight. She's the traitor Scorpios has been hunting for. It was never us, it was her."

"I…"

"Now, sweet Molly, will you come with me? If you don't, let me just remind you that no one will hear your screams here, darling. No one will come to help you."

"She's not going with you," Evelyn hissed and stepped in front of Molly, her arm spread out in front of her.

Senior cocked a thick brow. "You can let go of the pretenses now, Ms. Rose. The secret's out," he murmured, a mocking smile on his lips.

"I'm not fucking pretending. She is not going with you, Fitz. Whether you like it or not."

Fitz laughed darkly, his head thrown back as he did. "Why the change of heart, Evelyn? You wanted this. You said we forced you, but deep down, we both know you wanted it."

Molly watched Evelyn's side profile, her features unwavering, her chest heaving heavily as she faced off with Senior.

Evelyn simply shook her head.

"Such a shame."

Molly's stomach dropped at the sound of his low voice and she watched him move, move like a lion about to pounce, but his head was bent.

He was bent forward, his eyes far from hers. The power within her thundered, her instincts screaming at her to catch his gaze. To look at him. To use the power that rumbled deep within. But she couldn't, and before she realized it, he lunged.

Her hands shot out, to push him back, but his fingers wrapped around her wrists and his free hand found her neck, forcing her head forward.

She gasped, the tightness filling her chest as Senior held her by her neck. "I know your weakness, daemon. No eye contact, no power."

She hissed in anger, but only choked when he clenched tighter.

"You're coming with me," he said and stepped forward, forcing her to move with him.

"No, she's not, *bastard*," Evelyn's voice rang out loud and clear and she elbowed his face.

At the weakness of his grip, Molly jabbed his stomach and stumbled away, turning to catch the sight of the two rushing forward, colliding, their bodies meeting like a loud clap of thunder.

The two tore at each other's skin, bones shattering, blood splattering onto the snowy cement and Molly couldn't look away.

Senior swung his head forward and collided with Evelyn's own forward. She stumbled back, but kept her balance and punched him across his cheek, the sound of his cheekbone cracking.

Evelyn jabbed him with her knee and he gasped, staggering. Only to yank out a knife and stab her deep in her stomach.

Evelyn froze, her hands going to her where the blood gushed from her belly and she fell forward.

Senior wiped the blood off of his knife and sneered down at her.

Molly rushed forward and bent down next to Evelyn, feeling her pulse. Evelyn's dark brown eyes stared up at the black sky and white snowflakes landed on her cheeks, on the tip of her nose, melting into her skin.

Molly looked at the large gash, the blood freely flooding and tore her wool sleeve and put pressure on the wound.

"Mrs. Knight," Senior said, lowly. "Come."

Molly looked up at him, at her chance to destroy the man who was ripping Scorpios apart at the seams. At the man she wanted to strangle until she felt his life pour out of him.

Blood pooled in Evelyn's mouth and she sputtered, coughing, choking.

to crown a beast

She was dying…she had risked her life for Molly…even after she had done so many awful things, she had risked her life to save Molly's.

Either go with Senior now and kill him or save Evelyn…

Her thoughts struck her hard and fast and she raised her eyes, meeting Senior's eyes. A shiver of power spread down her spine and she felt the flare of strength. "Go. Run as far as you can and don't stop."

Senior's eyes dilated and for a moment, he didn't move.

He blinked and swallowed, turning and walking off. She watched him, her heart in her throat as he disappeared into the snowfall and darkness.

What was that?

What came over her was pure instinctual. She hadn't even thought of it before her eyes pierced his and he was moving away.

Her daemon powers…the trauma of Tensley's death…they were working. Fully working.

She took a shuddering deep breath and looked back down at Evelyn in her arms.

"Evelyn?" Molly whispered, searching her face for a sign of hope.

"I did it to save my family," Evelyn managed through a cough. "And then— then you're pregnant." Tears fell from her eyes and mixed with the melting snowflakes on her cheeks. "I couldn't hurt Tensley like that. He didn't love his father, so I could come to terms with that, but this… I just— I could never do this to a baby. Not after…" she said, stopping herself from saying more. Molly had many questions to ask, but they would have to wait. Evelyn was bleeding and it needed to be healed fast.

Molly's hands shook and she blinked back tears. In the middle of the night, in the cold beginning of December, Molly helped Evelyn back to the car.

She was a traitor, but she had saved her life…

"Evelyn," Molly whispered to her, trying to keep her conscious. She sagged against the front seat, a trail of dark crimson painting the black leather. "Stay with me. Stay awake. We'll be back to Scorpios soon." When she saw Evelyn was slowly falling asleep, Molly changed her plans. "Tell me more, about why you couldn't hurt a baby... you were going to say something but stopped."

Evelyn's eyes were half closed, her mind no doubt groggy, clouded over with exhaustion and her body's need to heal. "I... I got pregnant when I was younger. I was seventeen, naïve, forgiving," she started, her voice barely above a whisper, the words a mumbled mess. She took another deep breath. "It was an accident. The boy and I, we were fooling around at the time, nothing serious. But one thing led to another, and stupidity got me pregnant. Out of wedlock," she finished, but she was getting so drowsy, Molly had to lean closer to her to hear her last few words.

Molly's heart stilled and she glanced at Evelyn as she pulled out of the parking lot.

"When my father found out, he hid it from everyone, of course. It would be too scandalous for us. It would ruin us. Even though I was nothing more than a child at the time, had Fallen, or anyone one else, found out, I would have been killed without a second thought. You remember what happened to Beau and Valentina..." she said with a shrug, as if it was nothing more than a regular thing to hear. Which, sadly, in a world full of demons once ruled by a mad king, it was. "So in order to protect me, my father sent me away and I had the baby in a cabin upstate with my mother. But—" she sniffled subtly. "The baby died the day after I gave birth to him." Evelyn stayed silent for a minute lost to her own thought.

After a beat, Molly turned to look at the bleeding woman on, barely awake on the seat next to hers. "What," Molly swallowed with difficulty. "What happened to the baby? Why did it..."

"Die?" Evelyn said, her tone part sad, part sinister. "I never knew the reason why, and my father wouldn't allow an autopsy. He said it would be too risky," she finished, unable to look at Molly.

Her hands shook and she pressed harder on her stomach, but the shaking didn't stop. Finally, her bloodshot eyes looked up. ""Even though my time with him was too brief, I loved him you know. My son. He was everything to me. Isn't it amazing how something so meaningful, such as a child, a beautiful little baby boy, could come from something so meaningless. And I lost him."

"I'm sorry, Evelyn. I'm sorry for your loss," she said, and she saw the woman briefly nod. "Is that why you saved me? Because you couldn't see someone lose their child like you lost yours?"

"Yes," she said, and Molly knew those would be her final words on the subject as Evelyn dropped her head again against the seat, facing away from Molly, and sniffled softly.

Molly sat still, unable to speak. She thought of the fear of losing her own son every day and the fact that Evelyn had lost a child and had saved her because of her own loss sat heavy on her chest.

And the more she thought about it, the more she realized perhaps Evelyn wasn't who she thought she was. They all thought she was a whiny power hungry viper who lured men for their prestige amongst Scorpios. But maybe she acted the way she did because she had her own goals, her own vengeance to seek.

Molly didn't know how to feel as she drove back to Scorpios, driving with one hand and helping Evelyn apply pressure on the wound with the other. Her head kept getting blurry with thoughts of everything she had learned in the past hour, of the things she had witnessed with her own eyes. First, the image of Fitz Senior snapping his own son's neck without an inch of regret. Then, this new surge of power she hadn't known how to control, something she couldn't quite explain. And finally, Evelyn's revelation.

Once she knew Evelyn was in the hands of the doctor, getting the help she needed, Molly pressed a hand to her stomach and prayed she'd protect her son until her last breath.

MOLLY WATCHED ILLYA, on his hands and knees, as he built a crib. He grunted when the tiny screws jammed and she laughed, only earning a smile from him. She sat on the bed, slurping up homemade soup she had made that morning and studying the History of World War I. The last exam of her undergraduate year was coming up and she couldn't wait to have school off the list of things to do.

Last night was still fresh in her head and Evelyn was still being questioned. The members of Scorpios would have to vote soon on what they planned to do with her. As of right now, she wasn't sure what they would decide. Even though she had saved Molly, Evelyn was still a traitor to Scorpios.

After hours of instructing Scorpios soldiers how to proceed with the Rose family now in custody, jailed in the basement of the Knights' property, trapped in cells she didn't even know existed, all Molly wanted to do was sleep and forget everything. Evelyn had poisoned Tensley's father. She couldn't wrap her head around it and it made her sick to her stomach. Sitting down with Daphne to tell her what had happened broke her even more. Daphne's trembling mouth, her whimpers, her pleads.

Molly touched her chest, the pain heaviest there and breathed out softly.

Illya had spent the entire morning scolding her for not telling him what she was doing and how dangerous it had been.

She knew he was right, but she had to go. She had to try and help end this endless war with Ares to save Tensley's people.

"God, I can't stop eating," Molly said with a mouth full of rice and veggies.

Illya laughed, his blond hair falling into his eyes. "Well, you are five months—almost six months pregnant. Plus, it's a powerful thing you have growing in you, I wouldn't expect anything else."

Molly wiped at the corner of her mouth with her woolly sweater and grimaced. "This baby never stops wanting more."

"Definitely Tensley's son," Illya added and sat back up, glaring at the white crib.

Molly smiled at her belly, very noticeably round, even in her baggy sweater. When she glanced up at Illya, he had stood up and was stroking his jaw in deep thought, analyzing the crib. He had restarted several times, wanting to make sure the crib was safe, and even after she protested the second time, she couldn't help but grin.

And grinning usually made her cry nowadays.

Ugh, hormones.

"How goes the triangle of yours?"

Illya glared at her. "There's no triangle."

"Oh? You mean there's absolutely nothing going on between Stella, you and September?" she asked with a knowing smile.

"We're all friends."

"Right," she said dragging the word out before she blew out her cheeks and tried to focus back on her studying, but something else itched inside of her to tell Illya. She straightened and bit the end of her pencil, watching him glare at the crib once again.

"So I contacted Lance," Molly announced, lowering her head back to her sketchy handwriting just as Illya turned to face her.

"Lance?" He cocked a brow. "As in the warlock, Lance?"

Molly nodded, twirling her pencil. "I want to see if he has more information about daemons or if he knows someone else who does."

Illya frowned at that.

"Oh, don't give me that look." Molly frowned back at him and sighed. "I think it's about time I learn more about what I am. What I can do." She thought of the night before—what she had done to Senior and how she had made him leave. She wanted, needed to understand what that had been. How to manage it, how to wield it. "I'm seeing him today."

"You're supposed to be resting for the baby," he argued. "You need to stop trying to do so much and think about your son."

Her cheeks reddened, more so in anger. "I am, but I can't sleep, Illya. I want to protect my son. I want to get rid of Ares and Senior said something last night that really bothered me," she said, looking out at the city through one of the bedroom windows. "He said I still didn't know what I am. And parts of that are true. I know a bit more than I did back then, but that's all. I want to know what I am, all of it. I want to know what my son will be. I'm tired of being in the dark, I'm tired of not knowing my full potential."

She sucked in deeply, thinking of her time with Tensley and how even though he didn't have the answers to her daemon ancestry, she felt whole with him. She felt herself entirely with him.

Illya's brown eyes softened and he moved to sit down on the edge of the bed, his hand taking hers in his own. "If you really want to know, I can help you."

Molly felt the burn behind her eyes and her vision blurred. "Illya, if anything…" She paused, collecting herself and squeezed his hand. "If anything ever happened to me, if I wasn't able to take care of my son," she whispered and nervously licked her lips. "I want you to take care of him. To watch after him."

Illya shook his head. "Molly, I—what about September or your parents?"

"I'd obviously want them to help, but you know Tensley's world, you know how to teach him about your society, how to raise him in a world of heartless beasts and raise him to be kind and happy," Molly explained, smiling softly at

Illya's shocked expression. "I know Tensley and I know he would have wanted you, trusted you, to look after his son. Just like you look after me, I want you to look after my son."

Illya's brown eyes grew wet and red and he looked at the wall. With a deep, shaky breath he faced her and smiled. "I'd be honored, Molly. But you're not going anywhere, I'll take care of both of you. For however long you need me."

Molly's mouth trembled and she sniffled, and she leaned forward, wrapping her arms around him.

He in return, hugged her, warm and gentle, but everything she needed.

MOLLY SAT STIFFLY in the odd record shop, a teacup with an oriental design in her hand as she watched Lance sifting through his cupboards. He was the warlock who had helped Tensley after the hunters had attacked them a few months ago.

So much had happened since that time, Molly couldn't believe everything that had changed in only a couple of months. She, herself, felt like she had changed. And so had Tensley. They were all very different now.

"So, explain again?" Lance asked, sticking his head into one of the cupboards, his voice echoing.

Molly dug her nails into her knees. "Last night, I forced a man to walk away. I looked into his eyes and without even thinking, I told him to walk away. And he did. It felt—like an instinct. That it was a part of me. I can't even explain how I did it, it just... happened. I needed to think quickly, to act quickly, and my body just... took over," she said, gaze lost as she clenched her hands again.

Illya cleared his throat, shifting in the chair beside her and gave her a look.

"Ah, here it is," Lance said and yanked out a hardcover book. He moved toward them and perched on the corner of his unstable kitchen table. "After we talked last about daemons, I kept thinking more about it. I searched all of my ancestor's books and—I found this."

He turned the book around and Molly leaned forward, squinting at the fine print.

Illya frowned. "I can't read it."

"Right? It took me weeks to translate," Lance huffed dramatically as he pointed to the wrinkled pages. Molly stared at the art of men and women, their eyes wide and bright.

"They have my eyes," Molly breathed out, more to herself than for the others.

"Indeed," Lance began, nodding slowly. "Eyes are thought to be links to the soul. And you have rare eyes, Molly Knight. Very rare eyes. A daemon's soul is pure, it's powerful. That's why they shine so bright. Just like a demon's eyes turn black, black like the soul they are taught to cherish, to keep at all costs, from their very birth," he continued, with a shy look in Illya's direction. The demon stayed silent, unfazed. Then the warlock's eyes went back to the old, strange book. "I had to read the whole thing a couple times, some parts are still unreadable due to years and years of existence. But back to the important matters, this book, this particular part, recites the story of a daemon facing an event. A powerful but terrible event, something that could ultimately break their bright, pure soul. It then goes on to explain that when the soul of a daemon is broken, crushed, damaged, the power flares. It comes to life. But it can only truly happen if the daemon goes through a trauma, a moment where survival is critical. That," he said, a satisfied smile playing on his lips. "Is when a daemon's true powers are unraveled. What power the daemon could use before was nothing but a fraction of their capacity."

"A trauma?" Molly pondered over his words, trying to think back over every moment, everything that had happened since she'd first noticed a new surge of power within her. Her heart skipped a beat, as realization hit. "Tensley... After Tensley had his heart ripped out, when I thought he was..." she stopped herself, not wanting to say the words aloud. "I felt the power then. That was the first time I felt it with such vibrancy, such strength."

Lance nodded, stroking the dark scruff on his cheeks. "That would do it. That trauma fully awakened them." He pointed to her. "Those powers are constantly stirring inside of you now. They're a part of you. Like Medusa. If they look into your eyes, they're trapped."

Molly swallowed thickly. "But how was I able to force Fitz to do what I said?"

Lance paused, flipping through the pages. "Here. A daemon who's soul is awakened can access, through their gaze, power over others. To kill a daemon's soul completely they believed," he began and a chill ran down Molly's spine. "One must sever the head from the body and burn it."

Illya's hand landed on her shoulder and squeezed. "That's enough."

"No, Illya, it's fine," she told him. "I need to know everything." Her hand went to her stomach.

"Your powers are a part of you, now more than ever. It's like a sixth sense," Lance said, shutting the book. "It's not something that can be trained now. It's something in you. Forever. It will manifest itself when need be, but will never act against your will. It understands your emotions, you intentions, your desires. So you don't need to fear it being used on someone you love."

She felt over her stomach again. A comforting habit. "And the baby? Do you know anything about a half daemon, half demon baby?"

Lance's eyes dropped to her large belly and he stared at it for some time. "How far along are you?"

"The doctor said he's around six months," she told him, rubbing her stomach.

Lance hummed again. "I can sense it's a he now. A few months ago, I could only sense that there was something, something that wasn't you but somehow held a part of your essence, was growing inside of you. Now, I can tell it's well and truly a he," he said with a genuine smile.

Molly nodded with a soft smile. "You know, you were the first who made me think that I was maybe pregnant, it scared me to no end." She laughed and he laughed with her. Illya stayed quiet, but a small smile toyed with the corners of his lips.

"I'm sorry I scared you," Lance laughed some more. "But back to the baby. Considering it's a he, there's a good chance he won't be graced with your powers," he said, with a shrug.

"Most of the books I've read were theories from other warlocks and such, we have no real scientific information to speak of, unfortunately. However, most of those theories seemed to say most of the daemons that have supposedly existed and that we know of, through legends and myths, have been women. But very few stories depicted men. There were some that existed but not nearly enough to say men descending from a daemon bloodline truly had chances of wielding the powers.

"It still runs in their blood, but it isn't accessible to most of them. I'm guessing the lack of actual research isn't simply because daemons are rare, but also because the gene is unpredictable and doesn't seem to answer to any sort of rule or law when it chooses to show itself. You are the first daemon to exist for the last three hundred years. Why is that? Why didn't the gene show itself sooner, why did it choose you? We have no way to know," he finished, shaking his head slightly.

"I can try my best to find out more about the baby, what it could possibly mean to be half demon and half daemon, but I might not come up with much," he said, and Molly could see it frustrated Lance not to be able to say more, to learn more.

"Anything, anything at all is helpful, Lance," Molly said, softly. "I just want to be able to take care of my son."

Lance nodded softly.

"We should head back, Molly," Illya told her and she jerked her head up.

Illya helped her stand and walked them over to the door.

Just as he opened the door for her, Molly paused and looked back at Lance. "Call me if you find anything more about the baby. Please."

Lance smiled. "I will."

"Oh, and also, one last thing. I met a warlock at the court, she seemed more or less disturbed but she did say something about the baby, as if she could feel it somehow," Molly said, frowning as she remembered the warlock's words. "She said the baby had a heart. Whatever that means. Hopefully that could maybe help. Thank you for everything, Lance."

As Illya and her were getting into the taxi that would take them home, Molly looked back at Lance's store, where she could still see him standing there with a deep frown etched between his brows.

On their way back to Manhattan, Molly couldn't stop thinking of the moment Tensley's heart was ripped out.

The trauma had triggered her powers to fully awaken.

Illya walked her up to the apartment and began getting food out of the brand new, high hand fridge, asking what she wanted for dinner. She was too lost in her thoughts, overthinking every detail.

The doorbell rang and Illya turned to get it. Molly fixed her sweater and walked out after him, listening to a male voice speak.

"I need to speak to her," the voice demanded.

Molly peeked around the corner into the kitchen and she was greeted by the last person she expected to see tonight.

"Seto? What are you doing here?" Molly asked as she tiptoed closer.

Seto turned fully to face her, his features shadowed by the dark hallway, but she could barely read him.

"The mourning period for Fallen is over," he announced, cool and direct.

Molly frowned and Illya folded his arms, refusing to step back to let him get any closer to Molly.

"Your husband is to be crowned king tonight," he said, a glint of worry warring in his eyes. "And he requests your presence."

chapter twenty

ENSLEY'S CHEST ACHED, the pressure bruising his bones and muscles, sweat rolling down his nose and on top of his lip, brushing it off with the back of his hand. Anxiety riddled his body as he stood in the shaded hallway, the sound of the vicious court could be heard from beyond the golden doors of the throne room.

They were waiting for the beast to be crowned. To see their new king. He was waiting for his wife, hoping Seto managed to convince her to come.

If she didn't come…

He swallowed thickly.

The beast in him growled lowly, and it rumbled through his chest, the sound leaving the barrier of his lips. The man and the beast were still warring against each other, and he knew when he laid eyes on Molly, he'd be wild with want.

But she soothed him—both beast and man. She calmed him, like no other, and he needed her by his side today.

The tinge of pain sparked in his growing heart and he gritted his teeth, tugging at the high collar of his dress shirt.

"My lord," Lilith's voice carried through the hallway and she stepped forward, her black gown tailored to her full figure. A crown of thorns sat upon her red locks. She smiled at him, the tips of her white teeth visible. "It is time. To be crowned fierce king of all demons."

Tensley straightened, not letting her see his weakness, his pain, and stared past her.

"It's tradition," Lilith said softly and traced her silk-gloved hands along his forearm, placing her hand in the bend of his elbow. "It's tradition for the queen to walk beside her king. I will stand beside you in front of the court and vow to honor you. As your queen."

He glared at her red lips, too dark, too harsh against her skin and he jerked her hand off of him.

"I will walk alone," he said, lowly.

Lilith's features transformed into an ugly scowl. "I am your queen."

Tensley took a dangerous step closer, towering over her and let her feel the wave of aggressive pheromones suffocate her. "There is only one queen in my life and in my bed. And it's not you. I grow tired of repeating it to you, Lilith. Next time I need to repeat it, I won't be so gentle. And I may not use words to do so next time. This is your only warning."

Lilith's cheeks flushed in anger and she clenched her jaw so tightly he swore she'd bit it off. "So be it, *my lord.*"

"Tensley," a voice called to him.

A voice that was like a deadly lullaby to his growing heart and brought a familiar sting.

He turned, his heart sinking deep within his iron chest as if to protect itself from the woman walking toward him.

A heavy black cloak hung over her shoulders but he saw the tease of her lilac gown of lace and silk, clean and simple, but all the more arousing to him.

Seto walked beside her, but slowed down as soon as he neared Tensley.

The prince approached from behind them, a cold glare directed at Tensley. *Fucking good.*

The prince could feel the vortex of want and anger wrapping around Tensley's bones and knew not to test his patience.

Molly's mouth was the softest of pinks—so natural, so soft that he wanted to taste each lip separately and then ruin them all at once.

"You are not needed here, daemon," Lilith snapped, the aggressive sound brining Tensley out of his trance and his entire body tensed.

Molly stopped mid-step, her eyes going round in surprise, but then her brows dropped low and she returned her attention to him.

"She will accompany me," Tensley bit out, not bothering to face the snake behind him. "As queen."

"She is no queen," Lilith said, her tone raising, hands starting to shake with anger.

Tensley felt the reins on his anger break and he spun. "She is my queen, she is my wife. She is the one who will stand beside me in front of my court. Always."

His voice rang through the hall, leaving everyone in silence as his body shuddered with pure anger.

Lilith breathed through her nose and stepped back, finally seeing her place in his court. She was no queen, she was nothing to him, but a piece on an ancient chessboard left unused.

Tensley took a deep breath before he turned to face Molly. She had her head slightly bowed, but her eyes peeked at him through her thick lashes. Curious, a bit cautious, but calculating.

"There is only one queen in my life," he whispered, only for her ears, his voice shaking slightly. It surprised him, the sheer emotion the words contained. They hadn't been harsh, aggressive, demanding. If anything, they had been soft... caring, almost. He hadn't heard himself speak with such emotion in a long while. For months, it had only been anger. He cleared his throat and straightened to his full, powerful height. He watched her examine him—and he knew, somehow deep in his belly, deep in his chest, she could see his weakness. She could sense his ill state and her brows furrowed further. She didn't say it aloud, but she took a small step forward, closing the distance.

He breathed her in—her scent of sunlight and tulips and a sweetness that could never be bottled, and he felt his groin ache with need. No woman had this much control over him. It both frightened, enraged, and thrilled him.

Instead of gripping her hips and slamming her into his frame, he lifted his arm, awaiting for her hand to slide into the bend of his elbow.

She lowered her eyes and gently guided her delicate hand to rest on his arm. The single touch of her warm palm heating through the fabric of his shirt drove him wild.

He caught the pinched look on the prince's face, his eyes focused on Molly.

Tensley turned, Molly's steps matching each of his. The double doors of gold appeared as a sign of freedom and entrapment all at once.

The sound of trumpets blared and the noise of voices chattering followed after.

The doors swung open and all of the court turned to face them. He challenged each stare, each glare at his wife and he felt her shift closer to his side. His beast roared with pride.

The throne down the middle of the aisle glimmered under the chandeliers of crystals and with each step closer they took, Molly's hand grew tighter around his bicep.

The crowd hushed on either side of them, unable to look away from the sight of the king and his wife. A power wielded between them so deathly, so lethal, gods would die under their wrath. This was a king showing to a court full of corrupted wolves who he had chosen as his queen, their queen. Who held the power with him. Beside him.

Together.

He felt it in his bones, he felt in his veins as he marched forward. Her touch, her presence beside him fueled his strength.

As they neared the alter, all he heard in the room—in the palace, was her heart beating fast, hidden underneath her gown, hidden beneath her ribcage and nestled deep inside. Her shallow breaths sung to his ears and he turned to face the crowd, his head held high in authority.

His knees shook, but he didn't sit. He needed intimacy, he needed strength, but he wouldn't force himself on Molly. He'd survive through this until she wanted him as much as it fucking pained him.

Lilith and the prince proceeded down the aisle, joining the crowd at the front.

A lord stepped forward holding a sharp blade, sliding off a silk black cloth and bowed.

"My lord," the man spoke and Tensley took his time, his hand reaching down and gripping the blade, the edge cutting into his palm. An ancient blade from Fallen's father's ribcage. Said to be filled with a venom, with power, and his undying rage.

For the future king to soak in that venom.

He stood to his full height and faced the silent crowd. He undid the first few buttons of his shirt, revealing his chest, scars of the past and the recent ugly jagged scar across where his heart beat.

He thought of the legend of Fallen—of after he killed his own father and his brothers to take the throne, how he took the bone of his father's ribcage and sliced his own chest open. To show no fear of death, no fear of destruction, but to thrive in the bloodshed, the war outside and within one's self and to show his people his ability to conquer.

How the dismantled court of misfits and bloodthirsty thieves bowed to their king, chanting, humming a hymn of power and divine.

To crown a beast.

To crown a beast.

To crown a beast.

That same hymn the court now chanted lowly in unison and he felt the power rattle his bones.

To show the court no heartbeat inside of him, but Tensley felt the pounding of his own heart.

If the court saw his heart pounding, they wouldn't be pleased.

"With this blade of bone, I bleed for my court, my crown, my people," he spoke, voice composed as he took the vicious blade and dragged the sharp edge to his chest and sliced a line above his heart. The blood ran in thick, dark lines down his tanned skin and he smeared the redness along his thumb and pressed it to his mouth next, then smeared it across his forehead. "I vow to conquer armies and destroy kingdoms, all in the name of High Court. To savor victories and cherish losses. To devour traitors and to curse liars. I vow as the king to let the wrath guide my path."

A crown of glimmering gold sat on a white cushion and one of the lords walked forward, bending in front of Molly.

Molly's hands dropped and she glanced at Tensley. He nodded for her to go ahead.

She swallowed, gently lifting the crown off of the cushion and moved closer.

Tensley sucked in a harsh breath as her front touched his, her arms on either side of his head and she raised to her tiptoes to place the crown on his head.

He straightened his posture and couldn't look away from her. Her vivid eyes, soft and wide, took him in and he tasted her desire on his tongue.

"The king of beasts! The king of beasts! The king of beasts!" The court chanted, but all he saw was her rosy cheeks and those full lips beckoning to taste and that lion-heart battling inside of her.

They had crowned a new king. A king half of the court despised.

His eye's sought the prince, finding him scowling as if it was hard for him to be present at Tensley's crowning but nonetheless stayed. Controlled. Unmoving but watching closely. Tensley held everything the prince wanted.

Tensley placed Molly's hand back on his arm and he guided them from the throne room, the court following after. Too loud, too crowded.

He felt the wave of exhaustion, the shakiness begin in his bones. Now was not the time to be weak. Not when the entire court eyed his movements, his words, and breaths.

TIME PASSED SLOWLY as he sat on a throne, food overwhelming the long table in front of them. He felt the weakness consuming him and he struggled to keep his back straight. Molly sat stiffly beside him and from time to time he felt her eyes watching him.

He needed a cold bath to shock his system or to lie down in his chambers. He wanted to lie with Molly, but the entire feast she hadn't seemed as open as she had before. He glanced up, catching Seto's stare as he stood by the entrance.

He stood, ignoring Molly's heated stare on his back and met Seto by the hallway.

Tensley paused by his side. "Take Molly back."

Seto looked at him, his jaw clenching, but nodded.

Tensley marched back to his chambers, his own legs giving out, relying on the walls to help him manage to stay upright.

A hot dizzy spell took over him and he saw black dots filter his vision. His chest ached, it burned as if a flame sat upon his heart, endlessly burning for the one thing a beast shouldn't want.

Tensley threw open his chamber doors and gripped the bedpost. He tore open his sweat-stained shirt and tried to get to the bathroom, but ended up sitting down onto the bed.

He huffed, his chest a brutal heave of exhaustion and pain. "Fucking focus," he hissed to himself. He tried to think of Molly—of Molly's soft voice, of her full lips and those vivid, powerful eyes.

He thought of her sweet scent, of her blonde curls he wanted to run his fingers in and never let go.

He thought of her vicious heart.

A heart that once was his.

Oh, how he fucking wanted to claim that heart again.

He dug his fingers into his knees, thriving off another point of pain instead of the one burdening his chest.

"Tensley," that aching sweet voice called to him and in his haze, he groaned, looking up to find her standing at his doorway.

He tried to stand, but when he wavered, she jolted forward.

He raised a shaking hand. "Don't."

She paused, her hand retreating back to her chest. She stared at him, at his trembling form, at the sweat dripping off of him.

"You're in pain," she whispered.

"Because of this," he hissed, jabbing to his chest. "It aches for you. It burns for you."

Molly bit her bottom lip and that did nothing to keep Tensley strong. She seemed to be thinking over something, something that struggled within her. "Let me help you."

Tensley shook his head. "No."

Molly frowned and took another step closer. "You need me, Tensley. Just as much as I need you."

Tensley clenched his jaw and gripped the bedpost, his chest heaving. He regarded her, tracing her delicate features. "I'm too weak, dolcezza. If you touch me…if I touch you," he breathed, even saying it aloud testing his strength. "I won't be able to stop."

A dark glint flashed in her vivid eyes and she destroyed any space between them, her fingertips smoothing across his cheekbone. She breathed onto his parted mouth. "Then don't."

That was all it took.

chapter
twenty-one

TENSLEY'S STRONG HANDS gripped her hips and yanked her into his powerful frame.

His mouth found hers and the mere taste of his toxic tongue warmed her belly. Each kiss, she felt his trembling lessen and the strength grow wild in him. She smoothed her hands down his face and to his chest, pressing there, feeling his heart pound against her palm.

His hands slipped off her chin and when they grabbed a handful of her round derriere, she groaned achingly into his mouth.

He nipped, sucked and devoured her lips and he couldn't stop. She didn't want him to. She couldn't let him slip away. She'd be his strength, she'd be his power, if only he didn't stop.

He pulled her down on top of him as he landed on his back, his hands ripping the back of her dress so the loose fabric rolled off her shoulders. She felt his hardness against her thigh.

He yanked the front of her dress down with his teeth, exposing her heavy breasts. He paused and carefully, smoothing his large hands around each breast. She bit back a moan and dropped her head low.

"Beautiful," she heard him whisper and before she could say a word, his mouth caught one of them and he sucked.

She pressed her nails into his chest, laying half her body on top of him as he switched to the other one.

She squeezed her hand between her round belly and found his hardening length hidden in his trousers. He tensed, only to nip at her nipple.

Just as she undid his belt, he sat up, flipping her so she lay on her back. He stood at the edge of the bed and watched her, his eyes pitch-black with lust and power.

"I can't seem to shake you, no matter how hard I fucking try," he hissed, panting in-between. She saw the simple encounter between them had almost instantly given him a shot of power. His muscles flexed with lethal strength and the stiffness in his once trembling mouth was gone. With only one kiss, she had created a god of pleasure and power.

She didn't care how dangerous he was or how every touch she gave him could potentially be used against her.

She trusted him.

She trusted the man.

And even though the beast had said things about her she wouldn't forget so easily, she knew, deep down, that she could trust him too.

He lowered himself to his knees in front of her, the sight of a beast lowering for her, for his wife, for his queen, sent a burning sensation through her belly. Desire pooled. Heat consumed her. His calloused hands pushed the fabric of her dress up her legs, his fingers skimming her upper thighs. She shivered, biting her lip to stop a groan from escaping.

When she felt her lower region exposed and his fingers brushing across her tender folds, she couldn't hold the groan inside.

It had been a while for the both of them.

But they were about to change that.

It was when he licked up her length, up, up, up, with deliberate slowness, and teased the pearl where her desire pulsed wildly, that she completely lost herself.

"Oh—Tensley," she gasped out, withering on the bed, her fingers running through his thick hair.

He devoured her—worshiping her body in a way so feral, so pure, so wicked and beautiful.

Her orgasm was quick and harsh, roaring through her with an intensity she didn't know was possible, making her limbs seize and she threw her head back, panting.

Tensley stood, like a shadow flowing over her, his eyes dark as they shone with want and power. His eyes penetrated hers from above, a thousand wars shredding and conquering each other from deep within the darkness consuming them, but all were ruled by one need; her. He undid his trousers and she saw the two deep lines that ran front the lowest part of his hips and pointed toward the place where she knew his own desire pulsed, thick and proud.

Hers.

All of it was hers.

First she saw the hint of dark hair, then as he pulled them down, his erection sprang free. He stroked himself, slow and long, the crown an angry red of need.

"Say my name again," he hissed out between his clenched teeth, his hand still firmly caressing himself.

Molly swallowed slowly, the heat between them so thick it was scorching their skin. It felt as if the second they touched again, they would melt into one another. But she wanted to burn. She wanted to scorch him.

"Tensley," she breathed, her heavy breasts tingling, so tender, so sensitive.

His eyes darkened and the beautiful beast growled a warning.

He yanked a pillow from the bed and grabbed her hips, confusion fluttering inside of her until he angled her hips and placed the pillow there.

She fought against a smile by pressing her lips tightly together, realizing he was trying to make sure she was comfortable, that the baby wasn't putting too much pressure on her in their position.

He hovered above her for a bit longer. Eyes dark, hand tight, moves slow, lips parted, and breathing uneven.

Stroke.

Stroke.

Stroke.

His tongue came out slowly, gliding over his full, luscious lips. Molly almost moaned at the sight, ready to start begging.

Before she could do so, he went back to his knees, a vicious, sensual smile playing on his lips as his blunt tip poked at her core, deliberately.

She groaned, her hands going to his shoulders, fingers digging deep in his skin.

It would undoubtedly leave a mark.

She wanted him to ache like she ached, her whole body screaming, burning for him to enter her. To consume hers. To fill her once again.

To strengthen each other in the most primal way.

He watched her, examined her, his brutal full lips parted.

"Dolcezza," he whispered and she dug her nails deeper into his back at the endearment—so intimately, so softly and he lowered, pressing a soft gentle kiss to her belly. Her heart raced at the sight of the powerful beast peppering her belly with kisses. She breathed heavily, unable to look away as he lifted his head and leaned forward to capture her open mouth. One kiss from him was like a thousand brutal truths and she kissed him back.

He thrust forward, fast and hard, but it was everything they needed. Her nails clawed at his back, at his flexing arms, at his chest, pulling him deeper, so deep into her core it hurt. With the pillow supporting her, the angle was deep for both of them, deep enough they felt the burn.

They battled each other, warring against their bodies, but working toward the same goal, the same purpose.

She'd fight him, she'd wage war to get that iron heart back. Her fingers curled above his pecs, feeling the violent beat of his warrior heart.

His body powered forward, to a destroying rhythm and she matched him.

It was when his fingers skimmed her round belly, he slowed and his fingers couldn't stop caressing her.

Her eyes caught his and the look he gave her stole away her breath.

A god bowing to a mortal.

He stole her mouth into another kiss, but this time it was soft, tender, and long.

His mouth peppered gentle kisses against her, and soon, she felt the sting of pleasure approaching. She felt it in the way he grew fast and harsh, his grunts becoming louder and vicious, his hands going to either side of her belly and balancing himself over her.

"Tensley," she gasped one final time—and that was all it took to make the beast surrender.

He pumped, his cock pulsing and flexing inside of her. His warmth filling her.

He continued to thrust shallowly into her and he bowed his head, grunting lowly.

"Fuck," he hissed and when he didn't move, but stayed still, she ran a finger across the sweat gathering on his collarbone and down his pecs. The feeling of his harsh breath against her, the heaving of his chest—all of it felt beautiful.

Tensley slowly pulled out, then bent, grabbing his shirt and wiped her down.

He didn't say a word as he gripped her hips and helped her further up the bed, placing the pillow behind her head.

What surprised her was when he climbed into bed and laid down beside her.

His hand rested on her belly and she watched his jaw relax. Pure bliss swept over her and she couldn't fight a smile. She felt warm, she felt safe and cared for. She didn't want to close her eyes, in fear that all of this would vanish. Or tomorrow he'd return to the beast.

"I love you," she murmured to him and watched as his relaxed jaw once again clench tight.

In little glimpses, she watched him turn his head and caught the sight of his parted mouth.

His eyes met hers. "Sleep, dolcezza."

MOLLY WOKE TO a tender stroke on her belly and she blinked, confusion, and then realization flooding her.

The light streamed through the sheer curtains of Tensley's bedchambers and she looked down at her belly, lying on her side to find his large hand placed there.

She gently, cautiously, felt over his wrist, the veins visible. When he didn't jerk away, she placed her hand over top of his.

Tensley grumbled behind her, his hot breath fanning against the back of her neck and she smiled to herself.

In the bliss of morning, with the light flooding the room, her chest filled with a joy she never thought she'd feel again. Months ago, this was all she wanted and now, in his arms, in the morning, she felt whole.

But she knew—she knew the beast warred inside of him. It would still be a battle, but this single gesture, this secret, private moment they were having together, she knew he was close to the surface.

Molly traced one strong finger across his tanned skin a harsh contrast to her ivory stomach.

Then she felt a swift thump, and then another one. Tensley's body stiffened behind her as another kick bounced in her belly.

She laughed lightly, shocked, but thrilled.

The baby was kicking.

"Looks like our little monster decided it was time to wake up," she whispered, smiling at their hands joined, the faint movement continuing beneath their palms.

Tensley's fingers flexed, strong and long, and she almost cried out in happiness when he nuzzled his face into the crook of her neck.

Time passed slowly as the two of them stayed on the bed, not facing each other, but their hands placed on her stomach, feeling a faint kick every few minutes.

Her stomach grumbled and that snapped Tensley out of his lazy state.

Molly laughed lightly as she felt another kick from within, as if the baby agreed with her growling stomach.

"You need food," Tensley said and stood. She glanced back at him, his toned ass flexing as he grabbed his trousers and pulled them on. It was when he looked back, as if to check on her, her heart leapt into her throat.

Their eyes met, the heat she had seen in them last night was still there, sizzling, but there was also something new. Like he now wanted something else as well, something only she could provide him.

Something the man and the beast both craved.

She wrapped the sheet around her and stood. "Actually, I should probably go back to New York." She thought of everything she still needed to do and she had been gone far too long from Scorpios. The fear of another attack weighed on her, even when she tried not to think of the worst. The last few months Scorpios had become important to her and if anything happened, if any more of their men died under her watch, she'd feel responsible. Plus, the trial for Evelyn was today and the last thing she needed was to be late.

She grabbed the cloak she had worn when she arrived at High Court, and draped it over her shoulders, tightening it so no one knew she was completely nude underneath. Tensley had shredded her dress to nothing the night before, so the cloak was her only clothing option.

She turned to find Tensley standing stiffly by the door, his brows furrowed. "Stay here."

Molly frowned and moved closer. "I can't, Tensley."

"Stay here," he said again, clear and with gentle power. "Please," he added, with a foreign look passing through his eyes.

Molly shook her head and moved toward the door. "I'll visit again in four days. Scorpios needs me, they need a leader. I'll be back soon enough, just like we arranged, okay?"

Tensley stepped in her path, his large frame towering over her, the look in his eyes fierce. "No," he bit out. She blinked up at him, startled by his refusal. "I need to protect you and our son. I need you to be close." His jaw flexed under his tight bite and he lowered his gaze, huffing out a harsh breath. She saw the struggle inside of him—to speak what he feared to say the words he dreaded. "Stay here with me. I can take care of you, I can provide for you."

Molly's heart swelled to the point she felt it in her throat and she swallowed down her overwhelming emotions. "Tensley," she whispered. "I can't. Scorpios needs me. My whole life is there…"

Tensley's features darkened and before she could say another word, he stepped aside. She could tell by his behavior he was hurt and she realized her wording.

My whole life is there.

"Tensley," she said and reached for him, but he turned his back and moved to his whisky cabinet. She stood still, watching his back muscles flex as he poured himself a drink. "I'll come back in four days. I'll be safe."

He didn't give her a response and so she left, her heart heavy and her head filled with too many worrying thoughts.

chapter
twenty-two

THE ROOM WAS silent as Molly walked inside, fixing her large sweater over her belly. She assumed most of Scorpios thought she had maybe gained a little weight, not a baby. She wouldn't be able to hide it from Scorpios for much longer. Her only hope was to earn their trust and support before the secret was out.

Evelyn Rose stood at the front of the room, her hands chained in front of her, her dark locks messy and twisted. As much as she looked exhausted and worn down, she still held a fierceness in her eyes, a challenge to anyone who doubted her strength.

Mr. Rose stood along side of his daughter, a permanent scowl pressed to his thin lips.

Each man seated at the long oval table turned their attention to Molly, a stern, reigning silence that brought chills to her skin.

"Mrs. Knight," Connor, or Pudgy, as Tensley liked to call him, said as he gestured to a seat beside him.

Molly walked past the men and sat down, fixing her sweater around her front.

"You're late," one man spat, Fredrick. He was older, aged well, but he had a mean streak and an even meaner temper. He shook, not much, but enough from aging that she knew he wouldn't be in his position much longer.

There was an air to him of power and even Molly felt the sting of it in his voice.

"I had important matters to discuss with my husband, your Dux and king," she said, looking the older man straight in the eyes. Then her gaze turned, acknowledging the others. "Proceed," she told the assembly, voice strong, unyielding. She knew—just like Evelyn had said—she couldn't back down. She couldn't appear weak or little to these powerful men or they'd overpower her.

Fredrick's lip twitched and after a long, silent moment, he sat back, the leather squeaking under his weight.

Molly took a deep breath and turned to face Evelyn at the front of the room.

Molly nodded at Connor and he fixed the paper in his hand, clearing his throat. "We, Scorpios of High Court, are gathered here today to come to an agreement on the fate of Evelyn Grace Rose of Scorpios. She is on trial for poisoning the late Dux, Salvatore Knight, and committing the highest form of treason to our people."

Molly kept her gaze trained on Evelyn. She didn't lower her head, she simply stared, her shoulders tensing every few seconds as if the words were like bullets hitting her.

Connor folded the piece of paper and with a shaky hand, placed it on the table. He wasn't shaking from nerves though. She could feel the entire room was flooded with aggressive pheromones. It stung the air, poisoned it until her lungs burned.

But the woman trapped in the center of it all, no doubt being hit left, right and center by the aggressive feeling, stayed unmoving.

"The assembly will vote on the adequate punishment after the accused's final words are heard," Connor added. "Ms. Rose, you may proceed. I will warn you to be careful with your choice of words, they might be your only hope between life and death."

Evelyn's dark eyes shifted across the room, studying each member carefully. Her mouth twitched, the chains rattling as they swung between her wrists.

As Evelyn parted her lips, about to start talking, the doors to the congress room opened and slammed closed. All heads turned as Daphne Knight made her way to where Molly sat with determined steps. Her gentle features were warped into something feral, something fuming in anger and all of it was directed toward Evelyn.

"Mrs. Knight," someone spoke. "We are terribly sorry for your loss, but I am afraid you are not allowed to be a part of the trial."

Daphne didn't acknowledge them and kept moving with confidence, sitting down beside Molly.

"Not allowed to my own husband's murderer's trial. I'll be damned," she whispered to herself, irritated, eyes staying firmly on Evelyn.

It was the first time she saw the true life of a Dux's wife shining through Daphne. Composed, deadly, and powerful. A woman who was now facing the traitor who had murdered her husband.

Salvatore hadn't been the best of men nor had he been the best of father, but somehow, Daphne had still cared deeply for him. Perhaps, Molly thought, behind closed doors he had been a good husband to his wife.

But above all else, Molly knew he had been a good Dux to Scorpios.

Their Dux.

"Continue," Molly said, her voice leaving no room for argument.

The men cleared their throats and focused their attention back on Evelyn.

Evelyn's stance weakened, her shoulders pulling inward as she felt Daphne's eyes on her. It was like a constant whip of anger lashing at Evelyn's skin.

"I did it to protect my family," Evelyn bit out, gasping as the anger wrapped around her throat. "I did it to protect myself. They caught me. Fitz Senior caught me and told me he'd murder my family if I didn't work for him." She shook her head. "So I did. I fucking did it." Her gaze of darkness lifted and all Molly saw was a fierceness that would never die. Never burn out. "And I'd do it again," she added with a stern tone. Her eyes found Molly's, then Daphne's. "Look at me, and tell me you wouldn't have done the same. For your own family. For your children or your husband," she spat, a troubled look crossing her features. "Tell me you wouldn't have done the same," she said again, the words barely above a whisper.

Daphne's hand threaded through Molly's fingers underneath the table. Molly glanced at her, only to find a stern expression, but she knew more than anything that they were both pretending to be fine. To feel powerful, and strong. Yet, felt anything but in this instance.

But sometimes, pretending was enough.

Daphne needed Molly, and so she'd be her strength.

"We are your family," Fredrick snapped, his entire face filled with blood. He pounded a fist on the table. "You fucking betrayed us."

Evelyn sneered at him, a dark laugh escaping her lips. "Scorpios was never a family to me. All of you, you've turned your backs on me when I needed it most. Looked at me from above, as if I was always nothing more than a dramatic bitch. I lost too much because of Scorpios. I lost the things that mattered because of this sick world we live in. All of you, you wouldn't do shit to save the man sitting beside you. Or his family. You'd only save yourself. I only did the same. I saved myself and my family, damned be the consequences."

"That's not true," Molly's voice wasn't loud. If anything it was quiet, but clear and concise.

It was the venom, the power of controlling those around her and everyone stopped speaking, turning their focus onto her.

Molly squeezed Daphne's hand and glared at Evelyn. "You saved me. When you could have saved yourself," Molly said, and she heard a few gasps in the assembly. "You chose to save me, when Fitz Senior attacked. . You could have run, and never looked back. But you stayed. And you were stabbed…"

Evelyn's complexion paled, a deep frown marking her brows as if asking Molly if she really wanted her to tell the truth. Molly nodded almost subtly, and Evelyn licked her lips nervously, her answer taking too long for the men in the room.

One of them stood up from the side of the room, face marred with anguish. "Yes, answer the king's wife. Why!" he spat, voice booming. A few others joined in, wanting the accused to answer their question.

Evelyn's brows drew tight, hands shifting in her lap. "Because—" Evelyn paused and shook her head once. She steeled her expression and looked directly into Molly's eyes. "Because you're pregnant."

Dead silence took the room and Molly swallowed with difficulty.

Each men glanced between each other and back at her.

Molly felt her shoulders collapse against the leather chair and she tightened her grip on Daphne's hand.

It was out. The secret was out. And if the dead silence that had taken over the room was any indication, her next argument needed to be strong. She could see their trust disappearing by the minute.

"Yes, I am," Molly said and stood to her feet, letting Daphne's hand go.

Fredrick stood from the dark corner he had chosen to sit in, eyes fuming with unrestrained fury. "A pregnant woman. A pregnant human—" He laughed again, the sound like a snake ready to pounce on its victim. "Leading Scorpios.

What a farce. What has become of Scorpios, my brothers? It all became an absolute mockery when the Knights took over the legacy. I say we should—"

Before he could continue, Molly's voice boomed, crushing his to nothing. "I vow, to all of you and the members of Scorpios who aren't present in this room that a pregnancy will not affect the way I rule over Scorpios. I will not abandon Scorpios. I will not leave them now when we need to stay together and destroy Ares." She straightened. "We must stay strong and we are stronger together. And I vow—I vow to make those bastards beg on their knees."

Evelyn's nostrils flared, but she didn't say a word.

Molly took a deep breath. "But I am indeed pregnant. With the Dux, the king's child. A boy. So Evelyn Rose may have killed the late Dux, but she also saved the current Dux and king's wife. As well as his heir to Scorpios. You may want to take this into consideration when choosing the fitting punishment."

Molly sat back in her chair and took Daphne's hand again, breathing through her nose.

Fredrick let out an unsatisfied sound but sat back down, without arguing.

Connor cleared his throat, awkwardly. "Suggestions of punishment for Ms. Rose?"

All the men were silent as they looked at one another and then back to Molly.

Molly fisted her hand on her thigh and stared at Evelyn's blank expression, but she saw her throat bobbing. "Which options am I truthfully presented with here? I have no doubt the options were narrowed down to a few before the trial ever even began," she said with a pointed look in Fredrick's direction.

"Death," Fredrick began. "Or imprisonment in High Court."

Molly bit the inside of her mouth and straightened in her chair.

Just looking at the men in the assembly, nodding to each other as if those were the two options that seemed the most interesting, Molly knew she truly only had those two choices to choose from.

She stared at the woman—the strong woman ready to kill for her family, ready to take the blow. A woman caught in a web of blackmail and lies. A woman wearing the same mask Tensley once wore around her and others. She knew that deep inside Evelyn, hid something good. Something worth saving. Evelyn wasn't innocent, but she didn't deserve death.

She deserved a chance.

"Imprisonment." She watched as Evelyn's shoulders relaxed. With the trust the demon's had in her strength already fragile, Molly added with a powerful tone: "Let her relive what she did to Scorpios, what she did to a family, to his wife, to his children. Every day of her life, for a very long time. Death would be too easy." She let the venom roll off her tongue and into the thick air of anger and tension.

Evelyn stared at Molly for what seemed like a long time, as if she wanted to say more, but the men stood, one grabbing Evelyn's elbow and taking her away.

Molly stood with Daphne, the men watching them as they left the room.

Daphne opened the Dux's office door and Molly went inside first. As soon as the door closed, Daphne collapsed to her knees.

Sobs took over her entire body and she wept freely, uncontrollably. Molly bent and hugged her, letting her mother-in-law grieve, letting her show a moment of weakness.

Because she understood her pain. As much as she had Tensley still in her life, she had lost him. He had been ripped from her and she knew that pain well.

Minutes passed and Daphne wiped her cheeks, standing onto her feet.

She calmed herself with another breath and took Molly's hands. "I would have done the same thing," she whispered and Molly frowned at her. "I would have killed to protect my family, I would have done anything to save my husband." She dropped her gaze and squeezed Molly's hands. "You made the right decision, Molly. And I know you did it to save her from death. And if what you say is true, if she did save you and my future grandchild like you say she did, then I support your decision," she took another shuddering breath, hands shaking slightly with emotion. "I want to protect you, Molly. You are in danger. I know it's hard to let others help you, protect you. But people are out to kill you, because you are the most important person in my son's life. I know you're powerful, capable. But please stay here with me. With the soldiers."

Molly furrowed her brow and went to open her mouth, but Daphne raised a hand.

"Please, listen," she whispered, her eyes still bloodshot. "I want to protect you and I think having you here with Scorpios will ease my worries. The soldiers won't let anything happen to you. I won't let anything happen to you."

Molly lowered her eyes to their hands.

"You hold our future, our power, my son's baby," Daphne said, her voice full of unwept tears, but she took a deep breath and held it in with a soft smile. "You're part of my family, and I do not wish to lose anymore."

Molly paused and looked up, smiling back at her softly. She nodded.

MOLLY ENTERED HER apartment and sighed, removing her hat and mittens covered in snow.

With little touches, she had made the large apartment feel like home. As much as it could without Tensley. The furniture was a mix of traditional and classic, blend of warm and chic. Homey, friendly, and comfy.

She picked up an apple and took a bite, glancing at the work she had done in the apartment. She'd miss it, but hopefully she would only have to stay at the Scorpios property for a few months, until things calmed down, and the war with Ares hopefully ended.

Just as she took another bite, she heard footsteps from the master bedroom. Her heart halted as she edged around the corner.

"Illya?"

She peeked inside her bedroom and that same heart began beating fast.

Tensley sat on the edge of the bed, a stuffed teddy bear in his hands sat between his spread thighs.

His head was bowed, his fingers brushing over the smooth fur of the brown bear.

"Tensley," Molly whispered, tiptoeing in.

He still kept his head lowered, his eyes trained on the bear in his large hands.

When she thought he wasn't going to say a word to her, she moved closer.

"I could have given you all of this," he muttered and she paused, her eyes widening at the sound of his husky voice.

The sound went straight to her core.

His head lifted and he stared at the bedroom, focusing on the white crib Illya built.

Her heart pounded fast, in her own pain, at Tensley's pain.

"You still can," Molly whispered back.

He fisted the bear and laughed darkly. "You built our son a life. And I wasn't there to help."

Molly swallowed thickly and now it was her turn to lower her head. She could hear the pain in his voice even as it came out like steel.

"Did Illya help you?"

Molly paused and looked up to find him staring at her, his jaw line stiff.

She nodded. "He stays here. To help me. He comes to my doctor appointments."

Tensley nodded in return, moving his focus back to the teddy bear. She watched him closely, how his body tensed, how he examined the tiny toy in his large, powerful hands. Those hands that had burned her with pleasure and then the same moment caressed her with affection she had been craving for months just the same morning.

"When's your next appointment?" he asked, standing to his full height.

Molly blinked fast. "Uh— oh! Well, tomorrow actually," she said with a tentative smile.

"I'm coming with you," he said, his eyes piercing hers in a way that told her he was coming with her no matter what.

She caught her breath. "Okay." Standing next to him, watching him scan the room, noting each detail as his hands skimmed each toy, each item, she thought of earlier that day.

Of Evelyn.

Of his father.

She swallowed thickly. "We found out who poisoned your father, Tensley," Molly told him, tilting her head to see his profile.

He paused, his stormy eyes catching hers. He stared back at her, working his jaw. "And?"

She knew the anger stirred within him and she saw the man more than the beast take control.

His father even if he had been an asshole had been important to the man.

"It was Evelyn Rose," she told him, scanning his features for a sign of distress.

He continued to work his jaw and turned back to the room, as if unsure how to react. She saw his fists clench, saw his dress shirt strain on his back.

"I sentenced her to imprisonment in the High Court," she said after he hadn't spoken for a moment. When he still didn't respond, she took a step closer. "I know you would have decided differently—"

"It's what I would have done," he said, lowly, cutting her off.

She stared at the back of his dark head, hair thick and a slight wave curling around the back of his neck.

"Never doubt yourself, dolcezza. I would trust you to rule over my men," he said.

The compliment seized her heart and she fisted her hands. She needed to tell him. She needed to tell the man what she was withholding.

"Tensley," she whispered and reached out to skim her fingers along his palm. "Your father died."

She felt the air shift in the room, she felt the way his body tensed, and she heard the low growl from his mouth.

She blinked back tears and bit her lip, fighting from crying aloud. "I'm so sorry."

Tensley's hand gripped hers—tightly and he turned around. His dark eyes looked so heavy, so weighed down by exhaustion and sadness.

"I'm so sorry, Tensley," Molly whispered again and the warmth blurred her vision. She touched his cheek and he closed his eyes. Minutes passed and they stayed so close, so together, she heard his low breaths.

"You have nothing to be sorry for," he whispered back.

Tensley's eyes scanned her face, as if trying to memorize what she looked like. He lifted his hand and his fingers brushed across her cheekbones and up into her hairline. It was just a touch, just a skimming of fingers, but it made her heart stop, it made her shiver in delight and terror, and she leaned closer into his tender and dominating touch.

"I was coming to see you in four days," Molly whispered, her eyes dropping to his full mouth of sin.

His eyes darkened. "I couldn't stay away from you for that long." That same mouth met hers in a brutal kiss, in a kiss of worship and power, of adoration and lust, and she melted into him.

She gripped the back of his neck and his tongue played with hers, a moan fleeting from her mouth and into his.

He moved them back until he sat down on the bed and she straddled his hips.

His blunt length pulsed against her core and she ground herself against him.

He bit back a groan and cherished her.

They were addicted to each other—the beast may still be warring inside of him, but both of them enjoyed the pleasure and pain.

And just like the man she fell in love with, he destroyed her over and over again all night.

chapter twenty-three

WAKING UP NEXT to Molly was a blessing and a curse. He felt himself harden at the sight of her, curled up against him, her leg resting on his thigh, every once in a while skimming his swollen length.

Her curls glistened across his chest and each time he moved slightly, she moaned and moved closer.

He was addicted to feeling her next to him and the thought of returning to High Court without her sent a painful throb throughout his body.

When he heard her stomach grumble, he slid from her touch and crept into the kitchen. He made eggs and toast, sunny side up just the way he remembered she loved them and he made a fruit bowl.

Just as he poured some orange juice, he heard her footsteps and turned to find her walking into the kitchen. His eyes instantly dropped to her swollen belly hidden underneath his dress shirt and it did crazy things to his mind and body.

His beast growled his approval. His dolcezza was purely his and he had the evidence to show it. It was a primal, territorial feeling he knew some males were ashamed of, but he couldn't care less. He liked it.

"You made breakfast?" Still half-asleep, she tiptoed over to him and when she was only a footstep away, she touched his arm. "Thank you. I'm starving," she added with a soft smile, just as her belly growled once more.

He stared at her, his eyes going to her sweet, sleepy smile. He cleared his throat. "I was going to bring it to you in bed."

Her smile widened and she leaned into him, kissing his cheek. Just a single touch from her and he was an inferno. He wanted to take her on the counter, but he remembered how the entire night he had taken her—slowly, unrushed, kissing each inch of her until she fell asleep in his arms, still buried deep inside of her.

She needed to rest.

He pulled out her chair and she sat down, not without sending him another smile.

Her smiles were his undoing and the devil would have to save him if she ever came to learn that about him. He sat down next to her.

"Last night," she whispered as she bit into her toast and swallowed. Her gaze dropped when he turned to look at her. Slowly, she looked up at him and he saw the beautiful blush spread across the apples of her cheeks. "Was nice."

He scowled. "Nice?"

She laughed, covering her mouth. "Judging from your expression, I take it nice certainly wasn't the right word to use."

"No, it fucking wasn't," he hissed and cut into his eggs, glaring down at them. "Nice," he mumbled to himself, stabbing one of his eggs and she laughed some more. Whatever bit of heart he had squeezed at the sound, then pulsed vividly. Her hand slid onto his thigh and he froze.

"It wasn't nice. It was heaven and hell," he whispered to her, and her gaze caught his. "It was beautiful, it was dangerous. It was more than fucking nice," he added on the same tone. His finger caught her chin, strongly enough that she couldn't move her head, that her eyes couldn't look anywhere but straight into his own. "Admit it, or I might just have to go for seconds. To remind you. Right here, right now, until you admit it. And I won't be gentle about it."

"Is that supposed to be a threat, Mr. Knight?" she asked, with a ravenous smile. "If it is, a threat is meant to make people afraid of the outcome, not the opposite."

"It's not a threat, dolcezza, but a promise."

She laughed again, the sound oddly sensual and youthful at once, as her hand left his thigh to caress her stomach once more. Her eyes moved across his features and he wondered what she was thinking. "Can I kiss you now?"

Tensley frowned at her. "I'm your husband."

"My estranged king," she argued, shrugging playfully.

His hold on her chin dropped, and she stared back at him, a shy look took over her features. But she didn't look away. His hand swept up her neck and under her hair, gripping it into a makeshift ponytail. "And you're my queen. My queen who enjoys running away from me, making me crave her more and more with each visit until it fucking hurts. That's not very nice, is it?" he asked, his own voice filled with need as the tip of his nose brushed against hers.

His lips dove for hers and he kissed her like he was a dying man. As if she was going to be ripped from him again.

"Not very nice indeed," she whispered into the kiss.

A knock sounded at the door and he hissed, pulling back.

"Expecting someone?" he asked her, studying her reddened features.

She shook her head, trying to catch her breath.

Tensley stood, unfazed by the fact that he was only in sweatpants and swung open the door.

That damn hippie warlock was the last person he expected to see.

"Hey," Lance said, his beanie sat sagging on his head. "Long time no see, big guy."

"Lance?" Molly asked, moving behind Tensley. Her eyes brightened at the sight of him. "How are you? I wasn't expecting you today. Did you find out anything?"

Tensley frowned at the two of them. "Find out what?"

Lance shoved his way inside and eyed their apartment, nodding at each item like he approved of it. "Fancy," he whistled appreciatively.

"Lance?" Molly asked, standing behind him.

"Oh yeah," he said, clicking back into the present. "I did some more digging, it wasn't easy, but I managed to find some things that could potentially be helpful."

Tensley scowled. "Things? Helpful? What is this damned warlock talking about? Molly?"

"Lance was looking into information about the baby for us," Molly told him. She felt over her stomach again. "So, did you find anything about a half daemon, half demon baby?"

"Yes and no. Many of the things I found are mostly speculations, there are no facts to back them up, so hear me out," he said, shrugging as an apologetic half smile appeared on his lips. "I did notice the last time you came over to my place that your aura was perceptibly more dim, almost as if it had faded a bit. However, I did find one legend about the tale of a woman, it doesn't say if she was daemon or demon, but she was blessed with a child like yours growing within her womb. Half daemon and half demon. It said that the more the child grew, the more tired and weak the woman felt. And that's because the demon part of the baby only had one source of energy, of contact; its mother,"

Lance said, nodding vividly as if it was all crucial information. "Demons are demanding by nature, insatiable almost. They can never truly absorb too much energy. And so…" He stopped himself, biting into his bottom lip as he looked at Tensley nervously.

Tensley stopped breathing for a beat, waiting for what was to come, knowing he wasn't going to like it at all.

"Eventually, the tale ends with the woman dying because the baby drained the life out of her, but of course it's just a legend and is very unlikely to ever happen," Lance added, the words tumbling out of his mouth so fast Tensley barely managed to understand what he had just told them. And he guessed that was exactly Lance's intentions, because he sure as hell had just dropped a bomb on the both of them. Tensley's blood turned cold, fear wrapping around his heart.

He knew it was just a legend, and that most legends ended tragically for added impact and drama, but still… he looked at Molly, war raging inside of him. She looked at peace, serene. As if she knew the baby had been feeding off of her. As if without really knowing, she had known the baby had been taking more and more of her energy. But she didn't look worried.

"Plus, like I said earlier," Lance began again, uncomfortable with the sudden silence that had appeared between all of them. "The legend didn't specify if the woman was a daemon or a demon. But considering daemons are considered like an unending well of power and strength to demons, my guess would be that the woman in the story was demon. Which, in turn means there is no reason to be alarmed, and also would therefore mean the father was daemon. Was he only carrying the gene like your father, or could he actually wield the power, that is unfortunately left unanswered once more."

Tensley still swallowed with difficulty, feeling uneasy.

What if it was true? What if the baby could indeed drain the life out of Molly?

A low growl resonated within him. No. It wouldn't happen. She was fine, she was strong. Everything would be fine.

"So what about our baby? You talked about my aura being more dim than it used to be. What do you think it means?" Molly asked, and she gave Tensley a reassuring smile.

"Based on all of this, I think it means you're further along than you think you are. I'm guessing by the amounts of energy he's taking from you that he's bigger, stronger than anticipated as well," Lance answered, eyeing Molly up and down.

"By the amount the baby is draining your energy, he's growing fast. He's strong. You're probably further along than you expected."

"How much further?" Molly asked, her brow furrowing in worry. "Would you be able to tell?"

Lance hummed, stepped closer and placed his hands just an inch away from her stomach. Tensley itched to push him back, but didn't. "I don't pretend to be a specialist in the matter, but I can sense his own aura within you. My guess would be somewhere over seven months. He's growing fast, I wouldn't be surprised if you were to have him earlier than expected if he keeps growing at this rate."

Molly sat down on the couch, her skin ghostly pale, her hands on her belly, stroking the roundness, speaking softly to their son.

Tensley rolled his hands into fists on his thighs. After Molly had left High Court, his beast and the man battled inside of him.

They both wanted her.

They both craved her near.

If she just agreed to stay with him—

He shook his head. He wanted to protect his family, he wanted to see her.

The moment he tasted her again, felt her soft skin against his own, he knew he couldn't let her go. He would never be able to rid her from his system and he didn't want to.

"A baby in the middle of a war. The baby can't come now, not so soon. Not when it's so dangerous. What are we going to do…?" she whispered, gaze lost in the distance.

"The best way to keep you both healthy, to make sure everything goes smoothly with the pregnancy, is getting energy yourself," Lance added, his eyes darting to Tensley.

Molly's eyes looked up at him.

Neither of them had to speak. They both knew what that meant. Being more intimate. Another reason why she should come back with him to High Court.

"And what about him being a daemon… you still can't tell if he'll have my powers?" Molly asked, holding her stomach.

"I believe only once the baby is born we'll know for sure. If he has your eyes," Lance said, gesturing to Molly's wide eyes, "then we'll know for sure. But even if he never shows any signs, he'll still be half demon. There is no doubt he'll have the same needs and wants as a demon, whether he has daemon powers or not."

Molly nodded, dropping her gaze to her belly.

Tensley stood stiffly next to her and looked up at Lance. "Thank you."

Lance smiled and waved, leaving the two of them alone in the apartment.

Tensley sat down across from her, his hands between his spread thighs, thinking over how to fix everything. How to comfort her.

He stayed the night, lying beside her, but he hadn't been able to sleep. He watched her breathe shallowly. His fear was irrational, but he didn't want anything to happen to her. He didn't want to lose her again.

He was needed back in High Court though. He shouldn't have stayed so long. He shouldn't have stayed up all night listening to her breathing and her heart beat.

But he had.

When morning came, he kissed her lips softly, stirring her away from her dreams.

"I need to go back," he told her and she glanced up at him.

Her expression fell, but she didn't argue. "Okay."

He stood still, unable to walk away. Unable to turn his back on her again.

She held her stomach and stared back at him through her lashes. A look of want, a look of confusion.

He moved forward, a determination in his chest as he approached her.

Standing in front of her, those vivid eyes locked on his, the beast slowed.

The beast calmed and the man conquered.

A single look and he came undone.

But he simply bent his head and kissed her lips once. So soft, so tender and it was over.

"I'll be back, dolcezza," he whispered on those plump lips and he eyed them as they parted in a soft gasp. "Every night, I'll be back."

He turned, marching to the door, telling himself to keep walking, but he damned himself as soon as he reached the door and glanced back.

He was damned as soon as his heart had been ripped out of him.

He was damned to her.

TENSLEY MARCHED INTO the empty halls, shaking out of his cloak. His chest felt unbearably heavy. Leaving Molly and his child made his entire body ache. He wanted to be there for her, to be there for every single moment, to protect her and care for her.

The beast rumbled inside of him. Not out of anger, but of agreement. Each moment he spent with his dolcezza, he felt the pull, the weight of his heart growing. Seto had been right. It was only a matter of time before she fully tamed the beast.

He shook his head, growling lightly. It was happening too fast, but he had seen the signs. Even heartless, he was drawn to her.

Nothing.

Not even having his heart ripped out could stop him from having her.

"Tensley," a voice called to him as he neared his bedchambers.

He paused, glancing to his side to find the prince leaning against the wall. What caught Tensley's eye was the glint of the blade wedged between two of the prince's fingers.

The beast inside of him twisted with anger at the use of informal address, but he knew the prince well enough to know that he was probably looking for an aggressive response.

"The court is talking about the tamer of beasts," the prince said, his voice low to the point it was barely audible. "And how she tamed your heart." He gestured to Tensley's chest.

Tensley stood stiffly, his expression blank, but a fury burning inside of him as soon as the prince even mentioned his dolcezza.

"Talking of how easily their king will be ruled by a whore, how easily our kingdom of beasts will fade into nothing under your reign," the prince continued and took slow, even steps forward. His grin vanished and reappeared under the shadows. He paused a foot away and let his gaze wander. "And I have to agree with them. She truly did curse you."

Tensley gritted his teeth and stayed still.

"The beast has a heart," the prince said, his own mouth twitching in response.

"I don't fear the court," Tensley said, rolling his shoulders back.

"Ah, but you should," Lilith's voice rang behind him, yet he didn't bother to turn around.

The bottom of her gown whispered across the tiled marble floors as she entered his view, a twisted smile on her lips.

"That iron heart," she said, her eyes moving down to his chest—as if she could see through his cloak and shirt and muscle and bones and see the forbidden organ. "Is truly your curse." Her laughing eyes lifted to his and she shrugged, a laugh following after. "They do not wish for a king with a heart. Soon enough, they will realize this and grow brave enough to rally against you. And when they do, I'll sit back and watch. Because when they rip your heart out again, you'll be well and truly gone this time."

He simply stared back, but the smug expression on her face didn't sit well in his twisting gut.

"My dear son missed an important part of the curse he gave to your lovely whore," Lilith said, curling a red lock around her index finger.

Tensley glanced at the prince who stared at his mother, a pinched look on his face.

"If someone is to rip your heart out once again," Lilith began, taking a small step forward, but she invaded his space and her perfume suffocated him. "You will die. You will not come back. The curse not only forces a man to grow a heart, it also fusions the beast to the new heart. When you lost your heart the first time, the beast lived freely within you. It could live without the heart. But now that they form one, one cannot live without the other. Demons cannot live without the beast. So when they come after you, because they do not wish you as king, they will kill you, my brutal king, and your wife will be left unprotected."

Rage boiled in his veins and he fisted his hands beside him, eyeing the woman in front of him. If someone ripped out his heart…

"Now, sweet beast, I have yet to mention this little notion to any of my court," Lilith said, happily moving around him, a soft smile on her mouth. "And I will not, unless you agree to allow me to be your queen and to abide by my rules. Knowing this would put them at a great advantage against you, you and I both know they would not hesitate to use said advantage."

Tensley wanted to snap her neck then and there.

"You will not disobey me in front of the court, you will council with me first before anyone else, and you will not leave this court without my permission," Lilith said, raising her chin high, a venomous smile growing at the corners of her lips.

Tensley sucked at his teeth. He wanted to tell her to fuck off, that he wouldn't be threatened by her and the prince's knowledge of what was now one of his weaknesses, but he thought of Molly, of their son, and his iron heart.

If Lilith ripped it out, if the court knew of his death curse, it would only be a matter of time before they turned against him. He knew how they felt toward him, and how that wouldn't change.

"Fine," he bit out, glaring at her as she grinned back at him.

"Swear it," Lilith snapped, her eyes growing wide and wild.

He gritted his teeth. "I swear to abide by you."

The only woman he would ever swear to abide by was his dolcezza but if it meant protecting her and his family, he would do anything.

He would bow to a queen of snakes.

chapter
twenty-four

MOLLY PRESSED A hand to her stomach as another cramp pulsed. Over the past week and a half, the cramps had gotten worse and when she went back to the doctor, he said it wasn't anything to worry about.

The baby was getting fussy and she prayed everything was fine.

But she hadn't seen Tensley since he left her that day. He didn't return every night and she missed him.

She stroked her belly and continued brushing her teeth. It had been a few days since she moved into the townhouse. Daphne and the soldiers were constantly asking her if she needed anything and she hated it.

Ever since Scorpios found out she was pregnant, they treated her like something breakable. A soldier accompanied her to school, insisted by Daphne and she only agreed to make sure Daphne didn't worry too much more than she already did.

She spat into the sink and rinsed out her mouth, standing back up to look at herself in the mirror. If she was closer to seven months, she only had two months or so before the baby was born. That thought made her heart race. She had so much more she wanted to do before he arrived. So many things she wanted to deal with to make sure everything would be safe for him when he arrived.

Would Tensley be with them by then?

A knock at the door startled her and she opened it into the bedroom to find Donovan, Gabriella's oldest boy standing there.

His eyes were bloodshot and Molly brushed his hair to the side. "What's wrong, Donovan?"

He sniffled. "I can't sleep."

Molly smiled at the little boy, a little version of Tensley and she took his hand.

"How about I read you a bedtime story?" Molly asked and helped him up onto the king size bed. The same bedroom Molly and Tensley had both stayed in before he took the oath and became the Dux of Scorpios.

Donovan climbed up onto the bed and settled into the mountain of feather pillows, almost disappearing and Molly sat down beside him.

His eyes went to her belly and he gently touched it. "You have a baby in there? Just like mommy did before my sister arrived?" he asked, eyes full of wonder and fascination.

Molly laughed. "Yes. It's your uncle Tensley's baby. A little boy, just like you."

Donovan frowned, staring at her belly. Then he blinked and looked up at her with soft brown eyes. "I miss uncle Tensley."

Molly bit her lip as it began to tremble and she hummed softly. "I do, too. But he'll be back soon." She combed his hair back. "He misses you a lot, too, do you know that?"

Donovan lowered his lashes and a faint smile took to his lips. His hand went back to her belly and he stroked it with his two fingers. "Can I talk to the baby?"

Molly nodded, her smile uncontrollable as she watched the little boy lean down close.

"Hi baby," he whispered. "I'm gonna protect you. Just like Uncle Tensley would want me to. He always says I'm a strong boy. I'll show you how to be a strong boy too."

Molly rubbed along the side of her stomach.

Donovan turned his face toward her belly and gave it a gentle kiss, and she thought of Tensley.

How much she missed him.

Of how many things he was missing.

Another cramp pulsed in her lower belly and she squeezed an eye shut. Donovan sat back into the pillows and leaned his head against her shoulder.

"Can I sleep with you tonight?" he asked, oblivious, a yawn breaking up his words.

Molly brushed his hair back and forth, smiling at the sweet boy. "Sure."

With each stroke of her hand he fell deeper into a slumber and she watched his chest slowly fall and rise.

When her door creaked open, she sat up to find Daphne in the doorway.

A warm smile took to Daphne's mouth. "I'll let Gabriella know he's with you tonight."

Molly nodded, afraid to speak incase Donovan woke from his sleep.

Daphne shut the door and Molly settled into the pillows. Listening to Donovan's soft murmurs and feeling him snuggle closer to her warmed her chest. She wanted this life. She wanted this life with Tensley.

She thought of his promise, the one night in Paris—of a big house, of lots of kids, and how they would always be together.

Sleep ate at her and soon she too drifted.

Only to be awoken by a siren and shouts. Molly jolted upright, her heart pounding against her ribcage and Donovan stirred beside her.

"What's that?" he whispered.

Molly stared at the closed door in the darkness of the room and heard the pitter patter of footsteps thudding across the hardwood floor.

Whatever was happening beyond that door was not good.

"Stay here, okay?" Molly told him, struggling to stand up, her feet swollen and sore.

She tiptoed over to the door and peeked through.

Just as she looked out, Daphne appeared, out of breath.

She opened the door and stepped inside, shutting it behind her.

"You need to get to the safe room with Donovan and stay there," Daphne told her in a hushed tone.

Molly gawked at her. "What's going on?"

Daphne shook her head. "I'm not sure, but someone has entered the house. I'll be in there shortly. Go!"

Molly wanted to protest, to fight against her. She was Dux. She was covering for Tensley, but with the baby inside of her, she knew she couldn't risk anything.

"Okay," Molly said, calming herself. She went back to the bed and helped Donovan down onto his feet. He slotted his hand with hers and they walked back over to Daphne.

Daphne bent, kissing Donovan's cheeks and brushing his chin. "Be a good boy and help Molly, okay? Grandma will see you soon."

Donovan nodded, still half asleep.

Daphne stood, a glint in her brown eyes. Something Molly rarely saw from Mrs. Knight. "The safe room is just down the hallway and through the library. Donovan knows which book to touch, don't you?"

"Yeah." He grinned tiredly up at her.

"Good boy," Daphne whispered. "Now go and be quiet."

Daphne opened the door and they all tiptoed out. Just as they took a few steps down the hallway, Molly glanced back to see Daphne gone.

Donovan tugged at her hand and they continued. Once they entered the dark library, Donovan let go and walked over to the back of the room, his finger tracing each book until he stopped in front of a red one. He simply pulled it back and a built in door just a few feet away opened up in the wall.

Molly followed him inside and saw Gabriella with baby Isabella in her arms.

Gabriella bit back a cry as she stretched an arm open and Donovan snuggled in close. She kissed his temple and looked up at Molly.

"Damn Ares," she hissed.

Molly went to speak, but violent screams stole her voice and she moved further back.

"We're under attack," Molly whispered, all the blood rushing to her head. "Ares is here."

Isabella whined and Gabriella hushed her, swaying her in her arms. "Where's my mom?"

Molly blinked back at her. "She said she'd be here soon."

A dark look washed over Gabriella's features and her eyes grew bloodshot. "She's not coming."

Molly's heart shattered at the soft tone of Gabriella's voice. Daphne wasn't coming?

She bowed her head, a thousand thoughts storming through her. She looked back up at the closed door.

"I'm the temporary Dux," Molly whispered. "I should be out there."

Gabriella gripped Molly's wrist. "No, you shouldn't. Not when you're carrying the heir."

"I can fight them," Molly argued. "I'm a daemon. I shouldn't be here. I will make them beg before they kill another Scorpios."

Gabriella shook her head. "You can't risk it."

"Scorpios is a part of me now," Molly said and stood. "And I will kill anyone who tries to harm my people."

Gabriella's eyes grew wet, unable to speak, unable to look away as Molly turned and opened the door.

"Molly," Gabriella shouted as quietly as possible.

But it wasn't stopping her.

She was going to face Ares and destroy them once and for all.

They had yet to feel her fury.

chapter twenty-five

MOLLY CREPT INTO the hallway, shouts and glass breaking causing her breathing to quicken.

She knew the danger, she knew the risk, but she wasn't afraid. She wouldn't back down from Ares anymore.

Especially when she was protecting people she loved and her unborn son.

The shadows crawled up the walls as she approached the staircase. She glanced down, seeing figures of men move further into the townhouse.

Shouts erupted from downstairs, more destruction, a bang so loud her teeth rattled.

Someone screamed—and then there was a deadly silence.

She tiptoed down the stairs, watching the darkness of the hallway carefully.

The normal neat hallway that greeted her was a chaotic mess of blood and broken glass sprinkled across the hardwood floors.

to crown a beast

Here, it almost looked peaceful now. But just by the sounds, she could tell the attack had simply made its way deeper into the house.

They were gaining on them, and that could only mean one thing; Scorpios was losing more and more men.

Molly's blood boiled.

In one of the dark corners of the room, she saw one of their soldiers sitting by the wall and rushed to him. His entire face was swollen and beaten, and he held a hand to his throat which gushed blood.

Fucking Ares…

Molly tore her housecoat, creating a makeshift cloth that she pressed against the man's throat, hoping it would help in some way. Through the blood and bruises, she recognized his features. She had seen him a handful of times, bumping into him when coming in and out of the Scorpios household. But no matter how hard she tried, she couldn't remember his name, and she realized she wasn't even sure anyone had ever introduced them to each other.

The thought broke Molly's heart. This man was bleeding for Scorpios, bleeding for their Dux. He'd fought against Ares, to protect them, to save them…and she couldn't even refer to him by his name.

His eyes met hers—exhausted, thankful, but he didn't speak.

His hands were shaking from what Molly assumed was the lack of blood, his skin no doubt growing colder and colder by the second.

"What's your name?" Molly asked gently in the darkness, she wouldn't let the man go without knowing. He deserved as much.

The man opened his mouth to speak, and started coughing out blood and some specs of it sprayed onto Molly's housecoat, the white silk turning a deep shade of red in some places.

"Ge…George," he croaked out, barely managing the word out. "I'm sorry," he added, looking at her ruined clothing.

"There's nothing to be sorry about, George. It's fine."

She couldn't muster the courage to lie to him. To tell him that he would be okay, when they both knew he wouldn't. He had lost too much blood, and even if help rushed in now, she knew they wouldn't be able to save him.

She grabbed his hand, holding it reassuringly.

He didn't need false words, he needed someone to hold him until his last breath. She couldn't leave him alone.

He simply stared back at her and let his head sag to rest on the wall. These were her people and she wouldn't let them down. She would fight for them. Fight to win their power back.

After a while, the man's eyes started to close, his eyelids seeming heavier and heavier. His skin was positively chilling now, and she knew from the gurgling sounds that this was it. He was leaving them.

"Thank you, George," Molly whispered, grip tightening on the man's hand. "Thank you for what you did for Scorpios. Thank you for your courage."

When he took his final breath, Molly breathed out shakily, patted the dead man's heavy hand and let go.

Molly stood, continuing down the dark hallway, distant voices spatting back and forth ahead.

A lamp lit the shadowy hall and she heard a whimpering sound. She scanned the floor, until she found the source of the sound and her stomach dropped and she almost vomited.

Their men were dying. Scorpios was crumbling. Soldiers left and right were no doubts injured and desperately asking for help.

Hell, she had just witnessed one of them die while she held him in her own hands.

But now Molly was faced with the one sight she had dreaded seeing.

Not again, not again, not another...

Daphne…

She fell to her knees and gripped Daphne's face, bringing her head to rest on her lap. Molly barely managed to reign in a deep sob at the sight of her mother-in-law covered in blood.

"Molly," Daphne breathed out, a deep frown etched between her brows. She shook her head, struggling to breathe.

"Daphne, I'm right here," Molly whispered and swept her hair out of her eyes.

Daphne, of all people. Sweet, loving Daphne. The late Dux's wife, who had showed nothing but kindness to all of them. How could someone dare to attack her, dare to hurt her?

Molly saw red.

Fury.

Sadness.

Disgust.

It all flowed within her at once, hitting her so hard she could barely see straight. It wrapped around her heart, fed her stomach, and sunk into her brain.

They would pay for this.

She would make sure of it.

She would find Fitz, and she would make sure he died slowly, painfully. The way he deserved.

Because this was not fair. It wasn't fair.

Daphne hadn't deserved this, none of it. And now she laid in a pool of her blood, fighting to stay awake.

Those tender brown eyes now watching her closely. She thought of Tensley in that moment. The ache in her chest grew. He had already lost one parent, he couldn't lose another. He didn't need them the way children needed their parents, but she knew Tensley, no matter how hard he tried to hide it, cared for his family greatly.

So Molly wouldn't let that happen. Not his mother. He wouldn't lose her. He wouldn't.

Daphne gripped Molly's wrist, her hold weak, but her nails digging into Molly's bone. "Go hide," she said, swallowing difficultly. "Please."

Molly choked on a sob. "I'm not leaving you." She took a deep breath and slid her arms underneath Daphne's armpits, pulling her across the floor and into an office after making sure it was safe and empty.

Once the door was firmly shut, Molly raced to the desk and grabbed napkins, tissues, she clawed at the drapes that surrounded the big windows, ripping them, whatever material she could find and rushed back to Daphne's side, her knees hitting the ground painfully next to the older woman.

Daphne's breathing grew low and loud, struggling not to drown in her own blood.

Molly lifted Daphne's shirt and saw the puncture wound, a knife most likely driven into the side of her ribcage and had no doubt struck her right lung.

Molly wrapped the fabric she had gathered around her torso, tightly so the bleeding would hopefully stop.

Just as Molly went to stand, Daphne snatched her hand. The blood smeared across her palm, painting her skin crimson and Molly stared down at her.

Too much blood. There was too much blood on her.

Molly's body was a canvas of Scorpios' blood and she could feel the panic rising in her throat as her hands shook wildly. The growing panic was wrapping around her airway and tightening quickly.

No...

She needed to relax. She needed to take a deep breath in and relax. For Daphne. For the others that might need help. She needed to get herself under control.

She couldn't let them down. Not now. She couldn't...

Daphne's big eyes pleaded with her and Molly shushed her reassuringly.

"I'm not going anywhere," Molly told her, touching her cheek.

Daphne licked at her bloody lips. "Take care...of the family. You're going to be... a—a great mother, Molly."

The warmth burned the back of Molly's eyes and she glared down at Daphne. "You are not dying, Daphne. You are not dying, do you hear me."

A sad smile touched Daphne's lips, but she didn't say a word.

The door flew open, hitting the wall with a thud and Molly's body froze as she looked up to see Fitz Senior move into the room.

He smiled at her, drunk on blood and thirsty for more, his white hair a sore thumb in the darkness of the room.

"You, my lovely Mrs. Knight," Fitz said, his eyes strictly on anything but hers. To avoid her lethal gaze. "My favorite daemon bitch, are the next one on my hit list, and your time has fucking come. I've had enough of you."

When he lunged, she hadn't prepared herself. She darted out of the way and collided with the desk, gripping it as she turned to face him.

Just as he went to strike her, she caught his arm and shoved him back, but it wasn't enough.

She wasn't in the right headspace. She couldn't concentrate on what she needed to do. She'd seen too much blood, too many injured...

He gripped her wrist and threw her down onto the ground. All the air left her lungs and she watched slowly as his foot descended, aimed at her stomach.

She screamed when her arms shielded her belly, only for the foot to collide with her hand instead, shattering several bones in her fingers.

Her strength had been enough to stop Fitz's foot from making any contact with her stomach, but her hand now looked like a mess of broken bones. The pain filling her eyes with angry tears. She wiped them away quickly with her arm, her earlier wrath tightening around her heart once more.

Even through the pain, she forced herself back to her feet, ignoring her screaming body. Fitz shook out his foot, the impact with Molly's hand had no doubt caused him pain, and he seethed with rage.

Within the next thought, Molly was on Fitz, her hands wrapped around his throat, tightening and tightening. Her shattered hand was useless but the splitting pain she felt as using it didn't stop her.

She was waiting for the icy feeling of her powers to start boiling within her but they didn't. Lance had said they would, he'd said…

But all she could see and feel was red, powerful hatred running through her system, ravaging it.

She couldn't see past it, it filled her to the brink and she let herself drown in it.

Embrace it.

The hurt, the rage, the hatred, the disgust.

All of it.

She felt a piercing pain, from somewhere near the bottom of her belly, but she didn't let go.

Didn't stop to think about it.

All she could think about was using every last inch of her energy to strangle Fitz to nothing.

His face was turning blue, but that ugly, hungry smile kept growing, as he was proud of himself. As if she was doing exactly was he wanted her to do.

Fitz wasn't a stupid man, the dirty bastard knew to keep his eyes far from her own, and she wanted to growl in anger. He had learned his lesson from their last confrontation, that much was clear.

Then, too quickly for Molly to register, Fitz ripped her hands from around his throat, and pushed her away.

Her back collided painfully with a wall, but she managed to stay on her two feet. Fitz growled deeply, ready to attack once more just as the door swung open. They both paused, glancing over to see Lex in the entrance.

Her brows wrinkled, exchanging a panicked look with Molly.

"Lex," Molly breathed out. "Get away. Run. Now."

Senior though had already focused his attention on Lex. "Ah," he began, his nasty voice dragging the word out. "I remember you from the attack at the pit, little thing," he added, looking at her up and down, as his tongue ran across his bottom lip, making Molly want to vomit. "Who would forget a pretty bitch like you, huh? I still remember the taste of your skin, the taste of your fear as you were shaking in my arm. *Please. Please stop*," he mocked, imitating what Molly guessed had once been Lex.

Molly's heart halted and she watched Lex grow considerably pale.

"I knew you'd come back for more, lovely. But I'm busy now, you see. Wait in the hall for me, and let us finish what we started," he said, and his gaze turned back to Molly. "Let me finally have a bite of this daemon's neck because I'm going to rip it off her creamy shoulders once and for all."

Molly clenched her jaw. "Don't fucking touch her."

"You stupid whore," he hissed, and then laughed darkly. "Do you know what I'm going to do once I'm done with you? I'll rip that fiend baby out of your dead womb and I'll wave it like a limp flag in front of your *Tensley*."

Those words were like a thousand daggers to her chest, a spark igniting the rage to activate her powers.

Molly felt the sting of ice behind her eyes and the burn in her fingertips.

It was starting. Her rage was building, but she felt in control of her powers. Of the powers she finally understood. They were awakening slowly, pacing, waiting to be unleashed on their prey.

She would destroy anyone who harmed her family, harmed her loved ones, and she'd make them pay gravely.

Molly glared at the demon who had ruined so many lives, destroyed so many, including her own. He kept his head bowed, avoiding her gaze, but enough to still be able to appear like the powerful asshole he was.

"You will not touch my son," she snapped, letting him feel the air change, the anger filtering in-between them until it would suffocate him, too.

At last, the icy sensation came in waves and she let the power seize her bones, the blood pumping fast in her veins, all the way to her pounding heart. She almost fell to her knees in relief. All was not lost. She could do this, she could.

She knew he felt the change too—by the way his head tilted upward, that smug smirk wiped off his face, and his hands clenched beside him.

"Do you have any final words, Fitz?" Molly whispered, staring back at him, unflinching, unwavering.

Because she was the daemon, Dux of Scorpios and married to the king of demons.

"You'll beg me," Molly bit out and her eyes flashed bright, but not fast enough as Fitz looked away. "You'll beg me to end your life."

He laughed loudly, the sound like nails on a chalkboard.

"Scared to look me in the eye, Fitz?" Molly moved forward and he took a step back. "I may not know all the answers to what I am," she whispered, the surge of power pumping through her once again. "But now I know what I'm capable of."

Just as her hand darted out, he lunged, catching her broken hand and yanking her into him.

But she wasn't bowing down. Not anymore.

She jabbed her elbow with all her might in his thorax, cutting off his breathing for a long second, and he let go in surprise.

It only lasted a moment, but that simple moment was all she needed to feel the power raged inside her, ready to be freed, and she spun.

Her hands dug into his arms, drawing blood and before he could act quickly enough and tear his gaze away, she stared straight into his beady eyes.

They dilated from her power and his strength flooded out of him, and filled her.

"Beg me now, Fitz," Molly hissed, the icy sensation burning the back of her eyes. "Beg me to end you."

Fitz swallowed, but didn't look away from her.

He was entrapped in her spell.

"Please Mrs. Knight," he started, sounding almost robotic. "End my life, I beg you."

"This war is over," Molly said, her voice steel and iron and everything was Tensley inside of her.

Then he blinked and the pain she already felt from her stomach intensified — barely, numbly and she gasped.

"Molly!" Lex screamed, clutching her own chest.

And it was all it took for the power she had over Fitz to dim and for him to tear his gaze away from hers. "Naïve little bitch, you thought it worked, didn't you," he laughed viciously again. "I'm afraid this is just the beginning, little daemon," he hissed and struck her.

Molly stumbled back, crashing into the table, but as soon as her body hit it, she straightened, ready to attack once more.

Lex growled and rushed toward Fitz, stabbing his side, but it didn't slow him down. He swung his arm and threw her back, stumbling to the ground.

But it was the perfect opportunity for Molly.

He lunged, only for her to side-step him. She caught his eyes again—and this time she didn't waste a moment.

She yanked the knife from his hand and sliced his throat.

He gasped—and redness gushed from the deep cut, soaking his white dress shirt. Slowly, so slowly, he collapsed to his knees, then sagged onto his side, gaping at her bare feet.

Molly took even deep breaths, watching the last breath seep from his mouth, until he stilled completely.

Then she collapsed to her knees too and fell over onto her side—when she brought her hands up, they were coated in blood.

Her own blood, she realized.

Lex's hands rubbed up and down her arms, but she barely felt them. So numb, so cold.

"Molly!" Lex's voice hollered to her and she saw the worried expression on her face.

Molly choked, she gasped, she tried to stay conscious.

"My baby, my—" She put pressure on her side and leaned against Lex who hushed her, tried to speak to her, but it didn't matter. She couldn't think. All she wanted to do was run, to find help, to save her baby.

And Daphne.

"Daph," she tried saying, but stopped mid-word. She felt so cold, so empty. It was like all her energy was leaving her body at once.

Molly felt the rush of panic through her system.

A roar tore through the room like a great darkness had suddenly walked in and engulfed them all. The door crashed, being ripped from its hinges and someone screamed a name. But it didn't sound afraid, it sounded relieved. From somewhere near, she thought she heard Lex cry.

Someone bent down in front of Molly and she took him in. At first, her heart froze, thinking it was Tensley.

That he had come for her, that he was here and that he'd make everything okay, he'd chase all the nightmares and the pain away.

But it wasn't.

It was Beau. Not her husband. Not the man she loved.

He crouched down in front of her, his hand going to the wound on her stomach and he spoke to her, then to Lex, but Molly couldn't hear him. Everything was distorted, everything was muffled.

His dark features were warped into a frown and he shook with rage. Again, he barked something at her, but she couldn't hear over her own pants.

"He needs help," Molly said on a cry, the floor painted in her blood. So much blood.

Beau wrapped his arms underneath her legs and picked her up, a groan of pain escaping her mouth.

No, no! I'm not losing you. She had lost Tensley, she had lost so much, but she wasn't losing her son.

Not now.

Not ever.

chapter
twenty-six

T HE COURT BUZZED in the darkened hall as Tensley leaned back in his throne. Every night, before sleep, Lilith held a feast, a ball to celebrate the king, she would say.

To celebrate their new leadership together.

He bit the inside of his cheek at the thought and sneered at his court of snakes and wolves. They lusted after control and prestige. They dreamt of sinking their glistening gold and sharpened teeth deep into the power and never letting go.

He hadn't seen Molly for days now and as much as he craved her, he craved keeping her and his son safe more. No one was truly safe here.

He'd pay his dues to Lilith and find a way out of her grasp.

His heart pounded at the thought of her threat.

Of telling the court the truth about what could be found deep within the beast, beating wildly for his queen, once again.

And that without his new heart, he was a dead man.

It would be another reason for them to outcast him.

To destroy him.

And he knew their thirst for power would go straight to their head and soon, he'd have a pack of hungry wolves after him, clawing at his back.

Clawing at his heart.

They would, no doubt salivate at the thought of being the one to announce they had killed the king.

Tensley stroked his bottom lip, his eyes flitting to his side where proudly sat the queen herself.

Not his queen.

She was nothing but a queen of lies and bloodshed.

A queen that a beast might crave, but not him.

He craved a different queen. His true queen. One with blonde soft curls and vivid, breathtaking eyes.

To Tensley, the queen sitting next to him was nothing but temporary. The throne belonged to his Dolcezza and if she accepted it, he would give it to her on a gold platter.

But it didn't take a wise man to see the glint in Lilith's eyes. The dark, simmering want dancing in the depths of her soul.

It was only a matter of time before she grew restless and tired of playing around a beast with a heart and puncture his chest to take it out herself.

She wanted the power.

He knew she craved it more.

He knew that to her, he was a temporary misstep in the grand scheme of her supposed plan to gain complete power over his court.

He had no doubts she would try to kill him. It was only a matter of time.

So he waited patiently for her to make her move.

And when she did, he'd be ready. And he would rip her to shreds and never look back.

His hand rolled into a white-fist on the arm of his throne and he glared at the blunt laughter coming from the savage crowd. They ate like beasts, blood thick on men's beards, drunk off of aged wine and dark thoughts.

They appeared civilized, but he now saw what they hid underneath their gowns and suits.

Beasts thriving off of primal needs.

And a beast always craved some good bloodshed.

His fist trembled.

"My king," Lilith purred in his ear, her hot breath fanning his earlobe. He stiffened and didn't bother turning to face her. Her fingers skimmed down his bent fingers, feeling the slight tremble there. "You've grown weak again. Only a few days away from you and you become an addict begging for the next taste of her poison. Poor man you've become, look what she has done to you…"

He didn't acknowledge that, but it was true. Only a few days from his dolcezza and his body yearned for her.

But he would wait a thousand ages to touch her if it kept both of them safe.

"My king!"

His eyes shot to the man heavily breathing in front of their high table. The man swallowed thickly.

"What is it?" Tensley asked, narrowing his eyes at the man's disheveled appearance.

The man straightened, but he still couldn't even out his breathing. "My lord, Ares has attacked Scorpios again."

That iron heart inside of him dropped into his stomach, but he steeled his features, his mouth becoming a thin line of indifference.

to crown a beast

Even though his men, his family, his wife—were at risk of being ripped away from him, he couldn't show it to the court.

Couldn't show the emotions raging within him.

"And?" Lilith spoke, her voice ringing with annoyance. This news didn't interest the court unless they got to engage in the bloodshed.

The man swallowed again and Tensley growled lowly. He was beginning to believe it was all the man was capable of doing until he lifted his hand.

A white letter was slotted in his shaking hand and Tensley reached out, taking it. He tore it open, unrushed, but his heart was thumping as if he was dying inside.

His eyes skimmed the words.

It was short. It was to the fucking point, but its impact on him was brutal nonetheless.

His crunched up the letter and stood. At his sudden movement, the court hushed and turned, watching their king move from his table.

"My king?" Lilith called and he heard her heels click after him. "Where are you going? You cannot leave so hastily when the court is celebrating for you."

He didn't stop and continued marching into the darkened halls. "You have the court celebrate every fucking night, Lilith. Find yourself a pet to fucking play with, you're bored. I'm sure none of the court will care if I leave."

A hand clasped his bicep and he spun, barring his teeth.

"Oh. No. No, no, young beast," Lilith hissed, her features sharpened to the point she appeared as something purely sinister. "You do not get to decide when you go and when you don't. You will answer me. Now."

Tensley shook her hand off with one roll of his shoulders and glared down at her. "I'm going to New York."

Lilith's lips peeled up in pleasure. "I forbid it."

Tensley felt the wave of fury hit him.

"And if I find out that you've gone against my will," Lilith said, with the smile of a snake. "I will tell the court of your curse."

Tensley stood still, the options weighing heavily down onto him.

But it only took one moment to decide.

"Then damn me," he snapped back, his anger hitting her in violent waves and she stumbled back, caught off guard.

He turned away, feeling her own wrath battle his and she kept shouting after him. She screamed about him being a dead man.

She laughed about him being a weak man.

She raged about him being a foolish man.

But he didn't care in that moment.

Let them rip his heart out.

Let them have their bloodshed over a king of beasts.

Let her shout until her throat was raw.

Because all he could hear was that he was a loved man. And he needed to get to his family. To his men. To his wife.

The beast and the man both agreed that their wife and mate was above all else.

His chest burned at thought of Molly.

All that the letter held were three simple words.

Molly needs you.

But it was his undoing.

TENSLEY MARCHED INTO the familiar entrance of the townhouse shadowed in darkness, and each soldier that stood in the hallway stilled.

He continued forward, watching as each man stepped back, bowed their head. He drank in their fear—their anxiety as the king of High Court, king of demons, walked past them.

The beast had returned to his people, but he had returned a changed man.

As he turned the corner, he grabbed one soldier's sleeve and yanked him close. "Where is my wife?"

The soldier paused, his eyes widening in fear. He opened and closed his mouth, gawking at Tensley as if he had seen a ghost.

He wasn't a fucking ghost; he was far worse.

"Tensley," a voice called to him and he glanced over his shoulder to see Beau there.

Slowly, he released the soldier and turned to face his older brother. Dressed in all black, black hair unkempt, and laced with bruises on his cheeks and forearms, his brother had been at war.

"Take me to her," Tensley demanded, walking toward his brother.

Beau's expression pinched, no doubt displeased to be made his brother's bitch, but he didn't say a word.

He moved, like a dark shadow in the hallway and up the stairs.

Beau stopped at a bedroom door and glanced back at him. "Mother was harmed in the attack," he said, his voice low, holding little tenderness, but Tensley saw the glint of fury in his eyes. "They managed to heal her, but she's still recovering. She refused to leave Molly's side."

Tensley swallowed. Both his mother and his wife had been attacked and he hadn't been there to protect them.

To protect Scorpios.

Tensley opened the door and stepped inside the room, darkened by the heavy curtains, pulled tight so no light would shine through.

It looked like a fucking dungeon in there.

His eyes went straight to the bed.

Molly laid, underneath covers, her legs moving frantically and her breathing heavy and irregular.

"Tensley," his mother's voice rang out and he saw her seated in a chair beside the bed, stroking Molly's hair.

A few women gathered around Molly's side, trying to speak to her, trying to soothe her. Lex was one of them he noted. She didn't look worried though; she held a fierce scowl as if she was ready for war.

One of Scorpios' doctors stood on her other side, feeling her stomach with a monitor.

Tensley didn't waste time. He marched to the bed and sat on the edge. He examined her quickly—sweat pooled on her brow, her eyes fluttering open, her mouth parted as she panted, and her nightgown held a bright stain of blood on it's side.

His cursed iron heart squeezed in raw pain.

"The baby," she chanted, over and over, and Tensley's heart beat to her panicked voice.

"Molly," he whispered, making his own chant, overriding her's, his fingertips touching her wet cheeks. "Dolcezza."

She opened her vivid eyes and when she found him, she calmed for a moment. "Tensley?"

Her hands spread up his biceps and squeezed.

"I'm here, dolcezza," he said and kissed the inside of her wrist.

"She was stabbed," the doctor spoke. "The wound is not healing properly and we don't know why."

Molly wheezed and shut her eyes, rolling her head back.

Tensley scowled, bringing his hands to her stomach, feeling the wound on her right side.

"I'll heal her," he hissed.

He wasn't letting her go. He would protect her and their son. "Is the baby okay? Is my son okay?" he asked, eyes hard on the doctor.

"We just managed to find his heart beat, everything seems normal for now. It doesn't look like he's in any distress," the doctor told him.

Tensley nodded, then bent, lowering his mouth and peppering soft kisses on her stomach, on her side, feeling her tense and go limp, feeling the flutter of movement inside her belly.

His kisses mended the wound, mended her bruised heart, and he would take on her pain, he would take all of it away.

He straightened, his hands never parting from the sides of her swollen belly and gazed up at her.

Her cheeks had gained their rosiness back and her breathing became even.

He leaned forward, not caring about all the eyes watching him and her, and pressed his lips to hers gently, for a moment.

"She's stable," the doctor said and pulled Tensley aside. "But she's started having contractions not long after the attack. She's been having them for several hours now. We needed to heal her before going any further. It may be best for you to wait outside."

Tensley took a deep breath and looked at Molly. She was going to have the baby soon.

"Tensley," his mother said and touched his shoulder. He turned to face his mother. She looked pale, but she still smiled back at him. Tears glistened in her brown doe eyes. "Someone needs to speak to Scorpios. She will be fine. Lex will stay with her."

He nodded, stealing one last glance at Molly.

His mother and brother both followed him into the hallway.

"She killed him," his mother spoke after a stretched moment.

Beau folded his arms. "He could have killed you both. He almost killed Lex."

His mother just looked back at both of her sons. "Your father would be proud of you."

Tensley stiffened and stared at his mother. He could see it clearly, the way they stared at him. His mother, his brother, all of Scorpios. They stared at him like they were searching for the man and the beast within him.

"I should have been here," he said, shaking his head.

"You're the king now," his mother said, touching his shoulder. "You have other duties."

He felt the anger tighten around his heart. "My duty is to her. To protect my family. To protect Scorpios. A crown means nothing." He paused, taking a deep, shaking breath into his lungs, as realization hit him.

When he had lost his heart, he had lost his focus. His reason.

He had lost sight of what was truly important. Of what truly mattered to him. His thirst and lust for power had eaten at him. He had been no better than the snakes that called themselves a High Court.

He had been just like them.

But no longer.

He knew what truly mattered.

Not the stupid crown, not the stupid court, but Molly.

. "She's my crown, my court, my queen. Nothing matters without her."

His mother stared up at him, her eyes wide with shock.

"She truly did curse you," Beau muttered, regarding him closely. His dolcezza was stable. His baby's heart was still strong. Now, it was time to be the Dux.

He clenched his jaw and turned away from them. "I need to speak to my soldiers."

He continued to walk down the stairs, hearing their own footsteps follow him.

The soldiers gathered in the meeting room, faces drawn in exhaustion and anger, their stances stiffening as soon as he walked into the room.

Each man bowed, dropping low and he stood, watching them.

"Rise," he commanded, his voice like whiplash.

The men rose, silence spreading over the crowd.

He stood in front of them, studying each man slowly. These men fought for Scorpios and many not with them had died for Scorpios.

"I stand before you," he began, his voice clear and even. "Not as your king, but as your Dux."

At that, the men straightened further.

Tensley fisted his hands. "Ares has been defeated. By the hand of my wife and Scorpios." He paused, collecting his anger. "Scorpios has survived this hell and will prosper. We are made from ashes and acid and thorns. We do not beg. We do not give up. We fight, we conquer, we destroy. We are savages that cannot be tamed and will not be tamed. Scorpios—will forever stay in our society. They will speak of this dark time as a time of rebirth. A time of beasts conquering. I will bleed for each and every one of you until I have nothing more inside of me."

At his last words, the men roared in celebration, in agreement.

Tensley, in the chaos, left the room, feeling that iron heart heavily inside of him pounding.

He leaned against the wall and breathed through his nose.

"Tensley," a voice called to him.

He turned his head to see Illya Black walking toward him.

His best friend. His only friend. His brother. The man who had been taking care of his wife and unborn child when he couldn't.

"Illya," Tensley said, straightening and moving from the wall.

Illya regarded him, slowly taking him in and patted his shoulder. "The bastard returns at last. I was beginning to think I would have to play husband until the day I die," he said with a playful wink.

Tensley felt the corner of his mouth twitch. He didn't have the right words to say to Illya. "Thank you for taking care of her when I couldn't. When I wasn't the man she needed."

Illya's brow furrowed and he tightened his grip on Tensley's shoulder. "You are the only man she needs."

Tensley went to open his mouth, but Lex appeared in the hallway, out of breath.

"Tensley," she hollered. "It's Molly."

chapter
twenty-seven

T HE PAIN THUNDERED in every part of Molly's body, her bones aching, her muscles constricting until she cried out.

Dizziness came and went, blacking out her vision, the pain overwhelming her.

"It's too early," she heard someone whisper.

It's too early. Too soon.

She wanted to call for Tensley, but it was like her voice was trapped within her throat.

When her lips parted, all that came out were pained moans, and louder shouts when her womb seemed to twist from within. She couldn't speak, only to chant Tensley's name.

They tried to soothe her by combing her wet hair from her forehead, but it just made her angry.

It's too early.

She tried to tell her body to stop. To stop pushing, to stop the labor, but it was useless.

She knew the baby was big, she knew he carried his father's strength and her own, but would he survive this?

Would he be able to breathe in this world?

"Tensley," she managed to gasp out between contractions.

Her hands dug into the sheets, anchoring herself. The doctor spread her legs and examined her.

"She's eight centimeters dilated," he said to the other women around him.

Everyone moved fast, the noises around her seemed to be never-ending but all she wanted was silence.

All she wanted was Tensley.

TENSLEY SLAMMED OPENED the door and his lungs seized. Molly groaned in pain as she dug her nails into the bed sheets.

Women, including Lex and his mother, moved around the room, gathering more sheets and cold water.

Molly's eyes were squeezed shut and her entire face was bright red, her bottom lip wedged between her teeth in a death grip.

"Tensley," his mother said, walking toward him. She touched his arm. "It might be best if you wait outside."

Tensley gritted his teeth, unable to look away from Molly's painful expression.

When she cried out, a cry so raw, it burned his insides and his heart cracked.

"No," he bit out. "I'm not leaving."

"There's too many people in here now. You'd just be in the way," one of the women snapped, placing more pillows behind Molly's head and wetting her forehead with a cold washcloth.

His entire body shook. Shook from the rage inside of him, the anger at being denied, the fear of what he saw in front of him. His dolcezza was in pain, she was in distress, and he wasn't leaving her side.

"You'll have to kill me if you think I'm leaving her," he hissed and stepped around the women.

His mother grabbed his arm. "Tensley, think of her. Think of her and the baby."

Tensley glared down at his mother and steadied his breathing. He took a deep breath and pushed forward.

"Tell me what you want," he said, his voice low and deep, his power completely in the hands of his dolcezza.

If she didn't want him there, he'd go, even if it pained him.

Molly rolled her head across the feather pillows and fluttered her eyes open, weakly.

Her chest rose and fell rapidly, the pain visible on each part of her.

"Tell me," he bit out between his clenched teeth, baring himself to her once again.

Not as the beast.

Not as a man.

But as her husband.

As her heart.

"Tell me what you want and I'll do it," he whispered, aching to touch her, to steal away any pain he could.

Molly weakly parted her lips and her eyes drifted upward until those vicious eyes settled on his own.

"I want you," she breathed out, even that alone a painful thing to do.

She seized, bending forward, and that was all it took.

He moved fast, his hands going to her sides and he climbed in behind her, his large frame cradling her against him.

His hands found her belly and he stroked, back and forth, back and forth.

"Give me your pain," he whispered into her sweaty neck. "Give it all to me, dolcezza."

She bit out a distressed cry and dug her nails into his biceps, so deep it drew blood, but he didn't flinch.

"I'm right here," he said, peppering delicate kisses against her neck, against her cheek, against her shoulders. Anyway he could reach, he drowned her in kisses, in his power and rage and love, to take away the pain.

To soothe the ache in the only way a demon bastard could.

"Tensley," she gasped when he nipped at her jugular, her pulse fast and rushed. "Tensley."

She chanted his name back to him. It was the only word she spoke, but it was enough.

"I can't," she breathed out, falling back against him, her breathing ragged, shaking her head weakly across his chest. "It's too soon."

He shushed her and kissed her jaw line, tasting sweat and salty tears. "He'll be okay, he's strong. Just like you. My dolcezza is not weak. She's a thunderstorm. She makes powerful men bend to her will. I'll be your strength, your shield. I'll be your everything."

She sobbed into the air, her head tilted back against his shoulder and he gazed at her rosy cheeks, at her thick lashes resting there, at her bloody lips.

"You're the most beautiful, most powerful woman I've ever seen," he hissed and those vivid eyes caught his in a deathtrap. "I'm defenseless against you. Don't you feel it?" He pressed his chest into her back, letting her feel the throb of something so forbidden the gods would rival him. His heart.

He was unafraid of it now. If anything, it made him stronger.

Her breathing paused and her eyes widened.

"You cursed a beast," he whispered and brushed his own lips against her parted ones. "And made him bow."

Tears ran down her cheeks and she leaned her head back onto his chest.

"You can do this, Molly. You're doing great," he said one final time. "You're doing great, Molly."

When the doctor finally announced Molly was dilated all the way, and could finally start pushing when the next contraction came, Tensley kissed her sweaty cheek and smiled.

Freely. Happily. Nervously.

He had never, in his life, felt anxious, powerless, yet happy at the same time. It was a strange feeling, but one he wouldn't want to change for anything else.

His dolcezza was doing great, his son was doing great. And soon, soon he'd get to finally meet him.

His own flesh and blood.

His first born.

When the next contraction came, Molly pushed and pushed, red-faced, in extreme pain, but she kept going.

And did the same during every following contraction.

She was so strong. So, so strong.

He admired her.

Whoever said women were weaker than men because they had been cursed with a womb had clearly never seen a woman give birth.

It wasn't a curse. It was a blessing. A blessing that only showed how powerful and resilient women were.

Molly didn't bow to the pain, she didn't give up. She clenched her teeth and screamed through it.

Just like he knew she would.

She fought for Tensley and she fought for their son.

He continued to kiss her, to soothe her, to take away any pain he could.

She used him, she dug deep into his skin and pressed against his form behind her, but he didn't want it any other way.

He wanted to be her everything, to never leave her side again, and conquer together.

For what seemed like hours, they worked together, soothing and pushing, building closer to the end.

"She's crowning," the doctor announced, looking between her spread legs. "I see the head."

Tensley's heart pounded deep inside of him. "We're almost there, dolcezza. One more push. Just one more, ciccia. You can do it."

And when the next contraction came, she cried out, but she didn't stop.

She pushed, hard, deep, and he gave everything she could. Tensley gave her his strength, his power, his wrath, his soul and that iron heart.

At the sound of a baby's cry, Molly sagged against him and they both gazed up to see a tiny baby, covered in blood, held up above her.

The doctor placed their crying son in Molly's arms and her shaking hands cradled him against her bare chest.

She sobbed, a wide smile of shock and joy battling on her features.She stroked the dark thick hair on his tiny head.

Tensley brought his hand forward and gently stroked his son's back. His son. Their son.

His voice caught in his throat and he blinked back warmth. He tightened his grip on Molly, flushed against her and watched her care for their infant son.

"He's so beautiful," she whispered through a quiet cry.

A rush of emotions collided inside of him, but all he could do was watch.

"We just need to take the baby to make sure he's well," his mother told them, and carefully picked him up, handing him over to the doctor.

Molly relaxed against him, her head turning to the side and he realized after a few seconds, she was listening to his heartbeat.

He wrapped an arm around her, not caring about the sweat and blood between them as the doctor cleaned her up around her lower regions.

"What if he's not okay?" Molly asked, tiredly, as she tried to sit up.

Tensley held her to him and brushed her hair off her sweaty neck, kissing her there. "Rest, doclezza. We both need you to rest."

She hummed back to him, but didn't protest and snuggled against him.

He watched as the women and the doctor examined their baby, analyzing each expression to see if he could tell what they were thinking.

If his baby wasn't well…

He kissed Molly's head again and laid his cheek against the top of her head. "You were incredible, dolcezza. Thank you," he said, voice full of emotions. "Thank you for giving me a child. Our child. Our little boy."

Again, she hummed back but he caught the faint smile on her pouty lips.

"It must be because she's a daemon," he heard one whisper.

The doctor scratched his cheek and took the baby in his hands. Slowly, he turned and walked the baby back to Molly and Tensley.

Molly stirred from her sleep and took the baby back into her arms.

"He's healthy, a little tiny, but nothing alarming," the doctor told them, but Molly wasn't paying attention. Her eyes were glued to their son. "My assumption is because of the demon and daemon genes he's strong enough and healthy. I will want to see him regularly to keep an eye on him, but for now, he's healthy."

The doctor paused.

"What is it?" Tensley asked, glaring at the man.

The doctor cleared his throat. "He has a full heart. A human heart."

"What does that mean for the baby?" Molly asked, her eyes widening.

The doctor seemed to think about it, unsure of what the answer should be. "The truth is, we don't really know, Mrs. Knight. We've never encountered a half demon with a human heart. But it doesn't seem like it causes any threat to him, he's still strong, stronger than a human would be. I guess only time will tell. Perhaps, the more he grows up, the more we'll learn."

Molly breathed out slowly, no doubt nervous at the thought. "Scorpios won't like this. They won't like the thought of the heir to Scorpios having a full, human heart. What can we do?"

"I'll convince them otherwise. I'll make sure of it," Tensley told her and kissed her cheek. "Whether he has a human heart or not, he's still half daemon and half demon, no one will take that away from him. He's our flesh and blood."

Tensley dropped his gaze back to their son. The baby cried softly now and Molly cooed back to him.

His eyes fluttered open briefly and she gasped, Tensley's heart freezing. The vividness of blue peeked through his dark lashes.

"He has your eyes," Tensley whispered stunned. "He has daemon eyes," he repeated, his mind running a thousand miles an hour.

Molly bit back a sob and smiled through the tears. "He's a daemon and a demon," she said between stuttered breaths. "He truly is. He'll have my strength and power, not just the gene. A boy. A daemon boy."

Tensley smiled back at her outburst, but his own chest was tight with happiness.

"Lance won't believe it," she said, laughter in her voice. "Incredible..." she whispered to herself.

Slowly, Tensley laid his hand on top of Molly's and squeezed.

chapter
twenty-eight

THE LIGHT FROM the window hit Molly's eyes and she squinted. Exhausted and sore, she wanted to sleep, but she wanted to see her son. Their son.

She patted beside her on the bed where she had laid the baby, but felt nothing. Her heart seized and she sat up, to find the bed empty.

Just as she was about to get up and search, she saw Tensley standing by the window.

Their son was cradled in his thick arms of muscle and steel.

The baby whined, but didn't cry. He stretched his tiny, wrinkled newborn arms above his head and Tensley rocked him, holding him against his bare chest.

Skin to skin.

The mere sight of seeing Tensley holding her son was something she feared she'd never see.

It broke and mended her heart all at the same time.

The powerful, deadly beast gently holding their son.

She stayed still, afraid to spook him, afraid to turn away and miss this scene of raw tenderness and love from a beast that once didn't have a heart.

Tensley hushed his son and traced a finger down his tiny spine, calming him.

Molly swallowed.

Tensley's dark eyes darted to hers and he stilled, pausing for a second, only to continue rocking their son.

"I didn't want to wake you," he whispered, moving forward.

She couldn't speak. She couldn't look away from the man in front of her.

"I think he needs his mother though," he added, his voice husky and thick and everything that made her stomach flutter.

She lifted her arms and he walked over, placing the tiny infant in her hands. She cradled him against her chest and sat back against the pillows Tensley must have brought her. After the doctor gave the baby back, the women had helped her breastfeed for the first time and it damn well hurt. Soon, she had fallen asleep against Tensley. She had fought sleep, but it won and Tensley encouraged her to sleep. That he would watch after their son.

"Hi baby," she whispered, fixing his position so he lay across one of her arms. She unbuttoned her nightgown and brought his mouth to her breast.

She felt Tensley's eyes watching her closely.

He struggled at first, fussing, but when he found her nipple, he latched on.

She tensed from the uncomfortable pain.

"What is it?" Tensley asked, his brow furrowed in worry as he sat down next to her.

"It's just a bit uncomfortable," she told him, leaning back against the pillows. She braved a glance at him.

He was watching her closely, his dark eyes glued to her features.

Her cheeks warmed. This man had the ability to leave her speechless, to stir up emotions she never thought existed, and to make her heart ache.

"What?" she asked, frowning at him. She knew she probably looked like a mess. Her hair was greasy and her skin was sweaty and she definitely smelled. But she felt happy.

She had her baby.

Her son in her arms.

Tensley's thumb brushed along her cheek, slowly, painfully taking it's time, like branding his touch into her own flesh, and she blinked back at him, breathless.

"Are you sore?" he asked, scanning her body.

"A little bit," she whispered back, looking at him through her lashes.

"Come here," he said and she scooted slowly into his arms. He wrapped one arm around her waist and bent his head, his lips touching hers ever so slowly. "Let me take away the pain."

Molly fell into his arms, into his words, her baby nestled against her chest. The kisses were tender, so soft they felt like feathers against her mouth, but she felt the wave of endorphins spread up her limbs, helping to ease the tenderness.

For hours, he held her, gently kissing her, out of affection, out of duty to take care of her, their son falling in and out of sleep in the process.

"Is that better?" he asked between a kiss.

She nodded against his forehead.

"Molly," he whispered, his breath fanning across her hair.

"Hm?"

She felt him swallow thickly. "I found out more about the curse. More than you knew."

Molly held her breath. "What did you find out?"

He worked his jaw and sighed. "That if my heart is ripped out again...I won't come back. It's death."

Her stomach dropped.

"But you have nothing to worry about," he told her as he kissed her temple.

He moved back, perhaps to get a better look at her but Molly, her heart freezing, gripped his bicep.

He frowned at her. "What's wrong, dolcezza?"

She breathed out shakily and let go. "I'm just...afraid."

His ruthless brows furrowed into a deep line. "Afraid of what? I won't let anything happen to you."

Molly couldn't meet his eyes and shook her head. "It's not that..." She fixed the hold on her son and he cooed, snuggling closer. With another deep breath, she braved a look up at Tensley. "I'm afraid all of this is going to disappear. It's all too good to be true. I have you back—but I'm so scared of losing you again." Wetness filled her eyes and she lowered her head, stroking the baby's soft cheek.

Damn pregnancy hormones still ruling over her emotions and body, she wanted to say.

She couldn't wait for those to finally go away...

Tensley's large hand cupped her own cheek and raised her chin to meet his gaze. His own eyes were dark, holding a vicious storm within them.

"Dolcezza, I'm not going anywhere. Ever again," he bit out and as a tear slid down her face, his thumb caught it and he smoothed it into her skin. "No court, no gods, no duty will keep me from you. Not even death."

Molly's heart trembled inside her ribcage from the mere strength of his words. So powerful, so vicious, and deadly—a god would bow to them.

"This heart," he hissed, gripping her wrist and placing her palm against his chest to feel the thundering of his own heart. His dark eyes pierced hers and stole her breath away. "This heart is yours. All fucking yours. No one will ever take this away from me again."

She couldn't look away from where her pale hand laid, feeling the thump of his iron heart. Her iron heart.

It was back.

It was hers.

She sobbed openly, exhausted and happy and overwhelmed.

"Dolcezza," Tensley hushed onto her cheek before he pressed another precious kiss there. His tongue licked a few tears from her skin and then he kissed her again. "What are we going to name him?"

She giggled at that and Tensley's fingers swept across the baby's forehead.

"He looks like you," she said, touching his button nose and the baby cooed.

"All I see is you in him," Tensley whispered back.

When she looked up at him, she saw how tenderly Tensley watched him. So closely, listening, watching for any sound.

"Do you want to hold him?" Molly asked, shifting the baby in her arms.

Tensley looked up at her and he paused. Once he nodded, Molly placed the baby back in his powerful arms and he cradled him against his bare chest, leaning back.

Molly leaned back against his side, resting her hand on his chest.

She watched the two most important people in her life, the sunlight spilling in slowly over them.

"What about Salvatore?" Molly asked, stroking Tensley's chest in soothing circles. Tensley paused, his brows dropping as he stared down at his son. "After your father. I think you mother would love it," she said with a soft but sad smile.

Sad for the woman who had clearly lost a man she cared about so dearly.

Perhaps, Salvatore had been Daphne's Tensley.

Her smile turned amused at the thought.

The baby cooed again and Tensley brought his index finger to their son's little fist. The baby's fist opened and wrapped around that one finger.

"Salvatore," he muttered back and the baby gurgled, a faint smile appearing. Tensley laughed, breathlessly. A corner of his mouth quirked. "My little warrior."

She kissed his jaw line and he turned, capturing her mouth and in the warmth of darkness, the three of them lived in a fantasy.

Hours passed and Tensley waited on Molly—even when she tried getting something for herself, he would object and bring everything over to her.

Food for her growling stomach.

Pads for her postpartum bleeding.

Cream for her sore nipples.

When she finally announced she had found the courage to take a shower, he brought her a bag full of different kinds of shampoos, conditioners, body washes as well as a ridiculous amount of other products she didn't need. To which she laughed, saying if he thought she smelled and needed to take a shower, he only had to ask.

That only made him frown. And she laughed some more.

When the baby cried, he got up and brought the baby to her.

It was pure bliss. All of it.

She didn't want to let Tensley go, but the weight of the High Court sat heavy on her chest. She didn't want them to be separated. She didn't want to lose him again.

Each time he touched her, stroked her, kissed her, even just looked at her, she felt the warmth pass through her. The beast was tamed, and the iron heart was hers again, but for how long this time?

At the sound of the door creaking open, she turned to see Daphne tiptoeing in.

"Mother," Tensley hissed, unaware Molly hadn't been sleeping but watching him read over papers next to her. "She's resting."

He stood from the bed and stepped in front of the door.

"I just wanted to see my grandson," Daphne whispered back. "You've had them locked up for two days."

"They both needed rest. I needed to heal her," he told her and Molly's heart warmed.

"Childbirth is natural, Tensley," Daphne argued. "A woman's body was made to be able to give life."

Tensley sighed and folded his arms. "I didn't like seeing her in pain."

Neither of them spoke, but she saw the soft expression on Daphne's face as she looked up at her son.

"Both of them are healthy. Both of them are safe. You need to sleep, too," she told him, touching his arm.

"I'll sleep when it's safe," he told her. "I'm not risking either of them."

Daphne smiled up at him and touched his cheek. "You remind me so much of your father."

"I am not him, mother," he told her, softly, but Molly knew the hurt that strung in his voice. "Molly wants to name the baby Salvatore."

"Oh," Daphne said and looked over to the bed. The baby lay on Molly's chest, fast asleep. "Do you want to name him that though? I understand you and he weren't very close."

Tensley stayed silent and after a moment, he moved back to the bed. "If she wants to name him that, then I'm fine with it. Whatever she wants."

"She makes you truly happy, doesn't she?" Daphne asked from the doorway.

Silence, and then Molly felt Tensley's hand stroke her cheek and into her hair, brushing it to the side. "She does."

"Sleep, Tensley," Daphne said and shut the door.

Tensley continued to stroke her hair and she almost fell back asleep until his husky voice roused her. "You are my court," he whispered. His thumb pressed to her bottom lip and tugged. "You are my crown." His thumb stroked circles into her lips and then he leaned forward, pressing his own brutal lips to hers. "You are my queen."

Molly blinked back tears and tightened her grasp on her son, glancing up at him.

She sat up and kissed him, once, twice, and lost count.

"What if we name him Illya?" she asked against his mouth.

He paused and she sat back, trying to read his expression. "Illya?"

She rubbed his chest and smiled. "Yes. Illya Salvatore Knight."

His lips tugged into a ghost of a smile and he kissed Illya's nose. "My warrior."

DAYS PASSED AND baby Illya grew, faster than the doctor expected, but he was healthy. As Molly tucked him into his cradle, she couldn't look away. Every night she slept between them, but Daphne suggested they try the cradle.

Thankfully, Tensley hadn't left and had been dealing with both Scorpios and High Court as much as he could.

When he wasn't dealing with that, he was with her. She never would have imagined him being so involved with the baby—changing diapers, rocking him to sleep, bathing him, holding him. All he wanted was to be with them.

"Dolcezza," Tensley whispered into her ear and spread his large hands across her stomach. It was still flabby, but everyone told her breastfeeding would help lose the weight. Tensley would kiss her cheek and tell her just how beautiful she was constantly. "Come to bed."

"I will," she whispered back.

"I'll watch him," he told her as he took her hand, guiding her back to bed.

She frowned at him and forced him to lie down. "You need to sleep, too." She combed his hair back and he grinned at her. "What?"

"Are you going to be a bossy mother?"

She tried to frown, but the smile won and she smacked his arm. "You like me bossy."

"I do in certain places," he muttered and kissed her, his hand holding her thigh and moving her closer. "I received a letter."

"Hmm?"

"From High Court," he told her and she sat up.

"What did it say?" Her heart was in her throat.

Those dark eyes stared up at her. "The court knows the baby was born and they say he must be presented to the court, as per tradition."

chapter twenty-nine

THOSE VIVID EYES flashed—an angry, vicious tornado twisting within them.

"Tensley," she gasped.

"Don't worry, I'm not letting them near either of you," he told her, stroking her hair behind her ear.

She frowned at him. "They won't rest until they see him, Tensley. Simply telling them no will create more issues."

His jaw set. He knew she was right. The tension between him and the court, especially now between Lilith and him was not good.

Had she told them about the curse?

About his heart?

Would they try to kill him upon arrival?

She had sent letters upon letters to him saying he either returned to High

Court with the baby at once, or she would send someone for him.

He knew if they returned to court he'd be in danger.

And so would be Molly and the baby.

He didn't trust a single soul there.

"It's a custom for the child of the king to be blessed in front of the court, with the king and the queen present as well," he told her. "But fuck their rules and customs, I'm king now and this court doesn't rule me. I'm not risking taking both of you with me there. It's too dangerous."

"Tensley, I'm not letting you go there alone. If you go, then I go too. Especially now more than ever with your heart and the beast forming one because of the curse. I didn't know, I'm — I'm sorry Tensley… had I known…" she shook her head, a deep frown etched between her beautifully sculpted brows, and he reached for her, smoothing it out gently. "You're at risk now that Lilith knows. And she could be telling the whole damn court as we speak. But I'm… I'm stronger than ever. With my powers at their full capacity, I'm a true threat to them. But they don't know this yet, I can let them think I'm weak, let them think they can control me, so they won't suspect me to be any sort of threat. If they were to hurt you, Tensley… I—" she shook her head again, chasing away the words. "We can protect each other together. We're stronger together."

He stared at the rare woman in front of him, so tender, but so much venom in her bones and blood. She was what the gods would have fought for, would have waged wars and conquered cities just to glimpse at that tender venom.

And it was his.

He wanted to please her, he wanted to provide and protect her, and if she wanted to attend court with the snakes, he'd stand beside her.

His fingertips traced the edge of her face, sweeping into her golden curls and fisting them gently. "You're the tamer of beasts. Your command is final," he whispered, his gaze lingering on those rosebud lips. "But we have to be very,

very careful, Molly. I have no doubt Lilith wants me dead. And I wouldn't put it past her for you to be the next on her list. She's tired of us. She'll make a move, somehow. So we must be ready, we must be careful. I don't want you out of my sight," he said as his thumb came up to caress her bottom lip, dragging it out.

A glint of desire flashed in her eyes and she too looked at his lips. "I only tamed one beast. My beast," she said and placed her hand on his chest. He let her feel the roar of his forbidden heart.

He leaned forward, his lips skimming hers with a touch that just stirred his beast. He fisted his hands. He needed to be gentle with her and he would. He enjoyed watching her fuss over their baby, watching her brow furrowed when she was concerned she did something wrong with him. It had been like a rebirth of their love.

"We go tomorrow," he told her, resting his forehead against hers and he pulled her closer onto his chest. "I'll find a way to be here. As much as possible, dolcezza. I'm not sacrificing anymore time away from you. A court of snakes would never be more important than you are. But my only way out of this crown is death, and I'm not quite ready to leave my wife alone," he said with a wry, seductive smile. "I enjoy her a bit too much still. So we fight back, and we make that court kneel once and for all."

She squeezed those vivid eyes shut and a single painful breath passed through her lips. He gently stroked her jaw line, soothing her to open her eyes again.

When she did, they were wet and bloodshot and her bottom lip quivered, but she smiled up at him. "I love you. I don't care if it's forbidden, I don't care if it's a curse against you. I don't care. I love you so much," she gasped and big pearly tears rolled down her rosy cheeks.

He kissed her wet cheeks and licked away the tears. He smiled at her. "Curse me again, dolcezza. Curse me every day for the rest of my life."

He brushed his lips against her and they fell down onto the bed together. He held her, running his fingers through her hair and listening to her breathing, slow and deep.

Tomorrow, they were going back to hell.

Tomorrow, he was taking the two most precious things in his dark existence to the darkest realm.

Tomorrow, he would kill a queen if it meant saving them.

TENSLEY EYED THE crowd of worn men and women in front of him. He needed to speak to them. He needed to lift their spirits before he and Molly went to High Court.

He needed to be the leader he hadn't been for them in longer than he dared think about.

The boardroom was silent, all eyes on him as he stood, clearing his throat. His dolcezza had taken the reins while he was away, but this was his duty. His people to look after and he would never abandon them.

He nodded at his brother, Beau, who was standing a few feet away. Upon signal, Beau growled lowly, ever the beast, and the room shushed, all heads turning toward Tensley, waiting.

"Demons, members of Scorpios, I, Dux of Scorpios, stand before you today because we have all suffered greatly. Scorpios has been going through dark times, difficult times. We've been threatened with war and have fought against enemies, and in doing so, we've lost some strong, courageous soldiers from our family. We have also lost innocents. Friends, daughters, sons, husbands, wives, mothers... and like some of you, I share the loss of a father," he began, straightening, his eyes scanning the crowded room.

"Ares succeeded in poisoning some of us from the inside, of forcing some of us to turn on our own, but we fought back. We didn't back down. We, Scorpios, are born with brutal scars marring our skin and we grow up learning to embrace them. Because our scars are what make us stronger, they're what makes us more vicious to our opponents. Defeats and losses are not to be forgotten, buried in shame. They are to be embraced too, just like our scars, so that as a family, we can learn from them, so that together we can learn from them and continue to grow stronger and thrive.

"I may wear the title of king, but I will always be first and foremost a Scorpios. There is no royal blood running through my veins, but there is Scorpios blood running through them, and one can't forget their own blood. It lives within me, feeds my soul and fills the air that I breathe. They can break my bones, bleed me to death, it wouldn't change a thing. I am a Scorpios. I am one of you. No one, no king, no gods, can take what we are away from us. Even in death.

"The men we lost through this war, should be remembered with respect, and honor. We are brothers, we are one, and no grave in hell will change that. We strike, unprovoked!" he roared their motto, and the men and women in the crowed joined in with the same tone.

Tensley paused, rolling his hands into fists beside him. "But with each death comes a birth. A few days ago, we were blessed with one. With a child of Scorpios blood, running deep within him. My son, Illya Salvatore Knight, was born on Friday, February 3rd 2017, only hours after the bloodshed we went through as a family."

The crowd stirred at that, but quieted down.

"He has a heart, a human heart. One that beats and might beat out of love. But he's still a Scorpios. He still possesses our poison, our ruthless blood inside of him and he will be raised beside us. He will be raised like one of us, raised to be the heir. We will grow, we will rebuild, and we will rise like our forefathers.

No other group will rival us. No court will rule us, but ourselves."

The men cheered at that and Tensley turned, leaving the room.

A hand locked on his shoulder and he looked back to see Illya there.

Illya's bloodshot eyes pierced his own.

He didn't need to say a word and pulled him into an embrace.

An embrace of brothers, an embrace speaking so much more than words ever could.

He had given his best friend's name to their son, and Tensley would never regret his decision.

Illya was a warrior. He had gone through so much, had lost so much, but he had come out a survivor, always.

And Tensley would make sure his son grew to admire the man.

He'd grow to be a warrior too.

MOLLY FIXED HER hood again and held baby Illya closer to her chest as they entered the palace.

Tensley stood to her side, his arm brushing against her own. Every so often, he turned to look at her and she knew he was worried. The entire morning he paced, silent, deep in his own thoughts and she hadn't pried. They were going back into the heart of the beast.

The last place she wanted to be, but she'd do this. She'd please the court so they could leave them alone.

But what would happen after? Would they want more from them? Their son was technically the new prince. Would they want him present in court?

She scowled at that.

No, her son would stay with her. Away from the court of filthy snakes and wolves that wanted to feast on their young and dethrone their king.

She shivered at the thought and tightened her grip on Illya who cooed softly, his tiny fists curled to his chest.

Tensley's fingertips stroked the back of her hand and she glanced up at him. He stared, his features drawn into a blank expression, but it was his touch that told her he was there. They were together and he wouldn't let anything happen to them.

She smiled faintly back at him.

As they neared the throne room, Molly heard the court's voices—raised, powerful—and she remembered the day they banished her. She would walk in those doors next to her husband, their king, and her newborn son in her arms.

They had tried to damn her, destroy what little relationship she had left with Tensley, but she had risen and now she stood above them.

Seto stood at the double doors, his hands clenched behind his back and his head bowed as they approached.

His stern expression softened at the sound of the baby cooing, his arms waving slightly and Molly smiled at Seto.

She stopped in front of him and pushed back the white blanket wrapped around Illya, showing him the sleepy baby.

Seto didn't touch him, but he stared, slowly taking him in. "He's a fighter."

Illya grunted back and searched for her breast, growing irritated. Molly stroked his chubby cheeks.

When she stole a look at Seto, she saw the desire for the same thing. He wanted a child; he wanted to have a family with Prim. After everything they had been though, she hoped they would. They deserved to finally be happy.

"How's Prim," she asked with a worried frown.

Seto's eyes turned sad, heavy. "She… she's doing a bit better. Slowly, we are… we are getting there."

The court roared behind the doors and Molly scowled. "The beasts are restless, aren't they?"

Tensley placed a hand on the small of her back and glared at the doors. "They want to see him. Once they do, hopefully they will settle down."

Molly's lips thinned. She doubted that, but she figured Tensley was saying that to comfort her.

"Let's go," she told him, as she was now the restless one. She wanted this over with so they could go back home. She stole one last precious look at her baby and kissed his cheeks. It was terrifying how much influence, how much power this baby had over a court of thirsty demons.

"If…" Seto said, sounding hurried. "If anything was to happen. If any of you was to be in danger, I wanted you to know that you can count on me. To help you, to protect you."

Tensley nodded, his eyes saying the words he didn't.

He was grateful. Molly knew deep down that Tensley, no matter how strong he was, would take any help he could get to protect them, to protect his family.

Seto nodded back, then his eyes shifted to the guards on either side of the doors and they moved, pushing the heavy iron doors open.

The court hushed.

Molly stared at the throne room, glistening in gold touches and white marble slabs, eyeing the demons that lined each side of the aisle, leading down to the thrones.

She eyed Lilith and the prince at the end, standing opposite to Tensley and her.

Molly breathed out deeply, straightening her back in front of the court.

She wasn't afraid of them anymore.

She was the daemon and she would bow to no one.

Especially Lilith.

Tensley's hand, still warm on her back stroked once and then he moved them forward.

Together, with their infant son, the two of them, side by side, walked with ease and grace down the aisle.

Every single demon watched them in silence. No one cheered, no one spoke as they moved, her gown whispering across the marble floor.

Illya snuggled against her breast; completely unaware of the danger he was surrounded by.

As they neared the two golden thrones, Tensley's fingers tightened against her. She eyed Lilith, her gaze unwavering and Lilith didn't look away.

The prince stood further to the side, one gloved hand gripping the handle of his sword, an indifferent expression across his features. Tensley had brought a babe to court, his son, a future heir, and the prince was forced to stay on the sidelines, waiting yet again for his chance at the throne.

She wondered if the prince still held true to his promise. If once she returned the beasts' heart, he would receive the throne.

But if Tensley gave up the throne now how would they protect themselves from the court? He seemed to believe his only way out was through death. But Tensley had the power to bend rules, rules including his own heart, now beating against her back like a constant reminder he was there.

"My king," Lilith said, her eyes shifting to Tensley and she curtsied, lowering, but her head never bowing, her gaze never parting from his.

Slowly, she raised, a ghost of a smile playing on her lips. "We are pleased of your return."

Tensley simply stayed silent, his jaw locked tight and his hand massaging Molly's back. She wondered if touching her was more to calm him.

Illya cooed and Molly looked down at him, cooing back, swaying him a few times to calm him also.

When she realized how silent the court was she looked up to find Lilith staring at the child with a frown.

"Is that the child?" Lilith asked, turning her attention to Tensley.

"Our son," he told her with a bite to his words. "You wish to anoint and present him to the court."

She nodded once, her eyes returning to the baby in Molly's arms. She stared far longer than Molly was comfortable with and a flash of something dark glinted in her eyes.

A look Molly did not trust.

chapter thirty

LILITH SNAPPED HER fingers; startling Molly and a man came forward, carrying a bowl of holy water.

The man bowed in front of the two of them, his hands quivering as the porcelain white bowl shook, the water splashing.

Lilith hissed at him as she took the bowl and he bowed again, stepping away. Slowly, Lilith turned to them and smiled.

"We will anoint the heir of High Court, to bless him with steel bones and an iron soul. To wash him in our sins so he absorbs them into his new flesh and to be reborn a beast. May he honor Sonolios and chase his maiden into the darkness. May his blood be a sign of cruelty, not compassion," she recited, her voice loud and strong, echoing against the high cathedral ceilings.

Molly swallowed, fixing her grip on her baby and watching Lilith carefully. Each step she took, Molly's stomach tightened to the point of pain.

When she stood right in front of them, her gaze piercing Molly's, she gestured to Illya.

"Hand me the child," Lilith demanded. "His skin cannot be tainted by you anymore."

Molly gritted her teeth and gave her a sour look.

Murmurs filled the room, the court watching, waiting for one to move, one to strike.

Tensley stepped forward, half-blocking Molly and lifted his hand. "I will do it."

Molly breathed out shakily at that and watched as Lilith begrudgingly handed over the bowl. She flashed Molly one final look and stepped back.

Tensley turned to face her, his large hands holding the porcelain bowl, the water wetting the tips of his tanned fingers.

He edged forward, towering over her, the baby in-between their two frames and bent his head over hers.

"This is simply blessed water. Nothing that will harm our baby," he whispered to her and her shoulders relaxed. She glanced up at him through her lashes, seeing his bowed head, his dark hair falling over his eyes as he stared down at their son.

She wanted to kiss him then, the desire so strong she had to bite the inside of her cheek and tasted the iron blood.

Slowly, he lifted one hand and dipped his fingers in the water. She watched the water ripple gently, and just as slowly, he lifted them out, droplets of water sticking to his fingertips.

His hand moved and it hovered above Illya's dark hair. A few droplets fell onto his forehead and he wiggled in her arms. Gently, Tensley's fingers descended and smoothed across his son's forehead. The droplets rolled down his head, drenching his hair.

"Awaken the ruthless beast, to bless his bones and his blood with iron and steel, and to soak him in the sins of our fathers," he spoke, lowly, but with the dead silence of the court, every single member heard him clearly. One single stroke of his wet fingers on his forehead and he let his hand drop. "I'll take him."

Molly met his calm dark eyes and she felt the thunder deep inside of her. One look and she was his once again.

She passed the baby into his strong arms and he cradled him, without an ounce of worry when Illya cried out at the sudden movement. But soon he calmed, clinging to his father and turned to face the court, displaying the son of their king.

Each member bowed, a wave of men and women crouching to their knees and lowering their heads in respect.

Two people, however, didn't bow.

Lilith and the prince.

Molly's chest felt heavy at the mere sight of the demons on their knees in front of her husband and her son.

Tensley turned and came to her side, his head jerking to the side. "Come."

Molly frowned but followed him as he marched beyond the thrones and to the balcony, situated at the front of the stone palace.

As soon as they entered into the sunlight, the thick crowd below them roared so loudly Molly flinched.

The wind blew her hair in front of her face and her heart raced, eyeing the excited crowd.

"They came to see him," he told her, stroking Illya's back. When she glanced at him, he was watching her, his head lowered next to their son's. "The son of a demon and a daemon."

With that, he lifted Illya and the crowd roared, throwing their arms up. The power of their cheers vibrated through Molly.

The power their son already held, the fascination he generated in people, astonished her, but also made her stomach twist painfully tight.

Tensley cradled him back into his arms and when they turned away, he swept a kiss onto his forehead. A forbidden gesture, but it melted her heart until she could hardly breathe.

Illya stirred, whining and his eyes fluttered.

Molly glanced quickly up at Lilith, only a few steps away and simply gauging her expression told her what she feared.

Lilith had seen his rare blue eyes.

"His eyes," Lilith said, so loud the entire room behind her grew silent. "He's a daemon. He has the daemon eyes."

Tensley's jaw squared. "Yes, he is. Half demon, half daemon."

Lilith couldn't look away from the infant in his arms and it made Molly's stomach tighten in worry.

Tensley glared at Lilith and continued to move down the aisle, Molly at his side.

She'd protect them both.

With her life.

TENSLEY EYED EACH court member that dared to near him and his family. Lilith had insisted on yet another banquet, justifying it as a celebration of Illya's anointing. All he wanted to do was get Molly and their son home safe. The longer they stayed, the more dangerous the situation became.

Lilith appeared all sweet, but he wasn't a stupid man. He knew she hadn't forgotten about their last conversation.

It didn't look like she had told the court about the curse just yet, but he wouldn't put it past her to announce it when he and his close family were present.

He would protect them though. No one would approach them without his approval.

He watched as the prince sat across from him, his eyes dark with an anger that boiled beneath his skin.

Illya whined in Molly's arms. She was sitting beside him and at the sound, she brought him close to her face, speaking to him softly.

"Is he okay?" Tensley asked, lowly, his gaze fixated on the surrounding tables—of the members chatting between themselves, stealing glances at the high table.

Molly cooed at the baby. "I think he's just sleepy."

His hand crept onto her thigh and squeezed. "Both of you need rest."

She scowled at him, but her hand underneath the table squeezed his back. "Are you staying here?"

He clenched his jaw. "I'm not sure. I should."

She nodded, but he knew it tore her up inside, just as it did him.

"I'd give anything to fall asleep beside you each night," he whispered, stroking up her thigh and he felt her shudder under his touch.

He looked over at her and he could tell by the soft look in her eyes, she wanted to kiss him, to touch his cheek, but she held herself back. In front of the court, he was the beast, never the man.

But behind closed doors, he was hers.

Beast and man.

Completely.

Sinfully.

Hers.

Illya fussed and Molly sighed. "I think he's getting hungry, too. I'm going to go to your bedchamber to feed him, okay?"

Tensley pushed out of his chair. "I'll escort you."

Molly fought a smile forming on her mouth and he helped her stand, placing a hand on the small of her back. They stepped off the platform and moved toward the hallway.

"My king," Lilith's voice disturbed his thoughts and he looked to see her approach them. Her eyes went to the baby fussing in Molly's arms. "The members and I would like to see the baby. To judge for ourselves what power he holds."

Tensley's grip tightened and he glowered at her. "There will be no need. He is my son. Therefore, he is the prince."

Molly pressed the baby to her chest, not hiding her scowl.

Lilith smiled thinly. "If you wish to keep that crown upon your head, you will hand over the baby." She stretched out her hands and stepped forward.

Molly glared at her hands for a long moment and then shook her head. "You're not touching my son."

The crowd had quieted at the vicious sound of Molly's voice.

Lilith's smile twitched and she shook her hands out. "You will. You are not above this court. You are not above me."

"I am the king," Tensley hissed, stepping in front of Molly, guarding, shielding her from this fucking nonsense. "I am above you, and I say no. You are not touching our son."

"You are nothing but a mere pawn in my court. You hold no real power over these people, over me, and you know it," Lilith snapped. "I may have viewed you as a worthy king once, a worthy mate, but I can hear that wicked heart inside of you pounding, beating and it sickens me. It disturbs me how my dead husband ripped your iron heart out months ago and she's already infected you again. How fast you fall, how fast you bow to a whore, to a traitor." Her eyes shifted past him, but he moved so she couldn't see Molly. He felt the rage wrap around his throat and wrists, chaining him to the spot. He wanted to rip her head off. He wanted to shred her to bits and pieces.

"Back down," he barked, barring his teeth.

"The beast, your wicked-so-called king," Lilith said, so loudly, for every single member of court to hear, "has a heart. It pounds viciously inside of him, weakening him, making him crave things a demon should not. If he rules us, if he leads us, he will force us to damnation and disgrace. Think of your slaves, think of the filth that lives outside the walls of this castle. Workers, commoners, outsiders. They are no better than this king. What will they think if they see him ruling over us? What kind of image of us will this give them? That we are weak, that we are not above them, that our blood doesn't run purer than theirs. They will revolt against us, they will seek more power. We must not let them, we must not keep a king that reflects badly on our lineage, on our blood and prestige. "

The crowd murmured, casting glares his way.

She was turning them against him. She wanted him to bow down, to submit. He wouldn't. Not when he needed as much power as possible to protect his family.

"Within this reformed beast lives a heart that must be destroyed at once, for if it is, his life will be forever ended," she snapped and lunged.

He braced himself, lowering so she slammed against his shoulder and he shoved her back.

They propelled into the marble slabs, breaking under their powerful bodies and she scratched him deep across his cheek.

He shoved himself off the ground, the crowd parted on either side. He stole a glance toward Molly and saw Seto had gone to her side, protecting her in case any members got an idea to attack her.

But he knew she could hold her own.

Unlike the court. They had no idea what power rumbled beneath her bones.

Lilith, in her silky gown, held her head high, her delicate hands fisting beside her. "May the one to kill the king come out victorious once and for all," she roared.

"You want the beast," he roared back, rolling his shoulders back, the power thumping through him like a lightning bolt. "You can have him."

He moved—fast, uncontrollable, and struck—over and over—her body warring against his, slashing her nails across his stomach, his chest. Digging deep so she reached bones and muscles and tore.

"Tensley," he heard Molly gasp.

And then he gasped as Lilith dug deep into his chest—and clenched his heart.

Fuck.

If someone is to rip your heart out once again, you will die. You will not come back.

And now the queen of snakes had her hand wrapped around his pumping heart.

The fucking curse rippled through his mind. If she did, if she clenched his heart even tighter and pulled back, he'd be dead.

His heart pounded faster.

chapter
thirty-one

MOLLY'S OWN HEART clenched in horror as Lilith punctured Tensley's chest. Seto gripped her arm and held her back.

It was all too familiar.

She had seen the exact same thing happen before her very eyes only months ago.

Only this wasn't Fallen, this was Lilith.

And the man she loved would die if his heart were ripped out once more.

"Do not move," Seto hissed back at her.

Molly dug her nails into his back and gritted her teeth.

All the color left Tensley's face and he stood stiffly, and the fierce beast was now caged.

"Ah, your heart is strong," Lilith hummed and Tensley's brow furrowed in pain as her hand moved inside his chest. He tensed when her fingers squeezed.

"One small move and your iron heart is mine, little pawn. Forever and always."

The crowd grew deadly silent, witnessing the chance of their king's death.

Molly couldn't catch her breath and Illya cried in her ear. Panic clawed inside of her.

She had just got him back and now their future was threatened once again.

"Rip it out," Tensley snapped at her, the beast peeking from his dark gaze.

Lilith straightened her back and sneered at him. "I thought I would reign over your beast, but she has already destroyed him. Tamed him so he wields to only her sweet voice. Your son—your son is a daemon and a demon. He has potential and the court has agreed…that he will rule. That I will raise him and nurture him into a true beast. Any member of high court would tell you, a king's son is never his. He belongs to the court, and only the court can choose of his fate Just ask my son," she said with a wicked smile.

Tensley snarled at her.

She clenched his heart again and his entire body seized, his hands rolling into fists beside him.

"Mother," the prince hissed, moving into Molly's line of sight. He edged closer, one hand lifted slightly as if to reach out and touch her.

"Stand down," Lilith hissed at her son, her eyes swinging to him. "I will reign."

The prince scowled at her.

"Hand me the baby," Lilith spoke, her eyes focused on Tensley before her.

Molly frowned, bringing Illya to her chest as he grunted. She wouldn't give up her son, but Tensley…

Warmth gathered in her eyes.

When Molly didn't budge, Lilith squeezed Tensley's heart so tight he screamed out in white-hot pain.

Molly flinched as the baby cried.

"Bring me the baby or I'll rip his heart out," she snapped, her pear white teeth barred in anger. "And you can well and truly say good bye to your fairytale, little whore."

Molly stared at Lilith before she slowly glanced at Tensley.

He looked back at her, sweat building on his ruthless, heavy brows and on his top lip.

Tensley's gaze struck her deep to her core, to a place only he lived inside of and she clenched her jaw, aching to cry out in anger, pain and rage.

A look so soft, so tender even a beast would be moved.

A look that asked for forgiveness.

A look only one who knew they would die would give to the one they loved.

His wrath lurked beneath the surface, but his heart was there. Full and powerful and beautiful and in the hands of a monster.

"Don't move, Molly," he told her, his voice low, husky, everything she loved and craved. "Don't hand over our son, Molly. Never. I'll… I'd die for the both of you."

She glared at him and before she could speak, Lilith snarled back at him.

"Give me him!" Lilith roared, all the blood rushing to her face, the veins in her neck bulging in rage.

Molly glared at her, unable to move, unable to breathe, and the baby continued to sob.

Lilith snarled, stomping a foot and looked toward the crowd. "Take the baby from her. Now!"

For a moment, no one moved. Then a guard stepped forward, marching to Molly with determination.

Molly felt the icy sensation—deep inside of her veins, inside of her core and once the guard entered into her line of sight, inches away from her, she snapped.

Her eyes glowed and the guard stopped mid-step, his muscles freezing, his leg straining to move against her power.

But she wouldn't let him.

She took one step forward and raised her head, her eyes drilling into his and he lowered, onto his knees, grunting, groaning as she controlled his movements.

The crowd grew loud with murmurs and Lilith glared at the guard.

"Stand!" she commanded him, but he shook his head, unable to move, unable to speak. "Useless piece of trash, stand!" she roared again.

"He can't," Molly bit out.

Lilith barred her teeth. "Get her. Now!"

More guards moved toward her, but each time they neared Molly, she summoned that icy strength, forcing them to kneel in front of her.

She moved another step closer.

"You will remove your hand from around my husband's heart," Molly demanded, her voice soft, but with an edge of a threat no one could miss. "And you will kneel before us."

Lilith snapped her head back to Tensley and gripped hard, a brutal cry escaping his lips.

"Stay where you are, whore. Or I'll rip his precious heart out," Lilith said, watching Tensley's pain stricken face. "And I'll devour it in front of you." She licked her lips, as if she was imagining how it would taste. "Just like Fallen would have done."

Tensley caught Molly's gaze. "Stand down."

Molly shook her head, the icy sensation overwhelming her senses. She was on a warpath and she wanted blood.

"Hand over the baby," Lilith snapped once again, her footing becoming restless the more Molly neared, the more Molly stopped each guard summoned.

Only a few more steps and she'd be right in front of her.

"You tried to destroy us, you tried to ruin us," Molly spoke, fisting her hands beside her. "But you failed. Time and time again. I will never leave his side. I will never give up my son. Someone once told me that when none of the options sounded appealing, to create your own," she said, her eyes briefly falling upon the prince.

"His heart is mine," Lilith hissed and began to tug at Tensley's chest. Tensley's body shook in pain and Molly paused, her breath catching in her throat. "I am the queen. I am the queen of High Court and you hold no power over me, you fucking whore."

Molly smiled faintly and tilted her head to the side, her eyes still glowing vividly. "I am the queen and I will bow to no one. Including you. A viper like you. You may have venom Lilith, but so do I. Let's see whose venom is the more poisonous."

Sweat pooled on Lilith's forehead and her hands shook, but Molly could sense she was losing it. But she had to treat her like a cornered wild animal. One wrong move and she'd rip his heart out without a second thought.

Molly looked over at Tensley and his eyes were dark with the need to be brutal. To unleash the beast.

Just as Lilith tugged—Tensley gripped her jaw and snapped it to the side, forcing her to meet Molly's powerful gaze.

And Lilith froze, her mouth parting, her eyes widening—slipping under Molly's control.

Her hands went limp and Molly moved—

Lilith gasped, her body arching as someone plunged their own hand into her chest.

But it wasn't Molly's. And it wasn't Tensley's.

Prim stood behind Lilith, covered in her blood. Lilith's deformed beating heart gripped in her delicate hand.

"Sweet fucking dreams, Lilith. I hope they'll rip you apart in hell," Prim said with a tone so low, so menacing, so full of wrath.

Molly had never heard such an emotion coming from Prim and she wondered if she had dreamt it all.

Where she had come from, she didn't know. But she had a wild, dangerous look in her eyes.

The look of a woman who had been ruined and had grown a thirst for vengeance.

The prince moved fast, his boots stomping against the marble slabs and his hand slid across Lilith's limp neck and he crushed it—slowly, carefully, so every bone shattered into pieces.

"Goodbye mother," the prince hissed as he glared into her dull eyes.

The sound resounded in the room, as a heavy silence reigned over them all.

A stunned silence.

A relieved silence.

The court of snakes had one less viper amongst its troops, but she had no doubt that more would come.

More would show themselves now that the loudest was dead, someone else would take their lead.

Tensley yanked Lilith's hand from his chest, stumbling slightly as he held a palm over the hole.

Molly caught Tensley's arm and he instantly pulled her into his embrace, Illya crying between them.

Tensley kissed her mouth once—twice—again and again, his breath uneven, her own heart racing deep within.

"I'm sorry. I'm so, so, so sorry for bringing the both you into this, dolcezza," he kept repeating over and over, his head shaking.

"Shh…" Molly said, but the adrenaline was quickly leaving her body and she was starting to shake violently. "It's okay, we're… we're okay. We're okay."

When he wiped at her cheeks, she hadn't realized she'd been crying and smiled weakly up at him.

"We're okay, dolcezza," he whispered and kissed her.

When they broke apart, they gazed at the silent court.

Lilith's dead body lay sprawled across the broken marble slabs. Her gowns slowly turning a darker shade of red as her blood pooled.

The prince ran a bloody hand along his trousers and stared back at the two of them. She couldn't believe he had snapped his own mother's neck, but he had kept his promise. He had protected them.

Slowly, each member, both men and women, lowered to their knees in front of them.

Tensley's hand snaked around her wrist and squeezed between them and Molly gawked at the submission, at the bowing of the court to them.

TENSLEY STOOD BY the window as Molly nursed Illya. They had bathed together after the fight and the court was in a moment of quietness. Tensley had yet to tell Molly what he planned, but he thought it would be best for both of them.

Molly had summoned a healer and after the healer did as much as he could, Molly healed him with soft, sweet kisses and touches. He still felt sore, but he was alive and his iron heart still beat proudly inside of him.

As Molly fixed her dress and patted the baby's back against her shoulder, a knock came at the door.

"Come in," Tensley said.

The door opened and the prince walked in, bowing slightly, a look of indifference across his features.

"You summoned me, Knight?" he asked, his tone low and controlled.

"I have summoned you to discuss a personal matter," Tensley said, stepping forward. When the prince raised a brow, Tensley continued. "I no longer want the throne."

Molly's eyes snapped to him, widening.

The prince's jaw tightened.

"I have more important matters to focus on than a court," Tensley told him, his eyes darting to Molly and the baby for a split second. "I have been toying with the idea for a while now, but I didn't want to leave the position until I could find someone who I trusted to replace me. What good would it make if I replaced one tyrant for another. I wish for a better world for my son. A better world for demons. And I think you and I have very similar goals and wants."

The prince's hands rolled into fists at his side and he breathed out heavily.

"I only have two conditions. First, is for you and your court to leave my family alone. I will rule Scorpios, and you don't try and meddle in my business. You get your kingdom of beasts and I get Scorpios, my family. Neither of us rules over the other. Second, you revoke the law your father created about the heart of a demon. I trust you to be much more imaginative with your punishments," he said with a wry smile. "If you can agree to those terms, then the court, the throne, and the crown are yours."

The prince worked his jaw, scanning Tensley. After a long moment, he spoke. "You wish to give up the power for...her?"

Tensley's eyes moved to Molly who watched him closely, and his heart clenched tight. He looked back at the prince. "I would give anything up if it meant I could stay with them."

The prince nodded once at that and looked over at her. Tensley noted the look on his face. One of longing. The prince didn't want his dolcezza, but perhaps that same fierceness Tensley felt for her.

"You forget one very important detail however, Knight," he said, and when

r. scarlett

Tensley only looked at him, the prince's lips turned into a feral smile. "One must kill the king to become king. How does that play out in your master plan, huh?"

Tensley's smile became twin to the prince's. "I know men like you. I've seen them around. You're a wicked son of a bitch, I have no doubt you'll make the court kneel before you, whether you kill me or not. You're a born hunter, you love the chase, so hunt your kingdom down, and take it as your own. It's yours now. Your blood, your destiny, claim your rights and change the rules of the game. "

The prince's smile, grew more vicious, and something dark and wicked flashed in his eyes, before he clapped Tensley on the back. "I accept," the prince said. "You will not be disturbed by this court. I'll make sure of it."

Tensley nodded curtly. "Good. Let's announce it to the snakes then, shall we?"

The prince moved, stealing one last look at Molly. "It was a pleasure meeting you, little daemon. I shall be forever saddened I was not able to have a taste, as I'm sure you are delectable," he said as his eyes fell to her full breasts, tongue briefly licking his bottom lip. When Tensley growled deeply, the prince laughed, the sound resonating around them as he shook his head and left the room.

"Tensley?" Molly stood from the bed, her eyes wide. "You gave up the throne, the power. For us."

Tensley smoothed a hand across her cheek and into her hair. Then his head dropped toward hers and he kissed her lips. "I would do anything for you, dolcezza."

Molly smiled tearfully, and the baby cooed. Tensley leaned down and kissed his forehead.

"You are my court, my crown, my queen. Family above all else. That is all that matters to me," Tensley whispered and held them close, letting her feel the beat of his heart. "You have well and truly tamed the beast. Forever."

306

epilogue

one year later...

LLYA GIGGLED AS he crawled across the hardwood floors, determined to escape. Molly laughed and bent down, picking him up.

"You silly boy," she said and gave him a wet kiss on the cheek.

He only laughed more.

"He's a handful, just like his father," Daphne said as she grabbed a bowl of chips and avocados. She squeezed his cheek and he smiled up at his grandma. "I can't believe he's one today. He's grown so fast."

Molly swayed him as he perched on her hip. Their little warrior had grown up fast indeed. He was tall and chubby and had the sweetest dark curls on his head. His eyes—were just like hers and when he grew frustrated, they would shine bright.

At first when it would happen, Molly would try to teach him to calm down, to control his emotions, but he was still so young, it was almost impossible. So instead, she had found another solution. When he would do it, she'd flash her own eyes at him and it would make him laugh, his chubby little belly rumbling with the sound, and he'd forget he was ever frustrated about something. She knew she had plenty of time to teach him how to control his powers.

"Speaking of which where's his father?" Daphne asked, but still kept her complete attention on Illya. It was his strongest trait, one he had inherited from his father. He could capture everyone's attention in a room just with his presence.

Molly rubbed her cheek against his. "He's in his office finishing up some work before the party. I told him to be down here by five."

Daphne arched a brow. "That man is going to work himself to death," she said, and rolled her eyes. "And he keeps telling me he isn't like his father."

Molly examined Daphne's sad smile. She still missed her husband, and Molly knew that Daphne liked seeing Salvatore in their children, because it meant that in a way, he was still there, with her, beside her, through all the trials and hardships of life.

And Molly knew their child wasn't very different. She had caught Tensley staring at old family portraits of his dad a few times. He would only ever frown and wouldn't say anything, but Molly knew the pain was deeply nestled inside.

"I'll go get him," Molly said and gestured to Illya. "Do you mind holding him?"

Daphne grinned and shook her head. "Come to Grandma."

Illya willingly went into her arms, but he frowned as his mother walked away. He was attached to her and his father. It had been a struggle to get him to sleep in his own crib at first because he was so used to sleeping between both of his parents, snuggled tight. But Tensley felt they needed their own time together, that they needed their own space.

Molly was hesitant at first, worried their son might need her and she wouldn't be close to him.

But when Tensley had reminded her all the things they could do when the baby wasn't lying in their bed with them, Molly had eventually agreed to his demands.

But not without being very, thoroughly convinced first.

Molly smiled at the thought as she walked up the stairs of the summer cottage out in Cape Cod, eying the pictures of their wedding. Tensley had kept the promise he made before their wedding in High Court. He married her again in Manhattan, in a church, with a small crowd of their closest friends and family.

That had been five months ago.

September and Stella stood beside her and they would have came today for Illya's birthday, but Stella was beginning her Masters Degree in Law and September was backpacking in Europe for the summer.

Molly walked down the hallway and knocked once on his office door. His gruff response told her he was pissed off about something. She entered, smiling at him bent over his desk, papers scattered everywhere.

"You're late," she whispered.

His stormy gaze snapped up to her and he fell back into his leather seat, a hand going to his forehead. "Fuck, I'm sorry. I got caught up."

She perched on the side of his desk, crossing her legs.

"What will the guests think if their Dux is late to his own son's birthday party?" she asked, lips in pout. Then, mischief flashed in her eyes as she eyed him, as delicious as always in his tight, perfectly tailored suit. "On second thought, we could take advantage of the situation. You're already late anyway and your mother is taking care of the baby," she added, shrugging. "You, in that sexy suit. Me, spread out for you to feast on. A few minutes of bliss on your desk," she finished, and she almost sounded innocent. Almost.

His eyes went to her legs and his jaw ticked. "Oh you little temptress... Don't give me ideas now, dolcezza. With everyone downstairs, we'd have a hell of a hard time finding a kid friendly explanation as to why our guests could hear you screaming my name all the way from the office."

Molly's smile grew, then she shrugged again, falsely nonchalant. "You'd probably ruin my makeup anyway, and I spent a long time doing it. Might as well forget the idea."

Tensley's own smile turned feral. "Indeed."

She shrugged, smiling down at him. "You do it all the time."

He stood, stuffing his hands into his pockets, his jacket pulling back to reveal his fit body underneath. He stepped in front of her, his fingertips skimming her thighs. "Tonight, in here. You don't get to make suggestions like that one and not go through with them, dolcezza," he said, and his tone made her clench her thighs.

"Oh?" she cocked a brow and grinned at him, kissing his jaw. "Do I also get to decide how you take me? From behind maybe? We could let the beast have a little playtime," she went on a seductive whisper.

He growled and gripped her hips, forcing her to stand. "As you wish."

He kissed her softly, thoroughly, feeling across her cheekbones.

There was something she wanted to tell him, something she had been desperate to tell him for a little while now but was waiting for the right moment to do so.

But it wasn't now, not yet. She'd wait.

She would wait until tonight.

TENSLEY DRAGGED THE cigar from his mouth and let the smoke pass through his lips. Outside in the summer night, members of Scorpios and his family gathered in the darkness. Lights sprawled overhead and laughter echoed.

The men spoke of High Court. Of the prince's reign and the gossip of him claiming a woman as his and creating a scandal.

Politics and gossip that didn't matter to him anymore.

He did his job. All that mattered to him was coming home to Molly and his son.

He eyed them across the lawn as Molly held him on her hip. She had been a natural with Illya and every second he was home, he spent it with his son and her.

He never wanted to miss a moment and deciding to give up the throne had been the best decision he had made. He wouldn't have been able to see his family.

He would have missed so much and that made his chest heavy.

Gabriella stood next to Molly, her own Isabella on her opposite hip and Donovan moved between their legs, playing a game by himself. Senior Illya approached the group and smiled at Donovan, pretending to grab him. Illya had been a constant in their son's life, especially after the death of his own mother. He overheard Molly telling him he was always welcomed to stay with them. That he was family.

Tensley couldn't have agreed more.

Months had passed since the High Court and the passion between him and Molly hadn't died down.

The last couple of weeks though she had seemed strangely quiet when he came home at night. She seemed tired and he kissed her until she fell asleep, getting up through the night to soothe Illya when he cried.

He sometimes envied his son—for the childhood he knew he would have compared to his own. All he had known was a childhood of pain and horror. Illya's childhood would be his mother's sweet kisses and her soft laughter and snuggles.

"You're staring," Beau said beside him, taking another drag from his own belladonna, a demon drug. Both of them stood underneath the giant willow trees, away from the rest of the men.

"Yes, I am," he snapped back. He wasn't ashamed to say he enjoyed watching his wife.

Lex moved toward Molly, not before stealing an angry glance at the two of them in the shadows.

Tensley worked his jaw. "What did you fuck up now?"

Beau snarled. "I didn't do shit." He took another drag and glared at Lex as she turned to face Molly and hugged her, then kissing Illya. "I would just destroy her."

Tensley fought a grin. "Maybe she wants that."

"She deserves better than me," he hissed out. "You know what I am, how I am."

When the beast had ruled over Tensley, he had went through some dark times. But it could never be compared to the kind of hell his brother self-inflicted.

He had been through hell, had been scarred by the past events and years later, he was still recovering, painfully slowly. He hadn't had a Molly to heal him to curse him. But it seemed obvious to Tensley that Lex wanted to be Beau's Molly. She wanted to help him, to help him through it. If only he'd let her and stop his own self-destruction…

A man in his twenties, young but with a self-confidence to him—a soldier of Scorpios approached the group of men and gestured to Lex. Lex broke out in a smile. She went into the man's arms and he wrapped one of them protectively over one of her shoulders, whispering something in her ear. Whatever he said, it made Lex's smile grow even more as she looked back at him with a secret look.

Tensley waited for it with a wry expression, waited for what he knew was about to come. And sure enough; it happened.

Beau growled lowly, the dark, animalistic sound ripping through him with a force Tensley knew oh too well.

"Territorial, I see," Tensley said on a laugh.

"Shut the fuck up," Beau snapped.

The man and Lex spoke, her smile brightening. Beau growled again, his eyes growing dark.

"That bastard better fucking stop touching her," Beau snapped and stomped off toward her.

Tensley watched, amused as his brother wedged himself between Lex and the soldier. The soldier glared at Beau and words were exchanged. Tensley eyed Beau's clenching and unclenching hands at his side. He was going to destroy that poor bastard.

Lex stepped in-between and spoke to both of them, not before giving Beau a death glare that would surely freeze hell over. The man backed up, shaking his head and moved away. Lex said something to Beau and scowled at him, until she too walked away.

Beau, being a Knight, marched on after her.

Tensley smirked.

The party continued, the men chatting him up about the politics in Scorpios. Once Ares was dead, Scorpios had moved in and claimed that territory. Scorpios was massive now—with hundreds of men under his command.

As the party died down, people went home or retired to the house. It was then Tensley noted Molly and Illya were missing.

He searched the lawn and found nothing. When he went into the house and upstairs, he heard Molly's soft voice speaking to their son.

He tiptoed down the hall, opening the door to the nursery to find her rocking him in her arms, fast asleep.

Tensley moved slowly and when she caught his movement, she turned to him and smiled.

Tensley took their son in his arms and kissed his temple, stirring him awake slightly.

"My little warrior," he whispered and brushed finger's over the dark curls on his head.

He walked to the crib and gently placed him down, watching him settle into the mattress, a tiny, chubby arm sprawled over his head.

Tensley turned back around and slid his hands down Molly's sides, resting on her delicious hips. "Tonight, dolcezza, you're mine."

Molly giggled, the sound vibrating against his own chest. "Take me, Mr. Knight. Take your wife."

He growled, playfully, and bent, gripping her ass cheeks and lifting her up. She bit back a laugh. He walked them to the master bedroom, dropping her down onto the bed.

Her hands pulled at his belt. "Impatient?" he asked with a sinful smile.

She glared at him through her lashes. "Get naked."

He smirked, and helped her, throwing his belt to the ground and yanking down his pants.

His erection sprung free and she stroked him with one fist, licking the tip with her tongue.

He hissed, fisting her hair into a makeshift ponytail.

His hands ripped the buttons of her dress, revealing her full breasts and he yanked her panties to the side.

As soon as he touched her folds, he felt how wet she was. "Fuck, you're soaking wet around my fingers." He stroked deeply, her wetness drenching his fingers. Unable to resist, he brought one to his mouth and sucked it clean, growling appreciatively at the sweet taste of her.

He would never get enough.

"Oh god," she gasped and arched her back as his hand came back to her, caressing where her pleasure pulsed eagerly and her hand tightened on his cock.

"You want me inside of you?" he asked, his voice hard and dark, so full of lust.

She nodded viciously, rolling her bottom lip between her teeth.

He moved closer, forcing her thighs to spread open wide for him and bent. His cock touched her wet sex and he growled, his fingers biting into her thighs. He thrust fast and hard and she muffled her cries with the back of her palm. He took her hand away, wanting to hear all her sounds, all her cries and pleas. He wanted all of her. He wanted to consume her and devour her.

And with that thought, he pounded deeper, more roughly inside her, her full breasts moving to their harsh rhythm. He came down, taking one into his mouth, and biting a little harder than he usually would.

She had wanted to tempt him earlier that day with her seductive offers, she'd get what she deserved for that little stunt.

When she cried out from the bite, he smoothed out his tongue on her nipple, running it around and sucking once more.

He could feast on her skin for days and never grow hungry.

He knew he wouldn't last much longer. His balls tightened and her tightness clenched around his angry length.

"I'm gonna come inside," he warned her and he saw the glint of want flash in her eyes. That stirred the fucking beast. "Want me to claim your womb again?"

She groaned, arching her back and wrapped her legs around his hips. At his words, she clenched his cock harder, as if to trap him inside.

"Fuck," he hissed and kissed her panting mouth. "I want you pregnant. I want you full and swollen with my child again. To let those beasts know you're mine and will always be mine."

She gasped, moaning and nodding her head frantically. "You already have Tensley. You already have," she gasped, the words wrapped with a thick layer of bliss and uncontrollable pleasure as he kept thrusting fast, raising her hips so he could go deeper.

They both groaned at the new angle, the new depth.

But a frown marred Tensley's face. "What do you mean 'I already have'?" he panted, his own climax so close, as she kept tightening around him, squeezing him to death.

"I'm pregnant, Tensley," she said, eyes clenched tight as she too grew incredibly close to her blissful end.

And just like that, he exploded, the rush of pure pleasure overtaking him. His cock pulsed and soon his warmth spilled inside of her—deep and tight.

He stayed there, letting his essence root inside of her as her own pleasure exploded within her. His face came down once more, kissing her breasts as she relaxed.

He combed a few wet strands from her forehead and she gazed up at him. "What did you say?" he asked, and he had the biggest smile on his lips.

A shy, but happy smile took to hers. "I'm pregnant," she repeated.

Before Illya's birth, he had been worried he'd have to carve out space of his heart for his son.

But as soon as he had seen the wrinkled, little bundle of joy, he had realized he didn't need to make any room for his son. Because the heart didn't have any restraints. It grew. It simply grew bigger and bigger the more someone loved.

And as he kissed her slowly, lovingly, his heart grew a bit more. Growing for the tiny baby that grew within his wife. The child he already loved and would love until the day he died and hell would claim him.

His hand fell to her flat stomach and he rubbed it. "I love you," he whispered into the darkness.

When he looked into her eyes, they were bloodshot and her bottom lip shook. "I love you."

His hand felt over her collar, her body shuddering beneath him and his cock hardened still deep inside of her.

"You're mine, dolcezza. I sinned for you; and I'll sin for you for the rest of my life," he whispered again. "You tamed the beast, claimed the man."

And he claimed her again and again, until birds sung outside and the sun had risen and chased away the darkness.

The daemon tamed the beast.

acknowledgements

First off, I would like to thank every single reader who took the time to read this series. I've had such an exciting journey from writing *Vein of Love* to the last book *To Crown A Beast*. Each and every one of you helped made my dream possible of becoming a published author.

I would love to give a HUGE shoutout to Marjorie and Stephanie—my two alpha readers, but ultimately my best friends. To think a year ago we didn't know each other and both of you have helped me in ways I can't even express my gratitude. I love you girls so much and I'm so blessed and happy we met. Kind of like our khuis resonated or something (hahaha!) But seriously, I love you girls!

My dear Florida girls—Ann and Sarah. I think I should move just so we can hangout more! Sarah, you kick my butt when I need to get the words in and cheer me on and always are there when I need to someone to talk to! Ann—oh sweet, Ann. You are simply amazing and I'm soooo lucky I met you and that we can talk about hot men like Kova and Tensley.

Breanne—who wants me to write "The greatest human being on this planet, name your first born after her what a great name AMIRITE", Megan and Caley, you girls always have my back and listen to me when I have my doubts. I honestly would be lost without you girls and I love you each so much!

To my parents, who have to deal with me when I just worked a eight hour shift and demand to not be disturbed so I can get writing in. I love you each so much for always supporting me and helping me become the woman I am today.

To my family, thank you for supporting me and cheering me on and just being so amazing and loving.

A special shout out to Katie Levy for listening to me discuss every little detail at work about the books, and for pimping them out to everyone she knows. Love you girl!

To the bloggers and readers that always share or go beyond what's required of them, thank you so much! You help me so much by just sharing that one post and I truly cherish that.

To all those amazing authors that reached out and just wanted to help me, thank you so much from the bottom of my heart. Autumn Grey, K Webster, Leigh Shen, Charliegh Rose, Ella Fox, Lucia Franco, and Shanora Williams. I am so blessed to be surrounded by so many amazing authors and I can't wait to one day each meet you and hug you guys.

Made in the USA
Las Vegas, NV
14 December 2020